THE
BARREN

(Kelderan Runic Warriors #2)

Jessie Donovan

This book is a work of fiction. Names, characters, places, and incidents are either the product of the writer's imagination or are used fictitiously, and any resemblance to actual persons, living or dead, business establishments, events, or locales is entirely coincidental.

The Barren
Copyright © 2017 Laura Hoak-Kagey
Mythical Lake Press, LLC
First Edition

Cover Art by Clarissa Yeo of Yocla Designs.

ISBN 13: 978-1942211556

To My Readers

Thank you for continuing this journey into space with me.

Other Books by Jessie Donovan

Kelderan Runic Warriors
The Conquest
The Barren
The Heir (Jan 2018)

Stonefire Dragons
Sacrificed to the Dragon
Seducing the Dragon
Revealing the Dragons
Healed by the Dragon
Reawakening the Dragon
Loved by the Dragon
Surrendering to the Dragon
Cured by the Dragon
Aiding the Dragon
Finding the Dragon (Oct 2017)

Lochguard Highland Dragons
The Dragon's Dilemma
The Dragon Guardian
The Dragon's Heart
The Dragon Warrior

Asylums for Magical Threats
Blaze of Secrets
Frozen Desires
Shadow of Temptation

Flare of Promise

<u>Cascade Shifters</u>
Convincing the Cougar
Reclaiming the Wolf
Cougar's First Christmas
Resisting the Cougar

Chapter One

Vala Yarlen stood in front of the Barren Mother and tried her best not to fidget. If the leader of her citadel didn't sign the final documents, Vala wouldn't be able to join the colony transport ship leaving in a few hours.

And while she'd done her best to hide her desires for most of her life, the document in front of the Barren Mother would give her a new life on a new planet; a planet where both a princess and a human colony leader waited for her. Not because they wanted her as a servant. No, because they considered her a friend.

Her only non-Barren friends, to be exact. The Barren were females who couldn't have children and were pushed to the fringes of Kelderan society at a young age. Vala and the others were to be shadows and nothing more. They existed to help the sick and to voluntarily ease the sexual urges of warriors aboard the various Kelderan starships.

She'd never questioned the customs until recently, when she'd assisted the Kelderan princess to rescue a prince and his bride. After piloting a shuttle and being useful, Vala didn't want to go back to the shadows.

That was exactly what would happen if she continued living inside the citadel.

Unable to stand still any longer, Vala moved one of her feet. The much older female looked up from the document at the sound, her gray hair rustling against her shoulders in the process. "If I sign this, Vala, you'll lose the protection of the citadel. I can't protect you on this new planet called Jasvar. While humans currently occupy the planet, the Kelderans going to form their own colony there won't change their views about us simply because the human leader demands it. Males may end up taking advantage of you. Will you accept that risk?"

Vala stood taller. "I'm aware, Barren Mother, and I accept the risk. The sole princess of Keldera has requested my presence, and one of our highest honors is to serve the royal family."

The Barren Mother leaned back in her chair. "Formally, you are correct. It'd be an honor for any Barren to serve the princess. However, you do not have to accept the summons. I can make worthy excuses as to why you're needed here."

Vala had known the older female her entire life, even before she'd taken over leadership of the citadel and everyone who lived inside it. The Barren Mother had one of the biggest hearts and was also intelligent. If Vala wanted to refuse a royal summons, the Barren Mother would find a way to do it without causing offense.

Staying on Keldera with her own kind would be the easy path.

No. Part of the reason Vala had waited until the last minute to ask the Barren Mother's permission was to ensure she didn't back down from the once-in-a-lifetime opportunity. Vala wanted to leave the planet. But standing up for herself and going against expectations wasn't her usual way of doing things.

However, she needed to speak her mind now or risk losing her only chance at a fresh start.

THE BARREN

Taking a deep breath, Vala forced out the words before she lost her nerve. "I appreciate the offer, but I must decline. After seeing the stars and how life progresses outside of our sanctuary, I yearn for more. If I remain, I'll become an unnecessary burden. Let me be useful. Since I won't have the pressure of helping to populate the new colony, I can help the humans understand our people. They don't view infertility in the same way as the people of Keldera."

Many of the other Barren females living at the citadel would frown or take Vala aside to scold her. It wasn't a Barren's place to question ways or push boundaries. They were allowed to live by the grace and goodwill of the king. It was their duty to never forget that fact and to repay the king's kindness by serving Keldera to the best of their ability.

However, the Barren Mother was different from the others—her position required her to view all sides of an argument—and always was fair. Vala only hoped her honesty would help her case rather than hurt her.

The other female merely studied her before finally sighing. "You'd never be a burden to me, child. To be honest, I'll miss your smile and quick mind."

Vala's heart skipped a beat. "Does that mean I have permission to go?"

The Barren Mother signed the document with a flourish and handed it over to Vala. "Destiny has chosen you for great things, Vala Yarlen. I have faith you will live up to your potential and maybe exceed it. Just make sure to update us once in a while on your progress and accomplishments. There are many who care for you within these walls. You'll be missed."

Tears prickled her eyes at the thought of never stepping foot inside the citadel again, but Vala blinked a few times to push them back. To cry in front of the Barren Mother would be a great dishonor. "Thank you, and I will send as many transmissions as I'm allowed."

The older female waved a hand. "Gratitude is unnecessary. Hard work has earned you my respect. Now, hurry, child. You don't have long until they start boarding the colony transport ship, and your mother will be anxious to spend the last remaining moments with you."

She bobbed her head. "May fortune allow you to serve with honor."

"And may destiny shine light into your life to chase away the darkness," the older female finished.

Not wanting to think about how that would be the last time Vala ever said the formal blessing to the Barren Mother, she quickly bowed her head and exited the room.

It was time to find her adopted mother and somehow say goodbye to the only family she had truly ever known.

~~~

General Thorin Jarrell exited the Kelderan colony transport ship's main engineering room and headed toward his new quarters. There was still much to do before the ship's launch, but he needed a moment of peace if he wished to conceal his biggest secret. The lack of sleep and demands on his time had prevented him from meditating properly, let alone taking care of his unwanted sexual desires.

For a Kelderan, sexual desires were easy to control. However, Thorin was half-Brevkan—a violent, dishonorable race that was the sworn enemy of all Kelderans.

12

Being part Brevkan was more than a curse; it was dangerous. The genes of his rapist father wanted sex and violence above all else.

Thorin had managed to control his unwanted side for nearly three decades. He had come close a few times in exposing his violent side and being discovered, but through sheer strength and stubbornness, he'd kept his darkness in check. He sure as hell wasn't about to let it win after all this time.

Especially since the mission to Jasvar was Thorin's first assignment as the general in charge of a ship. He'd ensure the colonists and his crew would reach their destination in one piece, or die trying.

Picking up his pace, he was about to make the final turn to his quarters when one of his warriors in charge of security approached.

For a brief moment, the urge to rip out the warrior's heart and watch him die coursed through his body. The kill would make him feel better. Yes, he should give in and accept his true self. Life would be much more fun if the weakest were culled. Only the strongest should be allowed to survive.

Taking a deep breath, he ignored the thoughts and brought up every major battle he'd won defending his people from enemies. As a Kelderan soldier, Thorin had vowed to protect every citizen of Keldera with his life. He couldn't forget that now.

Drawing on the images of his successes, plus his years of training when it came to concealing his true emotions, he asked, "What's wrong? I'm to only be disturbed for emergencies. I hope this disturbance is warranted."

The warrior, Hinrick, made a fist and thumped it over his heart. "It is, sir. The king is waiting for you in the main cargo bay."

Thorin kept his surprise from showing. "I wasn't aware the king would visit us."

Thorin was one of the few who knew the extent of King Kastor's frailty and failing health. For him to board the ship meant he had something very important to discuss.

Hinrick answered, "He wanted it to be a surprise, but didn't elaborate any further. If we're to leave on schedule, your rest and meditation period must wait."

Images of battle, with Thorin ripping out another male's throat with his teeth, hit him. Followed shortly was the image of him still covered in blood and taking a female roughly from behind, glowing as he roared and branded her with his seed.

Only through a lifetime of practice did his eyes remain neutral, his runic markings a dark blue, and his cock soft.

For any full-blooded Kelderan, delaying a meditation session was not a big inconvenience. In Thorin's case, without meditation, the images and urges would only increase in intensity until he found a female or sparred with a male and possibly killed him.

Not for the first time, Thorin wished he were like his brethren, who were all full-blooded Kelderans.

But he wasn't. And if he wished to remain general of the ship, he had to dig deep to remain clearheaded.

Bit by bit Thorin packed away the images of battle and taking the faceless female. A second later, he answered, "The king must not be kept waiting." He waved a hand. "Lead the way."

As the warrior turned and strode in the direction of the main cargo bay, Thorin breathed in and out at a steady rhythm. He had worked his whole life to achieve the rank of general. He wasn't about to ruin it all because of a missed meditation session, no matter how intense or life-like the images would become inside his head.

By the time they arrived at the main cargo bay doors, the pulsing need had dulled to a gentle throb and the markings littering his skin remained dark blue, the color of peace and contentment. Only a novice warrior would allow any other color to show and reveal his emotions.

The males standing at either side of the cargo bay doors pressed their thumbs to panels on the wall. On a regular ship, access was freely given to the cargo bay. However, on a colony ship, doing so would only invite trouble.

He quickly looked at the tiers of walkways above, lining the walls of the cavernous space. Almost every level was full of spectators. All the gawkers quickly started moving again once they recognized him.

Thorin searched the area until he found the king sitting in an intricately carved chair just outside his personal shuttle.

Since it wasn't Thorin's place to note the paleness of the king's skin or circles under his eyes, he merely stopped in front of Keldera's ruler and bowed. "Your majesty."

Kastor's voice filled the space. "Sorry for my intrusion, but I must speak with you in private. Come, let us talk inside the shuttle."

Since the king possessed the most advanced and secure communications technology and could have easily used a view screen to contact Thorin, the topic must be something he didn't want to risk anyone getting hold of.

Thorin stood up straight again and waited for the king to rise. An older Barren nurse helped the aged ruler to his feet and up the stairs of the shuttle. The king was doing a good job of hiding it, but Thorin spotted the occasional wince and heard the grunts of discomfort.

Rather than waste time thinking of how the king risked the monarchy by leaving his palace and possibly exposing his frail body, Thorin glanced to the female at the king's side. Her graying dark hair, wrinkles, and sagging flesh denoted her as closer to his mother's age and too old for him to consider using to placate his sexual urges. However, Thorin needed to find a Barren of his own to use on the journey; regular sex would lessen his chances at losing control. The trick would be in securing one who would acquiesce to his needs and demands. Mainly, she needed to be blindfolded and bound. Otherwise, she might be able to guess his true parentage with sight and touch, and he wouldn't allow that.

As the king and Barren disappeared into the shuttle, Thorin took the last length of stairs two at a time until he reached the top. Once he was in one of the rooms with the king, the Barren left and shut the door.

Thorin bowed his head. "What is it you wish to speak about, your majesty?"

The king looked up from where he sat. "You're aware of the antimonarchy faction's cause gaining momentum on Keldera. I won't insult your intelligence by asking if you do. However, despite the best screening efforts of both the military headquarters and the council's security department, Keltor believes there's at least one antimonarchy troublemaker aboard the colony ship. He doesn't know who, or our security would take care of it."

Keltor was the king's eldest son and heir to the Kelderan throne.

Thorin nodded. "So you wish me to keep an eye out and discretely discover the sympathizer."

"Yes. The colony on Jasvar is the future of Keldera. If dissent takes hold on Jasvar, the humans may banish our people and send everyone back. If that happens, the strains of overpopulation will only worsen with time, and no matter what my son or I do, repercussions on Keldera will be severe. The pro- and antimonarchy factions will only increase their efforts, and I wouldn't rule out civil war."

The importance of Thorin's mission was more important than even he had anticipated. His failure would contribute to an eventual civil war.

"Who knows about this possibility, your majesty?" Thorin asked.

"Keltor, myself, and a handful of trusted officials. My younger son, Kason, vouched for your loyalty. I hope he wasn't misled."

"Of course not, your majesty. It is my duty to serve."

The king studied Thorin, and he wondered if the monarch would bring up Thorin's heritage. The only reason Thorin hadn't been imprisoned as a teen for his Brevkan blood was because of the king's favor and his repaying a debt to Thorin's mother for protecting the king's sister during an attack many years ago. To reward his mother's heroic efforts, the king had created a fake birth certificate which reflected a Kelderan father for Thorin instead of his Brevkan one.

For the king to even consider Thorin for such an important task meant that Thorin's former boss, Prince Kason, must have greatly praised his skills. Odd to think that considering he and Kason had never cared much for one another over the years.

Of course, Thorin's role in saving the lives of Kason and his bride probably played into the praise.

Kastor spoke up again. "Very well. Be careful of who learns about this. If you tell the wrong person, you'll be responsible for the ensuing trouble and will be dealt with accordingly."

And in keeping with Kelderan law, Thorin would be tried as a traitor and most likely executed.

He bowed his head. "I will take this duty as seriously as my mission to deliver the colonists to Jasvar. My life is dedicated to serving you and the people of Keldera."

"Good. And General Thorin, one last thing."

"Anything, your majesty."

"Once you arrive on Jasvar, ensure only the best warriors are assigned to watch over my children. If any antimonarchy sympathizers make it to Jasvar, Kason and Kalahn will become targets."

Kalahn was the youngest royal child and the only female. Both were currently living on Jasvar with the humans.

Thorin stood tall. "Kason is a former general, but regardless, I'll do my best to set up protection for him and Princess Kalahn."

Kastor smiled faintly. "Thank you."

Thorin tried not to blink. Kelderan royalty didn't display gratitude often. The king must be in poorer health than Thorin had imagined to so easily reveal his emotions. It was probably why the king wore robes that covered his body from his neck to his feet, the material hid his rune-like markings and the changing colors of his emotions. Even the best warrior slowly lost control of the color of his markings as the decades passed. For a king to show anything but steadfastness would question his ability to lead.

And as treasonous as it may be to think so, Thorin wished King Kastor would hand over the throne to his eldest son, Keltor, sooner rather than later.

He was about to ask if there was anything else when images of ripping limbs off enemies and tossing the parts to the corner burst into his mind. Shortly after, different ones of him pleasuring two females—one with his tongue and the other with his cock—took center stage.

The images became more vivid with each passing second. If Thorin didn't leave, he might burst into violence and jeopardize everything.

King Kastor's voice severed his visions. "Go, Thorin. You must take care of yourself."

The images in his mind faded slightly. After using every iota of strength he had to push them away and blank his mind, Thorin murmured, "Thank you, your majesty," before bowing one last time and exiting the shuttle.

Being so close to breaking, Thorin dug his nails into his palms until the stinging pain helped him to focus. He barked at the lower downs who tried to approach him. Unlike a meeting with the king, Thorin's second-in-command could handle just about any other issue that cropped up for the next ten minutes.

As soon as he entered his quarters, he went to the shower area. After undressing, he moved to the center of the area, and a spray automatically began.

Closing his eyes, Thorin begrudgingly allowed the images of him taking two females to flood his mind. He gripped his cock and allowed shame to flood his body as he gave in to his Brevkan urges and stroked. When the images flashed between battles of war and taking females—blood covering all involved in the encounter—Thorin increased the pace of his hand. As the females in his visions screamed his name and slashed his chest with knives to draw blood, he finally growled out his release.

After the last spasm racked his body, Thorin simply let the cleaning solution wash away his shame.

Although there wasn't enough cleaning solution in the universe to wash away the disturbing images of blood and sex he'd endured over the years.

He punched the wall, barely noticing the sting in his knuckles. Not for the first time, he wished the wall was the face of his immoral father.

Thorin should be grateful that his mother had kept him and raised him with love.

But in that moment, he was unclean and a barbarian. All he wanted to do was erase his father's life from his mother's past. Then he would no longer exist to burden her.

Of course he couldn't change the past. His mother's memory was failing and she may no longer remember who he was, but he would prove to her until his dying day that his honorable Kelderan half was stronger. He would succeed in his mission at any cost, including the king's most recent request.

Chapter Two

Vala hugged her adoptive mother. She took the moment to remember the warmth and peace Vala always found in her mother's embrace.

Such feelings of comfort she might never feel again.

Stop it, Vala. She had friends on Jasvar and surely she could make friends with other humans, too. She wouldn't be completely alone on a strange, new world.

After another minute, she released her mother and looked up at the female with a similar tattoo on her forehead, although her mother's hair was lavender to Vala's white. "They should be boarding the Barren aboard the colony ship soon. I need to leave."

Her mother smiled and cupped her face with both hands. "Rationally, I know that. But I have the strangest feeling this will be the last time you set foot on Keldera."

A few tears trailed down her cheeks. Vala quickly wiped them away. "Even if that's true, I will find a way for you to obtain passage to Jasvar at a later date. I promise you that, Mother."

"What do I always tell you, Vala?"

"Don't make promises you might not be able to keep."

Her mother nodded. "Exactly. I'm not even sure I'd make the two-week journey to Jasvar. Space travel takes its toll on a person in later years." Her mother lightly stroked her cheek. "I have lived my life, child. It's now your duty to live yours."

As she stared into her mother's blue eyes, Vala memorized every line and curve of her mother's face. "I intend to keep this promise. You'll see. The military and research scientists are always finding new ways to make space travel easier. I'm sure there's something to help get you to Jasvar." The audio system boomed with final boarding calls for the Barren passengers. Vala smiled. "And since I must depart, there's no time to argue with me."

Her mother snorted. "I will say that's a new excuse for escaping my hugs." She pulled Vala close once more. "I love you, Vala. You'll always be in my thoughts and dreams."

Emotion choked her throat. For a split second, she wondered if she could truly leave everyone she cared for behind. Even if things were brighter once Vala arrived on Jasvar and was reunited with her friends, the two-week journey would send her back into the shadows, where she would need to follow the letter of the law or risk her place. It wouldn't be easy, especially given her recently discovered assignment aboard the ship.

Before she could dwell on the difficulties ahead, her mother released her. "Go. They'll close the shuttle doors without you, Vala, and I won't have it. After listening to how much you enjoyed working with the princess and flying the shuttle, I know Jasvar is your future. Only there can you escape the restrictions on our kind and find your wings."

"Mother."

"It's true. I only want what's best for you." Her mother smiled. "And you don't have time to argue, either."

Taking a deep breath, Vala bobbed her head. "I'll send communications as often as I can." From the corner of her eye, she spotted the last few stragglers boarding the shuttle to the colony ship. "I love you, Mother."

"I love you, too, my darling Vala."

Her mother raised a hand in parting. After one more second of memorizing her mother's face, Vala turned away and somehow managed to rush toward the shuttle's stairs. It took everything she had to keep her gaze forward and not glance back once more at the female who had taken Vala in as a baby and raised her as her own.

Tears threatened to fall again, but Vala kept them at bay by remembering her shuttle flight not that long ago, when she'd helped Princess Kalahn and General Thorin Jarrell to root out traitors and rescue Prince Kason. The power to move through space again on her own, as a pilot, motivated her to not run back to her old life.

Besides, she made a vow to see her mother again, no matter what it took.

Once Vala boarded the shuttle, she took her seat at the back, where the other females in brown, flowing dresses with intricate tattoos on their foreheads sat—the section reserved for the Barren.

She recognized the female with dark hair and golden skin from her childhood days. But the female named Setla had her eyes squeezed shut and gripped the armrests with her fingers, which meant this was probably her first shuttle flight.

As much as she wanted to ask Setla if she was okay or try to comfort her, it was forbidden for her to do so inside the shuttle since several children sat with their mothers at the front of the ship. Barren were never to speak to or in front of children unless they were under their care or had been granted permission by one of their parents.

After all, you couldn't have the young ones asking too many questions.

Unless she wanted to risk ever setting foot on Jasvar, she would have to ignore some of her own desires until they reached the colony.

Not for the first time, she wondered how she'd been blinded by the harsh treatment of her kind for so long. Then she remembered most Barren lived in isolation, so it was easy to forget the outside world.

Reaching the back of the shuttle, Vala buckled in and looked out the window.

Soon the shuttle was in the air, and the yellow trees and black mountains of Keldera faded until the scenery was replaced with the darkness of space, albeit with pricks of light for stars and a few glowing planets in the distance.

The sight brought back memories of her piloting a shuttle with Princess Kalahn at her side, and later under Prince Kason's guidance. Who knew, maybe one day even females could command starships, including the Barren.

With that goal in mind, she closed her eyes and slowly contained her emotions. They would soon be arriving on the colony transport ship, and Vala needed all the peace she could muster. Her assignment wouldn't be easy.

After a glowing recommendation from Prince Kason and Princess Kalahn, Vala had been granted the honor of serving the general commanding the ship.

Unfortunately, the general in question was Thorin Jarrell. And judging by his looks of disdain and hatred during their previous acquaintance, he wasn't going to make her job easy.

Nevertheless, Vala would succeed. Even if she had to keep her head down and remain silent during her work hours, she would do it. Thorin Jarrell wouldn't take away her dream of freedom and hopefully eventual acceptance on the new colony.

The long shape of the Kelderan colony transport ship, painted in red and brown tones, came into view, and everything else fled her mind. The ship and its five thousand people was a new chapter for all involved.

She quietly wished for good fortune. They would all need it.

~~~

His peace restored temporarily because of his orgasm, Thorin exited his quarters and nearly ran into a white-haired Barren in her flowing brown dress. He growled. "Watch where you're going."

The female froze a second before standing. However, she kept her head bowed. Something about the shade of white hair was familiar. He ordered, "Look at me, Barren."

She slowly raised her head. He barely paid attention to the tattoo on her forehead. Looking into her black eyes, he clenched his jaw.

The woman who had invaded his visions for nearly a week after meeting her during a previous assignment stood in front of him—Vala Yarlen.

He had only managed to purge his dreams of her in the last few days. How dare she appear to tempt him again in the flesh. "What are you doing here?"

To her credit, the few visible runic markings on her arms didn't waver in color from dark blue. "I'm here to do my duty, sir."

For an instant, he wondered if his second-in-command had sent a female to help relax him; more than a few Barren willingly offered themselves to warriors aboard spaceships.

But Thorin quickly pushed that thought away. From his prior research into the female, he knew she didn't dally with any of the warriors. "I didn't call for you. Explain why you're here."

Whether out of respect or to defy him, he didn't know, but she bowed her head. "I've been granted the honor of seeing to your needs, General."

An image of Vala naked on her belly and blindfolded as he took her from behind flashed into his mind, but he quickly forced it away. In this case "needs" referred to being his servant, not his lover. "What I need is to not see you. My schedule will be sent to you daily. Ensure that our paths don't cross when you clean my room. Robot transporters can bring me my meals."

She deepened her bow and remained silent.

Good. If the female kept out of his way and didn't entice him with her black eyes and golden skin, he might avoid dreaming of her again. The thought of having a regular female to pleasure and claim was cruel since Thorin would never be able to take a bride of his own.

No one outside of the royal family must discover his true parentage or he would lose everything. For all he knew, the Barren would gossip about his skin glowing a faint blue to the others. Kelderans didn't glow as they found release and word would spread.

A small voice inside his head reminded him that his urges faded whenever he dreamed of Vala Yarlen. However, Thorin was a disciplined warrior and dismissed the idea. No general with ambition would ever take a Barren for more than a few weeks. And he certainly wouldn't trust a female with a secret that could

26

not only rip apart his life and career but could make his mother's remaining years full of shame and mockery for keeping a half-Brevkan bastard. Even if his mother's memory was mostly gone, she didn't deserve cruelty.

Then Vala's light floral scent finally hit his nose and a primal urge to drag her into his quarters and tie her to his bed coursed through his body. It seemed finding and rooting out an antimonarchy traitor or two might not be his most difficult task for the journey to Jasvar.

Taking a step back, he turned away from her. "You may clean my quarters. Whatever you see inside is confidential. Break your silence and you will be punished. Be gone within the hour."

Not wanting to chance hearing her voice or being bombarded by her scent again, he strode down the corridor. Each step caused her scent to fade.

After a few minutes, his calmness was wrecked with a new barrage of images. The recent onslaught included Vala on her back and looking up at him with desire as he glowed. No fear or disgust in her eyes, just acceptance.

Clenching his fingers and digging his nails into his palms, he banished the thought. No Kelderan, male or female, would accept his true self. Thorin could barely do so, and he'd had nearly three decades to get used to the idea.

No, he'd steer clear of the female, find a random Barren to sate his desires, and focus all his attention on his mission. Much depended on his success. The quicker he delivered Vala Yarlen to Jasvar, the quicker Thorin could busy himself with assignments and missions. Being a soldier was all he had. Her presence only renewed his dedication to serving. That way, he would be distracted from thoughts of a future or taking a bride.

Not that he wanted one.

The female was dangerous.

Thorin picked up his pace. If he threw himself into work, they might even launch a little early.

~~~

Vala watched Thorin disappear down the corridor. While he had a finely muscled broad back and walked with a confidence she yearned for herself, his orders and tone still rung in her ears.

She should be used to curt orders as most Kelderans viewed the Barren as second-class citizens. After all, a female who couldn't carry a child had no worth. The final stage of Kelderan marriage required a pregnancy. Without the sacred confirmation, a female could stray and make a fool out of her lord, claiming they weren't technically bound.

But for some reason, Thorin's disdain and dismissal stung. Probably because she had been a crucial player in him being able to save Prince Kason and the leader of the Jasvarian colony not that long ago. Without her help, he most likely wouldn't be a general in the present.

Still, it wasn't her place to question. If avoiding him would ensure a satisfactory recommendation and her place on the colony, she would do it.

Shaking her head, she cleared her mind and pressed her thumb to the small panel next to the entrance of the general's room. The door to Thorin's quarters opened. Stepping inside, she tried her best not to gasp.

The bedding lay shredded on the floor, the small mirror on one side smashed, and she swore she saw a dent in the wall made of nearly indestructible composite material.

If Thorin followed normal protocol, access to the series of rooms was restricted to herself and Thorin Jarrell. That meant he had done this to his own quarters. The stoic warrior had a secret, unrestrained side to him.

She only hoped he didn't do the same to the Barren who volunteered to share their bodies with him. Vala would have to keep an eye out and check. Violence against her Barren sisters was something she refused to tolerate. She might have little power over their fate, but she could possibly offer a shoulder to cry on and fake their medical records with an illness to keep them secluded.

Realizing she was judging the male without knowing him— something she suffered on a daily basis because of the special tattoo on her forehead—she pushed her judgments aside for the time being to complete her task.

Since Thorin had reminded her that the state of his quarters was confidential, she couldn't request maintenance to repair the damage. She should use the replicator to make new bedding. However, she had no idea if the replicator's logs were set to immediately purge after use or not. If they didn't, anyone in engineering or maintenance could see what was replaced, and replacing almost everything in the room could draw unwanted attention, especially if Thorin's outbursts were a regular occurrence.

So instead, she picked up the shredded bedding and laid it out on the mattress as neatly as she could manage. A small part of her wanted to see Thorin's face when he viewed the rumpled mess. Most would merely fold up the scraps and place them into the laser incinerator. But she was too determined to follow his order to the letter while also adding her own flair to it. She didn't think he'd scold her for something so trivial.

However, even if he requested an audience to admonish her, Vala would stand by her reasoning. Limited use of technology meant fewer records and generals tended to value discretion and intuition in their warriors. At least, that was the case from everything she'd read. In theory, Thorin should admire her dedication.

Still, as she lightly touched the dented section of the wall, she wondered what was behind his outburst. The second she'd received her assignment to serve him for the journey, she'd quickly researched further into Thorin Jarrell. All she'd managed to find before leaving were glowing reports of prowess in battle and dedication to his missions. There'd been no recorded history of violence. Not even his rank would erase his official military and peacekeeper records.

Glancing at the shattered mirror, tens of miniature reflections of her head stared back. Given the concentration of damage in the mirror, it had indeed been punched by a hand.

Yes, Thorin Jarrell was full of secrets. A part of her wondered what had caused him to destroy his quarters, let alone made him frown and look down at her when she'd only ever done as told.

Then she remembered her ultimate goal of living as part of the colony on Jasvar. She couldn't afford to stir things up by asking questions. Even discreetly diving into the more extensive records she could access on the ship might flag someone in the security department. It was best to leave Thorin's mystery alone.

Turning away from the wall and mirror, Vala moved into the cleaning and showering quarters. Before she could do more than note the drying clothes strewn about the floor, an unfamiliar musky scent invaded her senses. A vision of her naked and open to a male with a broad back and the toned physique of a warrior flashed inside her head. He moved his hips and pleasure coursed through her body. Her nipples tightened and throbbed before light flashed before her eyes. Something undefined but wonderful flooded her body, and she screamed.

As soon as Vala came down from the rush, she fell to the ground and the world turned black.

Chapter Three

Thorin sat in the slightly raised chair of the command deck and stared at the yellow-green swirl of color that was planet Keldera. While ensuring the colony ship made it safely to Jasvar was his top concern, he wasn't sure how long he'd have to stay on the foreign planet since he was to help set up the military command base for the Kelderan colony. Only once Prince Kason and his human bride, the female leader of Jasvar named Taryn Demara, gave the go ahead could he return the colony ship to Keldera with a skeleton crew.

In other words, Thorin had no idea when he would return to his homeworld.

If his mother wasn't hospitalized and still remembered him, Thorin would feel guilty. However, his mother had the best care he could secure. Him trying to coax memories that would never return only caused hurt to them both. Staying away was the appropriate solution. She had always wanted him to follow his own path.

Besides, he had never truly fit in on Keldera for many reasons he could never reveal.

Nahrenn's—his head pilot—voice cut through his thoughts. "Final predeparture check complete. The report from engineering clears us to launch when you're ready, sir."

Thorin sat taller in his chair. "Then set the coordinates and maneuver us out of the launch base."

"Aye, aye, sir," Nahrenn said before tapping a series of buttons on the large, flat notescreen in his hand.

While it was impossible to hear the engines whirring to life from his current position, the image on the view screen, of them moving away from the docking station ever so slowly, confirmed the journey had begun.

As soon as the ship cleared the overall maintenance and launch base and was safely in free space, Thorin stood. "Nahrenn, enter the coordinates to Jasvar and continue the journey until further notice. You have command of the deck. I have lingering matters to attend to that can't wait."

Nahrenn nodded, handed his notescreen to the next most senior pilot, and walked toward the chair. "Since we cleared the launch base without issue, things should be smooth for the next few hours, until we reach the nearest asteroid field. I'll reach out if anything arises before then."

Thorin stood and moved a few feet away. "Signal when we're an hour away from the field. I'll be working in my quarters on a special matter, but feel free to disturb me sooner if there's any sign of trouble."

Not waiting for Nahrenn's reply, Thorin exited the command deck and headed toward the nearest elevator. With their flight safely in progress, it was time to start combing through the records of everyone on board. Once he divided them into safe and potential traitor categories, he could begin his investigation for the king. He wouldn't risk discovery of the delicate matter by working in his small office off the command deck; his rooms would be more easily controlled and contained. The only people with access were him and the Barren female, and he'd make sure to keep any confidential information locked away and out of her reach.

Thorin arrived at the door to his quarters and pressed his thumb to the panel off to the side. It had been a few hours since his encounter with the Barren, so she should have finished cleaning and vacated his space. If not, he'd lodge a formal complaint and request another.

Sure, making the request now would prevent him from seeing her during the journey, but Thorin wasn't about to sully anyone's reputation just to make his life easier. Only a coward would choose that path.

As the doors opened and he spotted his shredded bedding laid out on his mattress, he should be angry that the female hadn't incinerated everything related to his earlier outburst. And yet, considering if the female had replicated a new one, engineering would have the log and while a long shot, they might possibly ask if everything was fine since replicating supplies so soon after launch was suspicious.

The Barren understood discretion. Maybe she was cleverer than he'd thought.

Pushing aside thoughts of her long hair and bared body from one of his visions, he moved to a drawer in the wall where he kept his personal notescreen. However, before he reached it, he noticed light shining from the cleaning quarters. Since it only came on when a life-form with a humanoid-sized heat source was detected, someone had to be in his room. Maybe the antimonarchy troublemaker had come to him, although he had no idea why.

Thorin placed a hand on the gun blaster at his hip and drew the weapon. Ensuring it was set to stun and not kill, he moved quietly and inched his way to the entrance. Once he reached the doorway, his eyes fell upon the unconscious form of Vala Yarlen sprawled out on the floor.

The lights sensing her heat source told him she was alive; the cooling temperature of a dead body wasn't enough to trigger the automation. The bigger question was why she was out cold on his floor in the first place.

Crouching down, he moved a finger to her neck and stopped when he was a hairbreadth away from touching her skin. Given her invasion into his dreams, her soft skin under his fingertips might cause his baser nature to take over.

No. Drawing on every bit of strength and restraint he possessed, he touched her warm neck to check her pulse.

Instead of focusing on the soft thump of her heartbeat, desire flooded his body. Visions of her naked, screaming his name in pleasure, and digging her nails into his back hard enough to draw blood, played out.

Vala's weak voice broke through the images. "General? What happened?"

He moved his hand away from her skin as if he'd been burned. "I just discovered you unconscious on the floor. I should be the one asking you what happened."

She attempted to sit up but quickly slid to the floor again. "I-I don't know. I came in here, smelled an unusual scent, and had strange visions before waking up at your touch, sir."

For a split second, Thorin's heart stopped beating. "Describe the scent."

She frowned. "I don't know, sir. I have nothing to compare it to. Not unpleasant, but strangely addictive."

Thorin stood and backed slightly away. "That's impossible."

Vala continued to stare at his feet for a few beats before finally meeting his gaze. "What aren't you telling me, sir?"

Thorin was torn between three actions: bolting from his room, imprisoning the female to silence her, and scooping her up to take her to his bed and live out one of his erotic dreams.

She couldn't know it, but Vala Yarlen's reaction to his scent denoted her as a less rosy version of a Kelderan's destined bride—she was a Brevkan's possession.

Little was known about Brevkan mating and courting rituals. However, during the throes of war, a few females on Keldera had experienced what the Brevkan called the claiming of a possession.

Only a Brevkan male's potential possession could smell their post-orgasm musk. And if the male in question wasn't present to relieve his urges and fill her with his seed, she would fall unconscious and wake up partially paralyzed. The few stories he'd found also pointed out that if the male left without ever possessing her, the female in question never walked again. Something to do with ensuring a female couldn't run away from a wild-eyed Brevkan male.

If Vala was indeed his possession, then he either had to sleep with her or leave her partially paralyzed for the rest of her life.

As the female looked to the floor again, he barely resisted swearing and debated what to do. It looked like his father's cursed genetics had surfaced once more to throw his life into chaos.

~~~

Vala focused on rhythmic breathing and tried her best not to panic. She could handle Thorin's tall, muscled form standing over her, even with the deep frown etched between his brows.

But as she tried yet again to move her legs, nothing happened and she had no idea why.

Her recent genetic health scan had revealed no known diseases or pending afflictions. Something was wrong.

She dared to meet Thorin's gaze again. Disgust warred with anger. With his black hair framing his chiseled, pale-blue face, he was both terrifying and glorious.

Even a few months ago, Vala would've meekly remained quiet and awaited the general's order on how to proceed. But after her recent interactions with Keldera's princess and her constantly prodding Vala to speak her mind, she couldn't help but blurt out, "What aren't you telling me?" As his frown deepened, she added, "Sir."

As he remained silent, Vala battled the urge to speak again. However, Thorin finally replied, "Telling you will have consequences. Namely, you'll be confined to my quarters for the entire journey and remain under my watch."

She swallowed. "I-I don't dally with the warriors." She should leave it there, but the rest of her thoughts spilled out. "I won't change my stance, not even for a general, sir."

What had she done? Speaking out of turn to any Kelderan soldier merited punishment, but to do so to a general was worse.

He could take her life and no one would be the wiser. High-ranking officers had the power to make people disappear.

When Thorin's voice echoed in the room, it was filled with disgust as he barked, "Neither one of us has a choice about the matter. You must dally with me."

If she weren't a Barren, Vala would state that she had no interest in him and his disrespectful ways. She wouldn't sully her body with his touch.

Unfortunately, the law prevented her from revealing her true feelings. She might not be able to move her legs, but she still dreamed of living on Jasvar and seeing her friends. She couldn't do that if she were imprisoned for a minor disobedience. She suspected he would punish her that way since if Thorin had wanted to hit her or worse, he would've done so already.

At her silence, he finally spoke again. "You have two choices. First, you leave my quarters and most likely remain paralyzed for the rest of your life. Or, second, I take you to bed, claim you, and keep you in my care until we arrive on Jasvar. Which will it be? Speak freely with me, Barren. I don't have time to dance around your hesitant words or actions."

She blinked. She'd never heard of a general giving a Barren permission to speak freely unless she were a mistress.

Aware her future and life hung in the balance, she risked following his order to speak her mind. "First, tell me why you're certain I'll remain paralyzed?"

He didn't miss a beat. "I just know. And before you suggest a medic will be able to cure you, I doubt it will work. Only I know the cause of your paralysis. Regardless of what either of us wants, either I claim you or you become even more of a burden to society."

She resisted wincing at his words. Being infertile was bad enough in a Kelderan's eyes, but a crippled one was ten times worse.

Thorin Jarrell definitely didn't tame his words to lessen their emotional impact.

Anger bubbled inside her. It was almost as if Thorin was determined to force her hand.

Not only that, it was as if he were punishing her out of spite. Maybe what she'd once taken as gratitude for helping him not that long ago, to root out the traitors and rescue Prince Kason, had really been a farce. After all, most males would see a female helping out a soldier as a sign of weakness.

Thorin prompted, "I need an answer. I have much to do, and your condition only delays more important tasks."

She wanted to narrow her eyes at his dismissal of her paralysis. Her years of training and caution faded. "The Barren are notorious about keeping secrets. Please tell me the cause and then I'll make my decision."

"No. If you don't tell me your choice in the next minute, I will make the decision for you."

"You can't do that. Even Barren have rights."

"I can and I will. Despite my reputation and what you probably have heard about me, I assure you that I'm trying to help you. I swear on my mother's life that I don't wish to harm you."

As Thorin stood tall, made a fist, and thumped it over his heart, her jaw dropped. A general never saluted a Barren. It was as if the king bowed to an animal herder—it defied logic.

Maybe he was being honorable. Only sharing her body would give her the truth.

She eyed Thorin's broad shoulders and bare chest. His markings were a dark blue, signaling calmness, which contradicted the emotions she'd seen in his eyes.

Her gaze trailed lower to the large bulge pressing against his tight warrior pants. Even if she agreed to his unusual demand, there was no way he would fit inside her. During her years of practicing medicine, she had seen a number of males' sexual organs. Thorin was far bigger than any she had seen before.

Thorin's husky voice garnered her attention. "Your eyes and flashing markings tell me that you aren't afraid of me, but merely curious. My decision is thus—you will remain in my quarters until you are ready for my claiming."

She looked up and swore Thorin's eyes glowed a second before returning to normal. She'd never heard of a Kelderan male's eyes doing that.

He spoke again before she could react. "I'll move you to my bed now. You have my word that I won't touch you more than necessary until you ask for it."

"Then vow it," she said before she could stop herself. After all, if he gave her enough time, Vala might be able to find a solution on her own and never have to experience Thorin claiming her body.

Thorin never blinked at her demand. "I vow it and will give up my general rank if I break it."

She somehow doubted he'd follow through, but his words eased her nervousness a little. It also gave her a small glimmer of hope that she could escape without an arrest record as well as her virginity intact.

Since he still waited for her to respond, Vala nodded. "Okay."

Squatting, he scooped her up and jostled her gently against his chest. His warm, muscled skin under her palms sent a little thrill through her body.

She frowned. The male was forcing her hand and making decisions without her. She should hate him.

Yet she couldn't resist tracing one of the markings on his chest, and Thorin grunted. Looking up, she waited for his reprimand. Touching a Kelderan's skin was intimate and Vala had no right doing so without permission. However, the only part of him that moved were his nostrils as they flared.

In the blink of an eye, he was across the room and gently laying her on his bed. The instant he released her, she shivered at the drop in temperature.

Thorin moved to the door. "I'll return with a hover chair programmed to only function inside these rooms. I will also fetch a more suitable blanket to keep you warm. Your thumbprint will be removed from the pre-approved personnel for my quarters, so there is no reason to try and escape. It won't work. Until I return."

She opened her mouth to speak, but Thorin exited the room.

As the door slid closed and locked, Vala hugged her upper body. She'd been a fool to allow his warm body to distract her from asking important questions when she had the chance. Namely, why Thorin had been surprised at her description of the smell and ensuing unconsciousness.

Maybe he hadn't paralyzed her on purpose.

Not that she would use that as an excuse for his behavior. She wasn't sure he understood honor, which was the crucial pillar of Kelderan warrior training.

The only good thing was that Thorin hadn't tried to take her straight away. She didn't completely believe his tale about her remaining paralyzed for the rest of her life unless she welcomed him into her body. Something else had to be going on, unless the general had a secret life of drugging females and convincing them only he could cure them.

She glanced down at her legs, but no amount of concentration made them move.

What if she never walked again? Life would be hard enough on a new planet, but Jasvar's technology was far behind the Kelderans'. And even with everything the colony ship was bringing to their new home, building and maintaining hover chairs would be low on the list of priorities.

Vala might end up having less freedom than she already had in the present.

No. She couldn't afford to think like that. After all, she'd only been awake for a short while. For all she knew, her legs could start working again within the hour.

However, just in case, she would spend what time she had doing research. Thorin would be busy taking care of the ship and its passengers. She didn't expect him to return anytime soon.

All she needed was a notescreen. Before departure, Vala had stored every medical tome she could find into her personal virtual storage area. She needed to delve into them to hopefully find the cause of her paralysis and then pinpoint any potential remedies.

Yes, finding a cure on her own was her top priority. She didn't have time to worry about her legs or the what-ifs in her future.

Besides, she needed a clear head when Thorin returned. Fear would only impair her brain and ability to think.

Because there had to be a way for her to regain her freedom and not dally with Thorin. After seeing the destruction of his quarters, she could only imagine what he was like when naked and free above her. A warm touch meant nothing if she ended up bruised and scarred for the rest of her life because of his violent side.

Chapter Four

Thorin marched toward one of the private recreation rooms. If he didn't expend some of his energy and unexpected lust at Vala's small frame against him, his Brevkan urges might break free. No matter how much he detested his current predicament, he vowed not to hurt or frighten the female. She shouldn't suffer because of his bastard, dishonorable half.

The only good thing from the whole mess was that Thorin could prevent future repeats of what had happened to Vala. He would have to either clean his room himself in the future or have a lower-down male do it. He couldn't give up orgasms to satiate his Brevkan half, but he could ensure no female was forced to accept him and his unclean genetics. At least the Barren couldn't be saddled with one of his bastard offspring.

Finally reaching the private room, Thorin entered and removed his weapons. "Computer, don't admit any visitors until the program completes. Only head pilot Nahrenn or security officer Xytor are allowed to interrupt via communications."

"Understood," the artificial intelligence, or AI, system answered. "State desired program and specifications."

"Hand-to-hand combat, level twenty. Search my records to prevent repetition."

The walls of the room turned a bright yellow, which instantly alerted his senses. A second later, a Kelderan male warrior several inches taller than him, with more muscle, charged into existence and headed straight for him.

Used to the program, he barely paid attention to the geometric look of the simulation. Thorin tensed his muscles and skirted to the right when the warrior reached him. He attempted to sweep his opponent's leg, but the warrior stepped to the side at the last minute.

Crouching down, Thorin lunged at the warrior and they both went to the ground. They rolled, but the simulated warrior managed to gain the upper hand, pinning Thorin before punching his jaw.

Tasting blood, Thorin growled before swinging his legs up around the male's neck from behind and flipping them over. He quickly released his opponent and stood. He waited for the warrior to charge again.

Just as the warrior moved toward him, the program paused. After two beeps, the AI system said, "Pilot Nahreen wishes to talk with you. Do you wish to receive?"

Thorin wiped the blood from his lips and cursed. He'd barely started to appease his violent side. He answered, "Allow it and cease program."

As the room faded to a light gray once more, Nahrenn's voice echoed in the room. "We're approaching the asteroid field, sir."

"I thought it was hours away?"

"Yes, General. However, the asteroid field is…moving in an unpredictable manner. I thought you'd want to be notified and see it for yourself."

Thorin's irritation eased. "I'll be there as soon as I can. End transmission."

Silence filled the room and Thorin went to the hidden compartment near the door to retrieve a towel. As he wiped away the sweat and blood from his encounter, he tried to recall a previous occurrence of when an asteroid field, or even a lone one, had moved unpredictably.

However, by the time he deposited the soiled towel in another compartment to be cleaned, he hadn't remembered anything from his years onboard starships or from his schooling.

While he would never wish for an opponent to appear and endanger his people, Thorin was grateful for the distraction. He might be able to forget about Vala for a few hours. The longer she spent alone and paralyzed, the more open she should be to accepting his offer. His father may have been a rapist, but Thorin would never lower himself to such a disgraceful act. He would wait for her consent.

After holstering his blaster gun on one hip and his short sword on the other, Thorin exited the room and headed for the command deck.

~~~

The longer Vala remained alone in Thorin's quarters, the more she plucked at his tattered blanket with her fingers. She hated being idle. Even during her rest periods inside the citadel, she had filled her time with flight simulations and rudimentary alien language courses. Neither of which could she do in the present without some sort of proper electronic equipment.

She'd gone back and forth about leaving the bed to search for a notescreen. If she left the bed, Thorin would know she'd probably gone snooping around since it was unlikely she could pull herself back up into it. He might be putting on a patient front for the time being, but violating yet another ship's code—invading a warrior's private space without permission—might trigger his temper.

And then who knew what would happen.

No. For once in her life, Vala was going to do something risky and forget about the consequences. Otherwise, she'd have to think about what Thorin might do to her if he tried to claim her.

Decision made, she used her arms to move to the edge of the mattress. When she leaned over, she could just reach the storage compartment built into the wall. She pressed against it and the drawer opened. Since it was empty, she now understood why Thorin hadn't put a thumbprint lock on it.

She scanned the room. Every set of quarters on board the ship had at least one notescreen for use. Given Thorin's status, she bet he had both a public and a private one.

She spoke aloud. "Computer, where's the public notescreen assigned to this room?"

"Public notescreen is located in storage bin 3A."

The computer's answer told her that Thorin hadn't taken away her AI access. At least, not yet.

The storage compartments were labeled in black lettering. Vala spotted 3A across the room.

Moving her body wasn't easy without the use of her legs, but the compartment was near enough to the floor that she should be able to reach up and retrieve the object.

When she had her legs hanging over the side of the bed, Vala hesitated. This was it. The mattress was built for a warrior male and the distance between the floor and the top was twice her own. If she had use of her legs, it wouldn't matter. But Vala didn't think she had the upper body strength to pull herself back up.

That meant Thorin would know she'd left the bed. Even if she wiped the memory of the notescreen and put it back where she found it, he would know she'd done something and probably interrogate her.

Her upbringing warred with her curiosity. Lessons as a child had drilled into her that Barren must be careful of their actions. Since their worth was almost nonexistent to the Kelderan race because of their inability to contribute to its survival, if they were deemed criminals or even perceived as ungrateful for the king's goodwill, they could be imprisoned or even executed. And if that weren't harsh enough, any Barren who mourned the loss of the erased members would suffer the same consequence.

In other words, the sentenced female in question became lost to history, never to be remembered.

For a few seconds, she merely sat still. She had no idea how lenient Thorin would be with her.

Then she dropped her gaze to her motionless legs. If she capitulated and accepted Thorin's claiming, she would probably lose her future anyway. No doubt he would banish her somewhere far away to protect whatever secret he was hiding. And yes, she had a suspicion the strangely addictive scent from earlier was key to what had happened to her, not to mention it probably revealed something about Thorin.

Something he didn't want anyone to know about.

The only way to possibly regain her future on Jasvar, as well as the power of choice regarding a male claiming her, meant that Vala had to find her own cure to her ailment, and quickly.

Ignoring any lingering doubts, Vala maneuvered onto her stomach and slid down the side of the bed. She landed in a heap and bit her lip to keep from crying out at her elbow hitting the hard floor. Once the pain faded, she used her arms to crawl across the room. By the time she reached the other side, a light sheen of sweat covered her upper body.

If she ever regained the use of her legs, Vala needed to add strength and endurance exercises to her regime. No doubt she'd need it on Jasvar, especially if Jasvar's female warrior leader—Taryn Demara—held up her promise to train Vala in the art of dagger wielding.

After catching her breath, Vala moved onto her rear and reached up for bin 3A. She pushed against it. Once it finished opening, she reached as high as she could and felt around the space. Her forefinger brushed against the edge of what she hoped was a notescreen. Pinching it between her fingers, she lifted and nearly cried out in relief when she saw the shiny, flat surface of the device.

Placing it on her lap, she quickly powered it up. When it didn't ask for a password, she clapped. She no longer had to wait at Thorin's mercy for information.

Logging into her virtual storage area, she ran a search on sudden paralysis of the legs. Over a hundred entries populated.

She scanned them and put them into different categories. Some were a result of plants, some gases, and other viruses. One of them was the odd one out and shared a keyword with the Brevkan.

Quickly dismissing the enemy race since Thorin was Kelderan, Vala went to work reading those related to gases. The strange smell was her first clue. She only hoped it was enough to find a remedy.

As it were, the clock was ticking. She had to complete her task before Thorin's return.

THE BARREN

Pushing aside thoughts of the male, Vala read the first entry.

~~~

Thorin finished his perusal of the asteroid-related data on the viewing panel on one side of the command deck. Nahrenn stood at his side. Thorin looked at the male. "Did you confirm this information?"

"Aye, sir. We ran several scans and launched a probe, which should be transmitting more detailed data back to us at any moment."

He looked back at the unusual statistics. If they were correct, the asteroids were moving in sporadic jerks, in no discernible pattern. Add in the fact they were closer together than they should be given past explorations of the star system by the Kelderans, Nahrenn had been right to interrupt his sparring session.

His first impression was that the objects gathered to their port side weren't asteroids at all, but some sort of living organism that had lain dormant for centuries. Some of Keldera's long-distance trading partners had mentioned similar situations. Thorin had always dismissed them as fabrications, used to entertain males on a long flight. Maybe he'd erred in doing so.

A different viewing panel beeped twice. The scientist manning the station said, "The probe's initial transmission has arrived."

Thorin moved to see the information. While he wasn't a trained scientist, all high-ranking officers in the Kelderan Army had sufficient knowledge to understand the basics.

He scanned the information and frowned. "Am I seeing this correctly?"

The science officer, Merctor, answered, "Yes, sir. Some of the objects are registering faint vibrations and even infinitesimal amounts of heat."

"Which means they aren't lifeless chunks of rock floating in space," Thorin stated.

"Correct, sir." Merctor looked from the viewing screen to Thorin. "In my professional opinion, we should inform headquarters on Keldera and request a research team as well as a few security escort fighters. If the asteroid-looking objects turn out to be enemies, a colony transport ship will become an easy, vulnerable target."

While all Kelderan starships had weapons and defenses, maneuvering a long colony ship and arming it for combat was akin to moving a mountain to construct a new road. It could be done, but it took time and a large amount of resources. By the time they moved into position, an enemy could have easily either captured or destroyed them.

Yes, the colony ship had a half-dozen small fighters to help with self-defense, but they might not be enough. Since this was Keldera's first attempt at a colony, there were many mistakes that needed to be rectified in the future. Thorin didn't think the rush job to launch the colonists had helped in planning, either. Thorin was at fault as much as anyone else. There hadn't been any enemies in the flight path from Keldera to Jasvar in decades. Peace had made everyone reckless.

Thorin took a step back and clasped his hands behind his back. He spoke to Nahreen. "Ensure we're at a presumably safe distance from the unknown objects, but still within the limits of our most powerful weapons." When his pilot nodded his assent, he moved his gaze to Merctor. "We should still be within secure communications range. Transmit your findings and notes to headquarters and ask for their orders. However, as we wait for their response, continue to monitor all probe transmissions and keep me abreast of the information. I will be in my quarters, devising strategies."

"Aye, sir," Merctor answered.

Satisfied his crew could handle the tasks set, he turned back toward the main viewing screen. Thorin preferred ships and males he could see to barely in-motion objects. Most advanced lifeforms made mistakes that a general could pounce upon.

However, if the small asteroid-looking objects were of lower intelligence, they might act on instinct alone, and that could make them extremely unpredictable.

After another long second, Thorin exited the command deck and headed toward his quarters. He hadn't lied about devising ways to handle the asteroid-like objects if they attacked, but until the ship was put on a high alert or was attacked, he also needed to ensure his charge was doing okay. Despite the circumstances that had placed Vala into his care, Thorin would do his best to take care of the female.

Realizing she'd be more comfortable if she could move about, he changed course. She should do well enough while he finally ordered a hover chair and put in an order for extra-large portions of all forthcoming meals.

The female needed the food, especially if she were to accept his claim and receive his wild Brevkan urges. He only needed to orgasm once to reverse the paralysis, but he doubted he'd be able to stop until exhaustion took them both.

He only hoped she would allow him to blindfold her and tie her up. Otherwise, he might witness her fear as she discovered what he truly was. And as selfish as it may be, he didn't want the image of Vala cringing in horror to haunt him for the rest of his life.

Thorin nearly missed a step. He didn't know why he wasted his time thinking of the female. His ship's safety was far more important. He had a feeling that discovering a possession could affect his ability to function normally as well.

And that was bad news. Thorin couldn't risk screwing up or people might end up dead.

He'd just have to make his visit quick and find another place to better study the data from the probes. He wouldn't allow the female to affect his ability to lead.

Chapter Five

Vala was starting to regret her decision to drop to the floor.

After hours of staring at her notescreen, she hadn't learned anything of value to remedy her situation. On top of that, the chill of the bare composite floor had seeped through the thin material of her flowing brown dress and into her bones.

Rubbing her bare arms for warmth, she eyed the replicator machine. She could easily ask the device to make her a blanket and pillow. True, she would have to clasp the edge of the receiving portal and pull herself up to retrieve them, but her request could send a warning message to security if Thorin had indeed revoked her clearance for his quarters. And because she was no longer authorized to enter Thorin's room, she would be placed into a cell and most likely convicted of trespassing and invading an officer's privacy.

As much as she wanted to believe Thorin's vow to help her, she wasn't about to entrust her freedom to a single salute.

She shivered and released her arms to drag her legs into a position where she could hug them against her chest. With each passing hour, her restraint and training had morphed into irritation and a desire to scold Thorin for abandoning her. Even if he disliked her, which would be odd since he wanted to claim her, Kelderan males were supposed to assist females in need.

But then again, she was merely a Barren.

Placing her forehead on her knees, she closed her eyes and let out a long sigh. Her trip to Jasvar should've been uneventful. In all her thirty-two years, she'd never been in a predicament such as the one she was currently in. Maybe she was being punished for wanting more than any Barren should have. Namely, a future of her own and the opportunity to emerge from the shadows.

And to think she'd given up her home and left behind everyone who loved her.

Only through years of conditioning to never display emotion outside of the citadel did she prevent herself from crying.

She had no idea how much time had passed or that she'd even fallen asleep, but the door opened and she jerked her head upright. Blinking at the male in the doorway, she murmured, "Thorin?"

He waited for the door to lock closed before he replied, "Using my name instead of rank is against protocol. That's even putting aside the fact you're on the floor with one of my possessions. Both are violations with consequences."

Vala was cold, tired, and for a brief moment, no longer cared about rules and restrictions on her kind. Since he already had ample reason to lock her up, she decided that Thorin needed to understand his behavior was unacceptable.

She pointed a forefinger at him. "You abandoned me without a word about what happened. I had given you the benefit of the doubt and restrained myself from judging you. But it appears that you're without honor. I might not be a warrior or valued member of society, but I am a living being. You have no right to treat me as a pet, humoring me when you feel the urge."

Thorin's eyes glowed before returning to normal. If she weren't cold and upset, she might think twice about it.

Instead, she frowned as Thorin finally spoke again. "I am as honorable a male such as me can be. But you, Vala Yarlen, are walking a fine line."

"Why? You should be happy. Now you can threaten to report me to security unless I allow you to claim me." She threw her arms wide. "Then proceed. The sooner we can part ways, the better."

He grunted. "No."

She frowned. "What? Why? I don't understand your response."

He closed the distance between them and crouched down in front of her. "You must accept me willingly."

She searched his gaze. She swore she saw a mixture of anger and shame in his eyes. But what would a general in the Kelderan Army have to be ashamed about, she had no idea.

His voice was low when he added, "However, I believe an innocent such as yourself needs a little coaxing. Forgive me."

Before she could do more than open her mouth, he lowered his lips to hers.

~~~

Thorin had expected to return to his quarters and find the Barren asleep in his bed. He would've found release in the cleaning area once more before gathering his personal notescreen and exiting to a safer place to do his work, while he waited to hear back from headquarters.

However, the instant he saw the female huddled on the floor as if she were a slave awaiting her master's whim to ease her discomfort, something had snapped inside of him.

His mother had been shamed for having a child without a male lord. She'd tried to hide it well, but Thorin had seen a similarly defeated look and posture in his mother many times when he was a child. Vala didn't deserve the same, Barren female or not, especially considering his own shameful origins had put the female in her current position.

Vala's anger only deepened his regret at what he'd done to her. Right then and there, he decided the claiming should be a pleasant one for her. If she allowed it, he would treasure her feminine body for what time he had. Because of the rules and restrictions of Kelderan society, neither one of them would ever find a lifelong partner—her for being infertile and him for carrying enemy blood—but they could at least enjoy each other for a short time. Dalliances between soldiers and Barren were common.

As he stared into her wide, black eyes, he suddenly wanted her to look at him with befuddled enjoyment instead of anger. Rumors said she never dallied with warriors. Maybe she had no idea of how pleasant the lead up to a claiming could be. He would have to show her.

He murmured his warning and kissed her.

With her mouth open, he easily slid his tongue between her lips. Vala stilled, but as he stroked his tongue against hers, her muscles relaxed gradually. He should pull away and not take advantage of her innocence. However, Thorin dared to thread his fingers through her soft, white hair and tilted her head for better access. When a small, cold hand touched his chest, the desire to warm her body and take care of her coursed through every cell of his being.

Images of her sleeping on his chest with her long hair fanned out behind her and a smile on her face flashed inside his

56

mind. It was as if he'd proven his worth and had earned the right to keep her.

He pulled back at that thought. The heat in Vala's eyes, combined with her kiss-bruised lips, sent a rush of blood to his cock. What he wouldn't give to claim such innocence and purity for his own.

Not that he ever could. He couldn't afford to allow anyone close enough to learn his secret. Thorin's career meant everything to him. Not even an innocent, willing Barren with a soft touch would persuade him to give it up.

"That is only a taste of what is to come," he stated.

She removed her hand from his chest and he fought the urge to guide it back. Her voice was husky as she said, "Oh."

He did something he hadn't done for a long time, and smiled. "With your permission, I can reveal another step toward a claiming. It would require you on the bed."

For a long moment, she gazed into his eyes with an unreadable expression. As the silence stretched, his smile faded. She was no doubt cold, hungry, and exhausted. He was a selfish bastard to revel in her kiss and ask for more.

Before she could say anything, Thorin scooped her up, walked over, and deposited her to the bed. Without a word, he went to the replicator machine. "Computer, synthesize a large, warm blanket. Size must accommodate a warrior's bed."

"Working," the computer stated as its internal parts hummed with activity.

He was determined to keep his back turned and allow the female to recover from his probably unwanted attentions. But he swore he could feel her gaze on his back.

Her soft voice finally filled the room. "What's the next step?"

He kept his back to her and shook his head. "Forgive me for mentioning it. The honorable thing is to serve you a meal and allow you to rest."

A part of him wanted her to dismiss his words and demand for more.

However, the longer she remained quiet, the more he wondered if she'd seen his eyes glow and had determined him to be something other than what he said.

No. There was no way she knew about Brevkan biology. True, all Barren were trained in medical sciences, but few bothered to study alien races.

Of course, Vala had surprised him in the past. He only hoped she wouldn't do the same regarding his father's people.

~~~

Vala's heart thundered inside her chest as she gazed at Thorin's broad, light blue back and the markings scattered across his skin.

She'd heard stories about how a male's kiss could warm your body and alert the senses. However, Vala had always dismissed them. She may not have dallied and bared her body to any of the warriors, but she had kissed a male or two inside the citadel. Recovering patients sometimes forgot her station and misinterpreted gratitude as desire.

But none of the brief kisses had made her want to wrap her arms around a male and feel his skin against hers. Touching her lips, she could still remember Thorin's strong, demanding actions. While generals weren't allowed to take a bride, they usually had Barren mistresses. With Thorin's skill, she wondered why he didn't have one.

The replicator machine finally completed the blanket. Thorin took it and walked to the bed. As he gently laid it over her body, his heat was near enough to warm her face.

If only he would look at her, she might gather the strength to ask for his attentions once more. Considering her research had revealed nothing of value and a claiming would allow her to walk again, she should do whatever it took to hasten the process.

Just as Thorin finished arranging the warm material over her body, she reached out and gently touched his face. She wasn't brave enough to voice her curiosity again, so she stroked his warm skin.

Thorin froze and kept his gaze averted.

Maybe she'd crossed a line. Touching a general's body without permission was taboo, and she'd done it more than once now.

Removing her hand, she started to turn away when Thorin's deep voice murmured, "Why did you stop?"

She did her best not to frown, but failed. "My touch was too familiar. I apologize."

One of his long fingers took her chin and gently forced her head to meet his eyes again. "I encouraged the action earlier. If anyone is at fault, it is me."

"B-but you're a general. You aren't supposed to have faults."

He smiled, and the crinkles around his eyes made her heart pound. When Thorin Jarrell wasn't scowling, he was handsome. And dare she say it, he looked as if he would be kind to her.

Before she could wonder where that thought came from, Thorin replied, "A general is a male like any other. Anyone who pretends to be flawless isn't worthy of the rank." He moved his thumb to just below her bottom lip and ran it back and forth. The motion relaxed her muscles. He continued, "I can't read your mind, Vala. You must speak the truth to me. Always."

She loved the way her name rolled over his tongue in his deep voice. "It's not a Barren's place to speak her mind."

His stroking ceased and he gently tightened his grip on her chin. "When we are alone, you are a female, nothing more. And despite propaganda to the contrary, most females speak their minds in private. I expect the same of you."

Of all the scenarios she had imagined about her trip aboard the colony ship, having a warrior—a general, no less—asking her to be honest hadn't been one of them.

She didn't expect Thorin's invitation to last, but she still answered, "Okay."

He shook his head, and she wondered if she'd made a mistake. "Okay isn't enough. You must tell me what you want. I can't take care of you if you don't."

"But only the Barren takes care of another Barren."

An emotion flashed in his eyes, but it disappeared before she could name it. "I will be the one taking care of you. As you rightly pointed out, you have worth, Vala Yarlen. And until you are hearty and whole again, I will see to your every need."

The fierceness of his tone made her pause. She almost wanted to believe he spoke the truth.

But she quickly pushed aside the foolish thought. Thorin only wished to claim her body and would say whatever it took to complete the task.

She must've remained silent too long because he spoke up again. "You're tired and need rest. Allow me one final kiss and I will leave you alone for a few hours. When you awake, tell the computer you're hungry and food will be sent directly."

A small flutter of disappointment churned her stomach, but she ignored it. Time alone would allow her to remember her station and possibly do more research.

Then her gaze fell to his mouth and she swallowed. Her dreams would no doubt be full of his hot, firm lips.

"Lay down," Thorin ordered.

She complied, and he flipped back the blanket to expose her upper body. "W-what are you doing?"

He traced her collarbone. "Kissing you. Have you changed your mind?"

Her curiosity overcame her fear. "N-no." He raised his brows, and she said more firmly, "No."

"Confidence suits you. I hope you show it more often."

Before she could speak, he leaned down and stopped above one of her breasts. Despite being clad, his hot breath made her nipple harden and the secret place between her thighs pulsed. He murmured, "Do you still want this?"

She didn't hesitate, "Yes."

"Good."

With a growl, he took her nipple into his mouth and gently caressed the nub through her dress. Vala cried out as pleasure coursed through her body.

From her own explorations of her body, she knew what teasing and tweaking the hard nub could do. But her previous pleasure paled in comparison to Thorin's heat and attentions.

~~~

As Thorin drew Vala's nipple deeper into his mouth, the female's hands threaded through his hair. As she clung to him, he licked and nibbled, loving how Vala dug her nails into his scalp. Before long, he hoped she would dig them into his back.

His baser half wanted her to draw blood and leave marks, but Thorin quickly dismissed the idea. He would never make such a dishonorable request.

Instead, he listened to Vala's moans and whimpers to judge how close she was to orgasm. His own cock was hard against his trousers, but for once, his instinct didn't demand him to spread the female's thighs and take her until he was sated.

Not wanting to focus on the irregularity, he bit her nipple harder. He longed to rip her dress and feel the tight, puckered skin against his tongue. However, he wanted her to have some dignity when he was finished.

Still, his Brevkan urges wanted him to caress her skin, touch her heat, and revel in her unique feminine scent. She was his possession—there should be no hesitation.

He growled, and Vala cried out at the vibration. She tensed before relaxing under him. Thorin nearly ran a hand up her thigh to touch her wetness.

But as she released his hair and tensed again, he knew Vala's temporary abandonment had ended. Even now, she was probably retreating to the protocols demanded of the Barren and feeling embarrassed when she shouldn't be.

Not wanting to push the female too far too quickly, Thorin released her nipple and counted to five. He wouldn't risk her seeing his glowing eyes again. While his body would emit a blue light at orgasm, his eyes betrayed him with lesser levels of desire.

He finally looked up, but Vala looked to the side, her cheeks flushed from her release.

Her innocence only reminded him of why he needed to be delicate with her or Vala might run away as soon as she had regained use of her legs.

And for some reason, Thorin didn't want that.

"Look at me, Vala." When she didn't comply, he added, "Please."

She took a deep breath and met his gaze again. What he wouldn't give to see her wild abandonment as pleasure took over.

Too bad he'd never be able to do so without giving away his heritage. "There's no shame in receiving pleasure from a male. Embrace it, Vala, and your release will become more powerful."

"It-it's not that."

He nearly growled at her stammer, but somehow resisted. "Then what? And remember, I need the truth. If I did something distasteful, you must tell me."

She looked away. "It wasn't distasteful." She paused and whispered, "Quite the opposite."

He softened his voice. "Tell me."

Even though she didn't look at him, her voice filled the room again. "It was the first time a male gave me pleasure, and I know the expectation is that I should return the favor, but without the use of my legs, I can't bow down and take you into my...mouth."

The image of Vala's hot, wet mouth around his cock only made him harder. Still, Thorin managed to growl out, "Toss aside any expectations or rules taught to you by the other Barren. I'll give you leave to explore what you wish, but at your own pace. But later, not now." He moved off the bed. "For the time being, you need to rest. The command deck should need me any minute now."

"I'm sorry to disappoint you, sir."

63

"No. Don't call me 'sir' when we're alone. My name is Thorin. Say it."

"Thorin."

He nodded. "Good. I shall return later."

Turning, Thorin retrieved his personal notescreen from a high-up storage bin and exited the room. As he took the long way to the elevator to cool both his cock and to tame his pounding heart, Thorin ran a hand through his hair. The action only reminded him of Vala's touch earlier, so light and delicate. The complete opposite of him.

What he wouldn't give to have such a pure-hearted female in his life. But that wasn't his destiny. Thorin's reason for existence was to protect his mother's people and prove they were his as well. Keeping the colony ship safe was one step in that direction. He needed to stay away from Vala to better focus on his duty, no matter how much he itched to do the opposite.

Yes, a Brevkan's possession definitely affected the male responsible because Thorin had no explanation for his recent actions. Being gentle and patient was foreign to him.

And bastard that he was, he hoped to prolong the feelings by trying to keep Vala around for a while.

Chapter Six

As Vala lay on her side, she knew she should be sleeping to recharge. But her mind whirred with one thought after another, meshed together with memories of her recent encounter.

Despite the fact Thorin was a muscled, hardened warrior, when she'd threaded her fingers in his hair, she'd felt in control. Every tug or scratch had prodded him to do more of what she liked.

And considering Vala had lacked any real power her whole life, the experience had been exhilarating. For a few minutes, the world had faded away. She wasn't a Barren and Thorin wasn't a general. No, they'd merely been male and female. Everything else hadn't mattered.

Vala pulled her legs closer and curled more into a ball on the bed. She needed to be careful. More than a few of her Barren compatriots had developed feelings for their various warriors. All of the arrangements had ended in heartbreak and confinement to the citadel. Displaying need or want was unfavorable. If she did the same, she could be confined until the ship returned to Keldera and banished to the citadel. She'd then never get to Jasvar.

However, there was still a way to solve her problems. If she found her own cure, she could reach her goal for certain. Less time with Thorin meant less time for desiring or wanting more.

The only real threat was if Thorin showed any more kindness and caring toward her, she might lose her resolve to do whatever it took to join the colony.

No. She refused to let that happen. Vala rose on her elbows and was about to figure a way down to the floor again to reach the public notescreen when she noticed the device on the shelf next to the bed. Thorin must've retrieved it at the same time he'd scooped her off the floor.

Surely he wouldn't have done so if he wanted to deny her access.

Vala plucked the object from the shelf and powered it back on. As it did so, the memory of Thorin finally looking up at her after her orgasm, a light blue glow emitting from his eyes, came back to her. After seeing it three times, she wondered if it was something a Kelderan male did when being intimate. Thorin was her first experience and she hated the unknown.

As the search prompt appeared on screen, she hesitated but finally typed in "male glowing eyes" into the space. Only one source came up and she frowned at the title. It was one she hadn't seen since her initial training years: *Brevkan Prisoners of War: Observations and Biological Discoveries.*

Tapping the resource, the relevant entry appeared. She read:

Even with sufficient care and sustenance, Brevkan warriors become antsy and irritable the longer they remain imprisoned. They soon disregard the observers and cameras—or even cell mates—and simply bring themselves to orgasm several times a day. While it's not unusual for a warrior to ease sexual frustration, the disturbing aspects occur leading up to and during orgasm. Their eyes glow the color of their skin, be it blue, red, or even yellow. However, when they find release, their bodies emit a light of the same color.

This is distinct to the Brevkan race, or at least according to the records and observations we have of other alien races encountered by the Kelderan Army.

While no prisoner will answer questions as to why they emit the light, many of the scientists in the facility believe it's to do with their pride in claiming a female and showing it off to their compatriots.

Still, it is merely a theory. Maybe persistent questioning will yield clearer answers.

Vala laid down the notescreen. The words "distinct to the Brevkan race" repeated inside her head.

Logically, that meant Thorin was Brevkan. However, his light blue skin tone, his markings, and even his facial features looked Kelderan. She was missing a vital piece of information.

She should be horrified that a partially, at least, Brevkan male had touched her. The war between the Kelderans and Brevkans had lasted decades. Vala had been a child when peace had been attained, but horrifying stories of rape, murder, and pillaging still circulated.

Vala stilled. Maybe Thorin was a result of rape. But if that were the case, she had no idea how he'd been allowed to serve in the Kelderan Army, let alone attain the rank of general. Even if his intentions were true, no soldier would listen to a half-Brevkan officer. Too many families had been torn apart or even lost during the Brevkan wars. Many people wanted revenge.

Then she remembered the sole Brevkan-related entry during her initial search for her sudden onset paralysis. Bringing up the search, she found the entry and clicked. Taking a deep breath, she read the entry from an official doctor's report:

Today marked the third confirmed unwanted pregnancy in recent weeks. The female had been raped during one of the Brevkan raids on our city. While the act itself is dishonorable and far too common in recent months, the female's detailed account leading up to the tragic event provided new information that I feel is relevant to all medical science.

The female claimed that she detected an unusual scent during her walk to her uncle's house. Unable to resist, she followed it to the source where she suddenly collapsed and fell unconscious. When she awoke, she couldn't move her legs. Even crawling with her arms, she didn't get far. The warrior returned to the area with a colleague. I will omit the struggle and simply jump to the startling end. Once the warrior left her to die, her legs worked once more. I have run a series of blood tests and am waiting for the biological make-up reports. Maybe if some of the paralyzing agent remains in her bloodstream, we can devise a serum to counter these effects. If the females carry a pill or vial of the counteragent, then they may be able to escape the enemy in the future.

The log jumped to a week later:

While my patient's identity will remain anonymous, I'm including the biological readings and some of my theories of how to counter the effects of the Brevkan paralysis component. I hope others will join me in finding a solution since we have no idea how long the war will continue. No female should carry the shame and repulsive genetic material of our enemies.

Barely glancing at the chemical compounds and formulas, Vala lowered the notescreen. Not because she couldn't understand them, she could. But she wasn't sure what to make of the doctor's account.

Unless Thorin had devised his own version of a Brevkan's paralyzing compound, which was unlikely, he was indeed part Brevkan.

More than that, he had to know about his parentage. Too many anomalies would show in his adolescent years, if her memory served her from her training, as a Brevkan approached adulthood.

And either he had done a flawless job of keeping his secret from anyone else, or there was something much deeper going on.

For some reason, she looked at the notescreen and reread the final line: *No female should carry the shame and repulsive genetic material of our enemies.*

The bias and judgment resonated with what Vala had endured her whole life. She may not be an enemy, but most Kelderans viewed her as a waste of resources and space.

In other words, she and Thorin both knew what it was to feel shame about simply being alive. Even if Thorin had preserved his secret, he was aware of the truth. He had said something about being the best a male like him could be, which made a lot more sense in light of her recent discoveries.

Vala leaned her head against the wall and stared at the ceiling. Logically, she should wash her hands of Thorin and try to use the doctor's formulas as a starting point to regain her freedom without him. And yet, a part of her wanted to find out the whole truth of Thorin's story.

She'd never imagined finding someone who could be more isolated than her kind, but at least she could live and love those who shared her defect. Thorin couldn't exactly seek out other Kelderans with a Brevkan parent and talk about his differences or challenges. Others would discover the enemy heritage and either seek revenge through murder or simply ostracize the targeted individuals.

No, anyone with a Brevkan father would probably risk their life to keep the dark secret.

While she couldn't do anything about how society viewed Thorin and others like him, she might be able to help a sole person. Despite her own wants, Vala had been trained to save and heal lives. Surely there was something she could do to help Thorin smile more or to at least convince him not to despise himself. She had no proof, but his words and actions made her think he detested his father's people.

The only question was whether learning about Thorin's past and probing to find out if she could assist him was more important than quietly surviving the journey to Jasvar without incident. The decision should be easy, but as she reread the entry about the Brevkan, Vala wavered.

~~~

As Thorin waited for headquarters to respond to his report, it took every bit of strength he possessed not to tap his fingers against the arm of his chair on the command deck.

Taking care of his ship was his first priority, but he couldn't help but wonder if Vala rested peacefully or not.

Apart from his mother, Thorin had never dared dream of caring for another person. Allowing people to get close to him could only end in disaster.

And yet, he couldn't forget Vala's dark eyes and long, white hair. She didn't have a choice but to allow him to take care of her for the next little while.

Of course, his Brevkan half only wanted to claim her whenever he was in the same room with the female. However, his honor refused to allow that to happen. He had made several vows to resist until she asked for more. Even if she never did, he would find a way to follow her wishes. The second he gave in to his barbaric half would mark the end of who he'd worked so hard to become.

The science officer Merctor's voice interrupted his thoughts. "General, about ten of the asteroid-like objects have vanished."

Thorin waved toward the front. "Magnify the screen, Fyzar."

Fyzar, the command deck's ranking operations manager, complied. But as Thorin studied the image, he couldn't tell the difference; there were too many of the asteroid-looking objects. "Can you share the coordinates of the missing objects to Fyzar so he can highlight their locations for us, Merctor?"

Merctor complied and a minute later, Thorin counted twelve little dots on the screen and said, "Are there any residual fuel trails to calculate their trajectory?"

"No," Merctor stated. "Nor are there heat trails or anything else to judge where they went. Only a handful of races has the ability to cloak their appearance so completely."

And Keldera didn't possess the same technology. "Is cloaking the only reasonable theory?"

"Teleportation is possible, but if it were used, it's unlike anything Keldera possesses," Merctor answered. "I'll have to analyze the area further to see if there is anything to point to teleportation use or not."

If someone had used teleportation, then Thorin's ship would be at a disadvantage. Keldera didn't have many ways to block teleportation abilities for large spaceships, and for what few options existed, none were aboard his ship.

And if they did start taking objects or people from his ship, it would be a declaration of war.

Not wanting to jump the gun and make a mistake that could cost thousands of lives aboard the ship, Thorin focused on obtaining the facts. "I want a list of all races rumored to have either type of technology. In addition, continue multiple sweeps of the area to ensure there isn't an infinitesimal trace overlooked in haste. Also, share all of this information with headquarters."

Fyzar spoke up. "Headquarters is calling us now, sir."

Thorin sat up taller in his chair. "Double-check that the line is secure before accepting their transmission. I need to divulge the latest development."

After a few seconds, Fyzar replied, "Secure, sir. Patching through the general."

A beat later, the image of the second most senior general in the Kelderan Army, Corvel Naytah, appeared on the main view screen of the command deck. The general spoke first. "We've received your information concerning the erratic objects you encountered and have also reviewed your request. As a precaution, we will grant you two fighters to escort you all the way to Jasvar."

"Aye, sir," Thorin said. "However, there is something else you should know." Thorin explained the disappearance of the ten objects and continued, "Do you still wish for us to head toward Jasvar, sir? Or should we return to Keldera until the objects are better understood and/or neutralized?"

The general glanced down, no doubt looking at the most recent details Thorin's ship had sent. Looking back up, he spoke again. "Hold your position until the fighters arrive and then continue the journey to Jasvar. However, I'm going to increase your escort to ten ships. If more of the objects disappear, then send a secure message flagged as urgent. You may have to take more drastic measures if the need arises."

"Drastic measure" was army code-speak for attacking an enemy with everything you had and possibly evacuating the civilians.

Thorin didn't like making offensive maneuvers without knowing all the facts. He just needed to have his crew focus their energies on the asteroid-like objects so that they could gather more information. "Understood, sir."

"Good. Headquarters will reach out to you if needed. The fighter ships should be there soon. Prepare your vessel for both the journey and a possible attack. End transmission."

The view screen returned to a scene of the asteroid-like objects at some distance. Thorin didn't hesitate to order, "Command deck to engineering, prepare engine warm-up sequence."

Enishi, head of engineering, answered, "Aye, aye, sir."

After a full stop, the engines would take half an hour to restart. Thorin only hoped nothing happened before then. He'd made a huge error in following protocol without further digging into the situation; he should've kept his engines at half power.

He could blame his Brevkan instinct for a millennia, but Thorin had let his concern for Vala cloud his brain. He would need to ensure he didn't repeat that mistake.

Since food and a hover chair would be delivered shortly anyway, he would leave her alone until his ship was out of danger. His own wants didn't matter. The needs of the thousands outweighed that of one male.

Looking at Merctor, he ordered, "Send several more probes and see if one can get close enough for a better surface reading, if not a sample of the material itself."

Merctor murmured confirmation of the order and Thorin moved his gaze to his pilot, Nahreen. "Research and ready evasive maneuvers that can be performed with only partial engine capacity. Even if we can't flee, there has to be a planet, moon, or other large object we can hide behind and use as a preliminary barrier until our own shield capabilities are restored."

"Aye, aye, sir," Nahreen answered.

Thorin keyed in a sequence on the screen on his armchair and brought up the detailed specs of his ship. While he had studied them in depth prior to his departure, there could always be something that he had overlooked. And when an unforeseen situation or attack occurred, the smallest detail could be the difference between life and death.

Chapter Seven

After three days with no sign of Thorin, Vala had contemplated escaping.

On the fifth day, she made it as far as the door, but cowardice made her use the hover chair to float back to the bed before she could attempt to open a panel to study the electronics.

By the seventh day, she deemed walking more important than escaping and had thrown herself into the formulas she'd found in the doctor's entry about the Brevkan. She even had a list of what she needed to make her first test serum.

If it were at all possible, she would walk again. As it'd always been, she could only rely on herself or her mother, but since her mother was back on Keldera, Vala would have to fend for herself.

And to think she'd felt sorry for Thorin and had wanted to show him some compassion. All her sympathy had brought was isolation and restrictions. The only resources she had were those she had downloaded the first day of her captivity and whatever was available on the public notescreen in the room. Not even the AI system would answer most of her questions. All Vala knew was that the replicator worked when asking for emergency provisions, but nothing more.

Oh, and she could confirm one more thing—the ship wasn't currently under attack. In that scenario, a red alert would sound in all quarters regardless of the restrictions placed on them. If it reached the point of an evacuation, her door would also open automatically, too.

In the end, she was a prisoner more than she had ever been in her life. As a Barren, she was able to move around freely and access the public data resources whenever she wanted. Now, she couldn't leave a room and had to be granted even basic privileges.

Stupid Thorin. She knew he was a general and was busy, but a simple message saying he had military matters to attend to would've been nice.

Instead, Thorin's absence confirmed how he had lied to her about saying she had worth. If he truly meant it, he would've kept her abreast of events and not kept her confined and isolated. His actions signaled she was little more than a pet or plaything to be taken out when he felt the need.

For the first time in a long time, Vala felt foolish.

"Well, that's what you get for trying to see the good in people," she muttered to herself. Vala would never reveal her theories surrounding Thorin's heritage since that would be petty and dishonorable. But if he still expected for her to wait around and welcome him with open arms, not to mention expect her to participate in a claiming, he had a surprise waiting for him.

If he ever showed his face.

With a growl, she looked back to her notescreen. She needed something to help calm her down and make her forget about the tall, blue-skinned general and his passionate kisses.

Vala pulled up the long-range communication message from Princess Kalahn and Taryn Demara. It had arrived her first day, before her communications had been severed. The message reminded her of why reaching Jasvar was important.

The video played and she smiled at the friendly faces.

Kalahn waved. "Hello, Vala. I'm still awaiting your arrival to help set up the female training program for the new colonists. Thanks to Taryn, my brother finally capitulated."

Taryn's Kelderan was broken, which was to be expected since Common Earth Language, or CEL, was her native tongue. "Easy. He like me."

Kalahn shook her head. "What she's trying to say is that she tried using her feminine wiles to convince Kason of my idea. When that didn't work, she surprised him with a dagger. He changed his mind fairly quickly." Kalahn spoke fast in CEL, which Vala had a hard time following, but Taryn snorted at the princess. *Kalahn finally continued in Kelderan, "I know you'll probably be busy on the colony ship, but make sure to keep up your flight simulation skills. While shuttles and ships are rare on Jasvar at the moment, your ship should be bringing supplies to help start up the industry here, albeit using Jasvar-specific resources."*

Taryn added, "Happy see you. We wait."

Kalahn spoke up again. "Yes, we're both anxious to see you. Sitting around and planning is boring. New colonists will definitely spice up the planet."

"No trouble Kalahn," Taryn said sternly.

Kalahn winked. "Just a little." Taryn understood and rolled her eyes. *Kalahn looked back to the recording device. "Before I go, we have a little present for you, Vala. See the secure attachment. We'll greet you when you finally arrive. Take care and try not to let Thorin get under your skin. Yes, we heard he's in charge of the colony transport ship. Just remember that he doesn't like anyone."*

The video ended. Even though Vala had seen the attachment before, she wanted something to distract her from thinking about Thorin, so she opened it again. A section of the Keldera-Jasvar Colony Agreement was highlighted:

All laws and rules specific to the Barren are null and void on Jasvar. This includes clothing restrictions, occupational limitations, and restricted housing options. They will be subject to the same laws as the rest of the Kelderan colonists.

She traced the words with her fingers and her eyes grew wet. The role of the Barren on the new colony had been unclear. But Princess Kalahn had come through with her promise to give Vala more freedom.

The video and attachment made Vala glad she hadn't given herself to Thorin and risked her place on the colony. There was much more than a future on Jasvar—she had a new start in life to be the female she wanted to be, rather than the one expected of her.

Not even a year ago would she have dared to think such a treasonous thought. Vala had a long way to go with regards to recognizing and voicing her opinions without hesitation, but she was becoming more honest by the day.

The one good thing about Thorin was he had also helped with that aspect. She might even prove to herself she could speak her mind if he appeared in front of her.

She wouldn't wait around for him, though. There were more important things to worry about.

Pulling up her formula notes, she went over the calculations and ingredients again. The hard part would be in obtaining them to perform her tests, but she was working on a plan. Because no matter what, she was going to help Princess Kalahn and Taryn on Jasvar. And to do that, she needed to walk again.

THE BARREN

~~~

Thorin should be grateful that events had remained quiet and peaceful ever since he'd given the order to resume their journey with the fighter escorts seven days ago. Yet as he pinned his virtual sparring partner to the ground and the hologram signaled defeat, his tension hadn't ease with any amount of physical exertion. If anything, each encounter had only heightened it.

"Computer, end program."

As his opponent and the yellow walls faded to the gray walls and floor of the actual room, Thorin stood and wiped the sweat from his brow. Despite his increased meditation practices as well as pleasuring himself several times a day, his hard cock pounded against his trousers, as if daring him to find the female who was their possession and to claim her as soon as possible.

No. He wouldn't allow his Brevkan urges to control his life. Vala was a female of worth who needed his protection, not the quick claiming that would probably end up hurting her.

Besides, once he had another taste of Vala, he didn't think he'd be able to leave her side until he completely sated his urges. That would only increase the risk to all five thousand-plus people aboard the colony transport ship if they were attacked and he couldn't respond properly.

Walking toward the exit, he stopped and retrieved a towel from a secret bin to wipe his body. No doubt she'd be angry with him for keeping her locked in his quarters, but she should eventually see that his actions were merely to protect her from something worse than an attack or even himself—the other Barren.

By now, he'd had to report to Vala's superiors that she was his personal mistress for the journey. And as much as he ignored the rumors and actions amongst the Barren aboard the ship unless it threatened the greater harmony of all, he knew others would be jealous of Vala's temporary station. While he was confident that she could handle simple jealousy, sometimes jealousy could resort to violence or even poisoning.

If others found out about her paralysis, she would become a target, especially since most of the Barren aboard the ship weren't from Vala's original citadel base. The rivalries amongst citadels intensified aboard starships; mistresses were often awarded favors. Their competition for a general's eye was nearly as strong as the competitiveness between merchant chains or even some warriors to thwart their compatriots.

His Kelderan upbringing meant that he would rather die than allow harm to come to her. Isolation was her best form of protection. Yes, he'd keep her that way until their arrival. Then he could quickly claim her and send the Barren on her way.

Tossing the towel into the dirty receptacle, he exited the room and headed toward his temporary quarters near the command deck. To keep up his ruse of taking Vala as a mistress, he went every evening toward his originally assigned quarters and entered the room adjacent his, which had a secret passage. But his main living space was currently down the corridor from his seat of command.

The instant he stood inside the cleaning area of his temporary quarters and the hot spray caressed his body, he gripped his swollen cock and closed his eyes. A picture of Vala, nude and on fours, filled his mind. As he stroked himself, he imagined taking her hard and making her scream. Unlike his visions before meeting the female, he didn't see himself covered in blood.

To be honest, all his visions recently had centered around the female as if he were merely a male and she a female, with violence nowhere to be seen. Not even battles or fights with other males had made an appearance.

Even in her absence, she'd become a sanctuary.

After spending his last drop, Thorin placed his hands on the walls and let the water wash away the results of his pleasuring.

For a long moment, he wondered what it'd be like to have a female who always kept his rages and violent urges at bay. Not only that, but one to share his secret and help relieve the burden he carried. With his mother's memories gone and the rest of his family dead, he and the royal family were the only ones who knew about Thorin's father. And he wasn't exactly on friendly—let alone speaking—terms with any of the Kelderan royals.

Vala could become that person.

Too bad he would return with the colony ship to Keldera once all the civilians and assigned warriors had been safely delivered to Jasvar and he'd finished setting up the military base. Vala would be foolish to give up her prized place on the Kelderan colony, where she would no doubt have more freedom.

Freedom he wished he could also possess.

A vision of him leading Vala through the purple trees of Jasvar, to the rumored giant waterfall, flashed into his mind. He slowly slipped her dress off one shoulder and then the other. The material dropped to pool at her feet, the sun shining on her naked golden skin. As she swayed her hips and walked into the water, Thorin ripped off his clothes, ran, and jumped in next to her. She squealed at the splash but quickly melted against his side as he hugged her against his chest.

Thorin's eyes glowed blue, but Vision-Vala looked at him with affection and no trace of horror or disgust.

As the spray from the shower head above him ceased, signaling the end of his daily allotted cleaning solution, Thorin stood and opened his eyes. The longer he stayed away from the female, the more absurd his dreams became.

If he wasn't careful, he might start to hope for what he could never have.

Still, since he'd both sparred and pleasured himself, he might be able to quickly check on Vala without persuading the female to kiss him or more. And who knew, maybe his visions would become less frequent once he saw her in the flesh.

Glancing to the time keeper on the wall, Thorin had about an hour before he needed to join the warriors during one of their training sessions.

He was still working his way through his initial list of antimonarchy suspects. The training session in an hour would finally give him a chance to investigate the final few warriors he suspected of possible ties. If they all turned out to be innocent, he'd move on to start investigating his list of civilians.

Before he could talk himself out of it, Thorin quickly dressed and headed toward his former quarters. With each step, his heart beat faster in anticipation.

The action reminded him of the possible dangers. Thorin quickly went to work fortifying his mind and clearing his head of emotion. If he couldn't arrive calm and collected, he would keep walking and avoid Vala.

And for some reason, the thought of not seeing Vala's face again sent a rush of disappointment through his body.

Warning bells went off inside his head, but Thorin ignored them. After all, he was a seasoned warrior. He could certainly handle a brief visit with a beautiful female and leave unscathed.

~~~

Vala sat in her hover chair next to the replicator as it answered, "Access is prohibited for Vala Yarlen for the requested materials."

She tapped a finger against the composite material that formed the arm of her chair. "Emergency provisions are allowed."

"Correct, but the eye drop solution is not part of that list."

"Tell me what is."

"Accessing." The machine whirred a second before repeating the same answer she'd received a hundred times before, "Access denied."

She sighed and looked to her notescreen. "Computer, replicate a burn emergency kit."

"Working."

As the computer didn't stop and tell her no, Vala must've finally found something else she could have.

She glanced at the scattering of vials and bottles on the bed. The replication only seemed to grant her emergency kits. If she couldn't find some of the key ingredients in her theorized formula, she might have to resort to more drastic measures.

Because if she didn't regain use of her legs soon, there would be lasting effects to her muscles. If they atrophied, Vala didn't want to endure physical therapy and miss the chance to fly a shuttle on Jasvar for longer than she had to.

"Burn emergency kit complete," the computer stated. Just as Vala looked at the object next to her, the door behind her unlocked and swished open.

Since she had expected one of the service robots to bring her latest meal, she didn't turn around. "Leave it next to the door."

The door closed and locked a second later. She was just about to ask the replicator to make something else when a familiar male voice filled the room. "Shall I stay standing next to the door?"

She whipped her chair around. Thorin stood bare chested in his tight warrior trousers.

Blinking, she pinched her arm, but Thorin didn't vanish. She was awake.

When he smiled, she frowned and moved toward him. Her years of training and understanding of her place in society vanished. "You left me."

His smile faded. "But I am here now."

A few days ago, Vala would've merely bowed her head and let the matter drop. But fire burned in her belly and the words came out before she could stop them. "Is that supposed to erase your treatment of me? You claimed I had worth, and yet you left me with no access or contact with anyone." She waved around the room. "You locked me in a prison."

"Barren are used to solitude. Besides, I was protecting you."

"Barren may be isolated from nondefective Kelderans, but we have friends and family within the citadels."

"You are not defective," he growled.

"Are you saying that so you can earn my good graces again? Because that's not nearly enough. I want my freedom, sir."

Thorin's eyes flashed. "My name is Thorin. And there's only one way to regain it, but that must wait."

"No, I won't ever accept your claiming."

Thorin raised an eyebrow. "Then you will remain paralyzed. Is that what you want?"

"Of course not. But I won't stay this way." She picked up her notescreen. "I discovered the cause of my paralysis."

He stilled. "You are mistaken."

"Am I? You are part Brevkan, correct?"

For a long moment, Thorin didn't move or even seem to breathe. When he finally spoke, his voice was low and dangerous. "Be careful of what you say, Vala Yarlen. I control your future."

At his threat, she increased the chair's distance from the floor until she could look Thorin in the eyes. The fire roaring inside her drowned out all reason. "I will not resort to petty insults or stereotypes, even though you seem to apply them to me. You are more incompetent than I when it comes to how to interact with people. Being distant and pushing them away, or lording authority over them, may work with others but not with me. I assume the royal family knows of your origins, yes?" When Thorin remained silent, she had her answer. "Then you need to be careful, sir. Because Princess Kalahn is waiting for me on Jasvar. And even if she doesn't know the truth, I suspect her brother, Prince Kason, does since all the male heirs are privy to Keldera's secrets and classified information. On top of that, Prince Kason's bride is also waiting for my arrival. If you punish me unnecessarily, they will take my side. In that instance, your future becomes uncertain."

She didn't know if Taryn and Kalahn would go to such lengths to help Vala, but she kept her face free of concern. The bluff was worth trying.

Thorin shook his head. "The colony agreement prohibits criminals from joining the colony. Not even you are immune. I could easily have you arrested."

She leaned her face closer to his. "And when they find me chair-bound, what then? Even without me spilling your secret, others may look into my account of how it happened and figure it out themselves."

He growled. "No one will find out."

Her heart thundered inside her chest, but she was too angry to acknowledge any fear. "Why? Are you going to kill me and make it look like an accident?"

"I would never harm you intentionally."

She blinked at his words. "What?"

"Now who's judging whom? No one will find out because you will walk again soon enough."

He leaned closer until his breath caressed her cheek. Rationally, she knew she should move away and order him out.

Yet his heat and scent comforted her in a way she couldn't explain.

No. She wouldn't let the dishonorable male fool her.

She turned her head, but Thorin's breath remained hot against her skin. His voice filled the room. "Now that you know the truth, I understand your aversion to kissing me, let alone being in my presence. However, all I need to do is come inside you and you will walk again. If you lean over the bed, I can ease your condition quickly with minimal touching and disappear. I'll return your freedom and ensure no one tries to harm you. You will never see me again."

At the disgust in his voice, she chanced a glance at Thorin. The shame and hatred in his gaze eased her anger. A flicker of sadness and concern washed through her body.

The powerful warrior hated who he was, and Vala had only fed his demons.

Still, he had abandoned her and she wouldn't forgive him so easily. But to allow him to think she didn't want him for circumstances beyond his control was wrong. "My anger has nothing to do with your genetics, Thorin."

At his name, Thorin reached out and touched her cheek. When she didn't flinch, he asked, "Why? My father was the enemy and forced himself upon my mother. I'm a product of shame. Don't feel obligated to protect my feelings."

"Don't do that."

"Do what? I only speak the truth."

"No, you speak what others expect you to say. When you do, they win. Never let them win your mind, Thorin. If you don't fight for yourself, no one will."

~~~

At Vala's words, Thorin searched her gaze for deceit or platitudes. Before his mother's sister had been killed during a Brevkan raid toward the end of the conflict, she had also said he shouldn't allow others to determine his worth when he was a child.

Yet as he risked stroking Vala's cheek, her expression remained fierce. He didn't dare to hope that she didn't find him repulsive.

Instead, he focused on her words. "What did others do to you to merit such a response?"

She shook her head but didn't try to dislodge his finger from her skin. The brush of his skin against hers only reminded him of how soft she was.

Vala answered, "Don't try to change the subject. I know my place in our society, but their view doesn't dictate my worth. I do what I must to stay out of prison, but I don't allow the actions or words of my life outside the citadel to take hold in my heart or mind. You should do the same when it comes to your Brevkan half."

"We both know that I can't do that. Unlike you, I don't have a refuge to hide with others like me or can afford to act without worry. One glimpse of my glowing eyes and half of the people near me would try to kill me."

He mentally cursed at acknowledging one of his Brevkan physical traits.

Wanting to distract Vala from his comment, Thorin spit out, "Besides, after the amount of pain my existence caused my mother, I deserve a life of isolation and penance."

She inched closer to him until he could feel her breath against his skin as she said, "I disagree. You being alive and raised by your mother tells me that she cared for you. She had other choices. After all, many females abandoned their half-Brevkan offspring to the Barren during the war."

He frowned. "Since when?"

She raised an eyebrow. "Did you expect us to share this secret and allow the army to retrieve the babies and possibly execute them? Not even the royal family knows about this. There are more Kelderans who have Brevkan blood than you think. They are raised as a Barren if female and can pass as a Kelderan. Males are given to the army as adults if they look Kelderan and feel they can control themselves. If they look more Brevkan—for example, if they have red skin which no Kelderan has—they are sequestered in secret enclaves at locations I don't even know about."

Thorin knew the Barren often accepted unwanted children. It was the only way some of the females would have offspring to raise of their own since there weren't enough infertile babies to give to each Barren female who wanted a child.

But to take in Brevkan bastards? Impossible. "Your claim seems improbable. Otherwise, you would've recognized me for who I was when my eyes glowed."

"Just because I learned the secret by mistake doesn't mean I was involved in raising the abandoned children, male or female. All of them would be grown by now since the war ended decades ago. Besides, only a Barren Mother knew where the children had been raised. The females raising the boys would've known the signs and also would've helped the males to control themselves. I never had any contact."

"What do you mean you discovered this by accident?"

She looked to the side. He cupped her cheek and forced her gaze back. She murmured, "Before I condemn myself, am I talking with General Jarrell or just Thorin?"

He didn't hesitate. "Just Thorin." He grunted. "Tell me. I don't like when you keep secrets from me."

Thorin resisted backing away from Vala. The female owed him nothing. Why would he state such a thing?

However, she spoke again before he could act. "Before being assigned to any ships, I often took care of the elderly Barren back on Keldera. One time, a female was quite ill with a high fever. She spoke often about a few of the children she raised. More than once she pleaded with them to treasure the gift of life instead of resenting it; they were loved and her children. When she recovered, I talked with her in private and she told me everything. However, it was a secret that I couldn't share with anyone or it could risk the lives of all those living in hiding. And despite the fact I should've reported it when applying for a starship assignment via requirements in the contract about full disclosure, I kept all of this to myself. Until now."

"So I could find others like me, possibly even aboard this ship?" he whispered.

She shrugged. "Perhaps. I imagine they've found ways around genetic scans, same as you, which means they could've joined the colony. To be honest, that makes sense to me. There are many of us who wish for greater freedom to be our true selves. The Jasvarian colony is that rare chance to do just that."

At the longing in her voice, Vala's revelation took a backseat. He didn't want to cause her any more hurt.

Not to the female who was more accepting of his heritage than anyone since his mother and aunt. More than anything, he wanted to ease her anger and settle things between them.

He threaded his fingers through her hair. "I didn't consider that your isolation would be a form of punishment to you."

He expected her to push away his arm, but she merely placed a hand on his bicep. Her warm touch caused his belly to flip.

Thorin was on dangerous ground.

"Then tell me why haven't you visited before now?" Vala asked.

"I couldn't."

She raised her brows. "Explain."

Thorin was the ranking officer aboard the colony ship. He had no reason to heed her order.

But at her gentle touch against his arm, combined with her curious gaze, he couldn't help but say, "You are a temptation and distraction. I can't risk the lives of everyone aboard this vessel."

Her brows knitted together. "You aren't making any sense. If you want to assuage my anger, then tell me the whole truth, Thorin. Does your keeping away have to do with what caused my paralysis?"

He liked it when she used his name. He had a feeling that if he didn't tell her everything, she would never speak his name again.

There were many reasons for him to refuse the female and simply walk away, especially since he currently had a new secret goal—to find others like him who led secret lives.

However, it had been years since his mother had been cognizant enough to discuss his Brevkan-half. While unfair to Vala, he wanted to unload some of the weight off his shoulders.

Still, he wouldn't touch her while he did so. He couldn't risk one of his urges to surface and make his actions unpredictable.

Or, worse, he frightened or disgusted her.

Thorin stepped back and walked to the opposite side of the room. To avoid the questions in Vala's eyes, he kept his back to her as he spoke. "My Brevkan-half recognized you as my possession—a thing to be claimed and to accept my seed. When my instinct recognizes a possession, I exude a specific pheromone that only affects the possession in question; I'm unaware when I do so and had no idea I even could as a halfling until I found you unconscious. The paralysis is to ensure you can't run away and escape my intentions."

Vala's soft voice filled the room. "Is that why you kept your distance? Because you feel the urge to claim me?"

He gave a cruel laugh. "It's not a set-up for a claiming, but rape. Full-blooded Brevkan probably can't resist the pull. I can barely contain it as I am."

"But you did. More than that, you're doing it again now."

At her words, he glanced over his shoulder. Vala's expression was kind and patient. He blinked at the unexpected emotions.

He had never thought himself worthy of kindness, but Vala's words from earlier, about acting the way others expected of him, resonated inside his mind. Maybe he deserved more than he gave himself leave to expect.

An image of her naked with her legs wrapped around his waist flashed into his mind.

Severing eye contact, he faced away from her again. "If you could peer into my mind, you wouldn't think me so honorable."

"Our minds are private places. All males have indecent thoughts. I've heard many a fantasy whispered during a fever."

He shook his head. "It's not the same. I can't control my visions and many of them are barbaric. If you saw even a glimpse of one, it would give you nightmares."

The hover chair's electronics hummed, signaling movement. But he resisted looking back at Vala.

However, when her hand touched his shoulder, it took all of his training and experience to prevent himself from jumping. Her voice was like a caress over his body as she said, "You are not your father, Thorin. If you tell me the whole truth about why you stayed away from me, it will prove you're an honorable male."

He did meet Vala's gaze. "How are you so sure?"

"Because my gut tells me so."

As he stared into Vala's dark eyes, Thorin debated what to do. The more he talked with the female, the more he yearned to know her better.

However, they were destined to part ways within weeks. He should do everything in his power to push her away.

Then she moved her hand to lightly brush his cheek with her forefinger, and his restraint faded. Even if it were only for a short while, he would confide in Vala Yarlen and enjoy her company. After all, it would give him something to recall in the future, when he needed to think of positive memories to chase away his barbaric visions.

He turned and faced Vala. "I stayed away from you because if I attempt to claim you, I don't think I would be able to leave your side until I was completely sated, if that is even possible. You tempt me, Vala, in a way no other has before."

Chapter Eight

Vala hadn't known what to expect from Thorin, but him all but saying she was irresistible made her heart pound harder.

As much as she had made plans in recent weeks to become a pilot and a part of society in the colony, she had never imagined a male would find her addictive or irresistible. Not because she was unattractive, but rather most males wanted a female who could eventually continue their line and ensure their slice of immortality through bearing offspring.

Yet Thorin had stayed away because he wanted her too much, infertility and all.

Any residual anger melted away and she smiled. "I like this version of Thorin Jarrell much better than the jerk of our first few encounters."

He cleared his throat. "I had no choice. Your beauty threw me off guard and I needed to drive you away. I couldn't risk you seeing my eyes glow with desire or even my body glow in orgasm."

"That assumes I would've accepted you in the first place."

He bowed his head. "My apologies. I should not be so presumptuous."

She frowned. "Don't do that, Thorin."

"Do what?"

"Put distance between us. My whole life I haven't been able to speak my mind freely, and I suspect it's been the same for you. Let's both be honest and open."

Fear flashed in his eyes. Vala's heart ached for the male so afraid of himself. He murmured, "I'm not sure that's wise."

She moved closer and leaned forward in her chair. There were many reasons she shouldn't, but Vala reached out to touch Thorin's warm chest. When he didn't step back, she ran a hand down his hard, defined muscles.

He sucked in a breath, and she met his gaze again. His irises glowed light blue. "Your eyes."

He closed them and tried to step away, but Vala reached out to hook her arms around his neck. "Don't hide from me. If you promise to be forthright and honest about yourself, I will do the same."

Keeping his eyes closed, Thorin gently laid a hand on her upper back. Even though it had to be her imagination, a tingle shot down her legs to her toes. After a few more beats, he opened his eyelids. She was disappointed that they were merely blue again, with no glowing in sight.

He replied, "I want to be open and honest with you, Vala. But I can't risk the people aboard this ship."

She tilted her head. "I'm not sure I follow. Tell me what you mean, Thorin."

At his name, Thorin rubbed her back in slow circles. All she wanted to do was curl against his chest and revel in the warmth of the male who wanted her.

His voice was gravelly as he answered, "I want you more than any female before, that's the truth. However, once I start to claim you, I won't be able to stop if you later have hesitations."

"I don't believe it. You have an enormous amount of self-control. I don't think you'd hurt me."

"Believing something doesn't make it true."

She lightly caressed the back of his neck. "I agree, but I think there's more to it than that. What haven't you told me? Has something happened to the ship I should know about?"

He smiled. "You are intelligent."

Vala resisted sitting up tall at the compliment. She wouldn't allow Thorin to distract her. "So something did happen. Tell me."

He explained about the strange asteroid field and the disappearing pieces before adding, "So while everything is peaceful for now, there's always the possibility of an attack. On top of that, all of my free time must be spent on a special assignment."

"What assignment?"

The markings on his chest flashed from dark blue to white and back again. Since white signaled worry or indecision, she had a feeling his assignment was classified.

And while Thorin may not be quite as open with words as she wanted, the flashing of his markings spoke volumes. As a highly trained warrior, he would only allow it to happen in front of those he felt comfortable with. After all, to a warrior, displaying emotion exposed a weakness to pounce upon.

His eyes widened before his deep voice finally filled the room again. "You might be able to help me. But in order to do so, you need to be able to walk again."

She brushed the back of his neck with her nails. She swore he let out a barely audible moan, but she focused on the situation at hand. "Stop talking in vague statements and maybe I can help. As you already acknowledged, I'm clever. I also can walk in the shadows with few people paying attention to my movements. That's a valuable asset to have."

He growled. "You shouldn't be ignored so completely."

"Focus, Thorin. Tell me your mission and allow me to help, if I'm able to. I might even bend over the bed and allow you to claim me quickly so that I can walk again."

His voice was strangled as he replied, "You shouldn't tempt me."

She dug her nails into his skin. "Just tell me the facts, and then we can decide what to do."

"Fine." He leaned over and whispered into her ear. "I'm looking for antimonarchy troublemakers aboard the ship. Intelligence suggests some are among us."

Vala may have been sheltered in the citadels, but everyone on Keldera knew of the increasing tension and confrontations between the various political factions. Some wanted a government ruled solely by the people, whereas others believed the royal family's guidance was necessary to help keep everything under control and to help maintain peace.

She kept her voice low. "I could be your eyes and ears, Thorin. There are many places where my presence won't cause a stir. Not to mention many speak their minds with little heed to any Barren listening."

When he didn't reply, a sense of doubt came over her. Thorin may be telling the truth about desiring her, but most Kelderan males rarely viewed females as worthy allies. Even though she and Princess Kalahn had helped Thorin succeed in identifying traitors and rescuing Prince Kason recently, it may not have been enough to sway Thorin's long-held beliefs on gender roles.

Thorin moved his hand around to her front, to where her hip met her ribcage, and it took everything she had to listen to his words instead of lean into his touch. "I see the merit of your suggestion, but I worry you'll become a target. The jealousy among Barren on a starship is legendary."

She leaned back and raised an eyebrow. "And who says those things?"

"Other warriors, but—"

"Exactly. Usually it's the warriors who injure or poison the Barren out of jealousy and then say it was one of us who did it. As the law stands, any Barren who speaks up against an officer is automatically assumed a criminal until proven otherwise. You can imagine how often that happens."

Thorin's markings flashed black, signaling anger. "It's dishonorable to take advantage of a female in such a way, let alone harm her."

"I don't disagree. However, we have two vastly different views on society. Honor is conveniently forgotten when a male's genitals are involved, especially when it comes to dealing with females considered expendable by most of the planet."

As Thorin searched her eyes, Vala wondered if she'd voiced too much of her opinion too soon. Thorin saying he wanted the truth from her and accepting it without anger were two different things.

When he finally ran his hand up her side and brushed her long, white hair over her shoulder, she relaxed a fraction. She murmured, "You did say you wanted honesty."

The corner of his mouth twitched, but he didn't smile. "I didn't think you'd be speaking of male cocks so soon."

Heat flushed her cheeks, but Vala refused to look away. She changed the subject back on topic. "So, as you can see, I have nothing to worry about from the other Barren. And if you disavow me as your mistress, then males will try to woo me into bed instead of poisoning me. After all, they'll want to prove they're better than the general."

He growled. "That might be worse."

For the first time in her life, Vala was tempted to roll her eyes in the presence of a warrior. "While I may have to act coy around them to prevent rumors, I have no wish to bed any of them."

"I need to hear why, Vala."

His eyes glowed blue, and her face burned because of the desire in his eyes. She may be innocent in the way of males, but she had seen that look on many a warrior right before they disappeared with one of her Barren sisters.

She cleared her throat and drew on her recent experiences of showing a backbone. "I have no interest in them. That's all I'll say for the time being."

She waited for Thorin's eyes to narrow or for him to order her to tell him the truth.

But all he did was nod. "I respect your right to silence."

She blinked. "Truly?"

"Yes. It only encourages me to try harder so that I can earn your full trust."

As they stared into one another's eyes, Vala wanted nothing more than a chance to unpack all Thorin's secrets and share her own. She'd seen firsthand how arrogant Prince Kason had transformed into a more easygoing and teasing version of himself simply because of his love for his bride.

No. She wouldn't hope or dream for anything more than a few days of closeness and losing her virginity to Thorin. She would join the colony and he would return to Keldera.

And as much as she wanted the closeness of a lord and for him to call her his bride, Vala wanted freedom more.

She finally made her mouth work again. "So, will you allow me to assist you in your mission? I proved your fears about the other Barren and warriors unfounded. Besides, my help will most likely increase your chances of success."

He opened his mouth to reply, but the communicator on his belt beeped three times, signaling a call.

After staring into her eyes for one last second, he moved away and said to the room, "Computer, accept call and patch through."

A male's voice she recognized as Ryven Xanna, the ship's head trainer, came onto the line. "The men are assembled. Do you still wish to join us and lead the meditation?"

"I will be there shortly. We can use the waiting time to test their patience," Thorin answered.

"Aye, aye sir. They will be ready for you," Ryven replied.

Thorin said, "End call," and turned back toward her. "I'll consider your offer. Once I'm done with the warriors, I'll return and provide my answer. Although I must be very clear that if I accept your help, I will need to claim you quickly in order to correct your condition."

Afraid her voice would crack, she merely nodded. Thorin frowned and closed the space between them. "Don't take my response as a slight. Every general must weigh the pros and cons of a situation. It'll also give you time to think about what I must do to you, because no matter what it takes, I won't force you to accept me. My Brevkan half will also probably take over, meaning the coupling will be rough and fast. With all the facts presented, the decision must be yours and yours alone whether you will accept the claim or not."

She bobbed her head again. "I understand."

"Good. Then I shall return within the next few hours. Until then, will you stay in this room?"

"Thank you for asking and not ordering."

He raised an eyebrow. "So is that a yes?"

"Yes, I'll remain here for now on one condition—allow me access again."

Thorin hesitated, and she wondered if he'd say no.

Then he gave a curt nod. "I'll reprogram the room's permissions as I leave."

She smiled. "Thank you."

"Of course." He moved to the door. "Think carefully about helping me, Vala. If I do accept your offer of help, you'll need to do more than accept me into your body. You'll also put your life in danger and possibly become a target if the troublemakers discover your intentions."

With that, Thorin exited the room and the door locked behind him.

Vala sighed and placed her hands on her hot cheeks. She already knew what her answer would be if Thorin decided to accept her help. The threat of being discovered by an enemy didn't faze her because rooting out troublemakers would help protect her friend Kalahn and most likely everyone on Jasvar as well.

However, when it came to rectifying her paralysis, Vala wanted more than a quick encounter with her facedown on the mattress and Thorin touching her as little as possible.

Not just to fulfill her own wishes, either. She had a feeling Thorin had never taken a female face-to-face, afraid of what would happen when his body glowed. Even if the fact wasn't widely known that the glowing was a Brevkan trait, it wasn't a Kelderan one.

And for some reason, she wanted him to embrace his difference. Maybe then she would have an easier time doing the same for herself as a member of the colony.

Of course, the hard part would be gathering the courage to ask Thorin for what she wanted. No doubt the distance apart would calm her mind and erase the previous easiness they'd shared. She only hoped he wouldn't become the unfeeling, disrespectful male from a few weeks ago.

Closing her eyes, Vala hummed one of the Barren meditation practices. She had time to prepare for Thorin's return and was going to do everything she could to ready herself in both mind and body.

~~~

As Thorin walked among the warriors currently sparring with one another, he tried to focus on his target, a male named Beltor. From the male's movements and flawless execution, Thorin deemed him a warrior with potential. The difficult part was determining if Beltor did so to curb suspicion and to advance to become a high-ranking spy, or because he wished to one day become a general who could protect his people.

Thorin wouldn't be able to make a decision until after practice when he would take the male aside and talk with him in private. While uncommon for a general to single out one warrior, it wasn't unheard of. Regardless, he needed to get the male alone. Thorin had perfected deceit to conceal his heritage, and one benefit was that he had become good at reading people. Very few could lie to him undetected.

Although he should amend his thought to be only good at reading other males. He still didn't know what Vala's closed expression had meant right before he'd left her room.

Two hours had passed and their entire encounter felt more like a dream than reality. Between Vala's revelation surrounding other half-Brevkan children and her not showing disgust at his glowing eyes, it was too much good news for him to avoid being skeptical. Something would go wrong, if his past experience was anything to go by.

Time apart would allow him to see if she would still accept the truth of his heritage, let alone if she would want the same closeness with him once more. He didn't dare hope she would allow him to claim her.

As much as her help would be beneficial to his cause, Vala needed to make the decision on her own about losing her virginity to him. With her being his possession, it wouldn't be gentle or drawn out. And bastard that he was, a part of him was eager to experience it with her.

The golden-skinned, silver-haired form of Ryven Xanna walked up to him, and Thorin quickly tucked away all thoughts unrelated to the training session. The trainer had earned a reputation as the best for many reasons, ferreting out secrets was one of them.

Ryven stopped next to him, a faint smile on his lips. "While I'm honored by your visit to one of my training sessions, are you sure you don't wish to challenge a few of the warriors to a battle session?"

While Ryven smiled more than any warrior Thorin had worked with in the past, he was aware that the male had been suspicious of him until recently. After all, Ryven had been childhood friends with the former general Prince Kason, who had only warmed up to Thorin after he rescued Kason and his bride. "Given recent events, I think it's unwise for me to possibly incapacitate any warrior and decrease our numbers."

"I would say you're cocky, but I have yet to see anyone but Kason defeat you in a battle session." As an afterthought, Ryven added, "Sir."

"Do not take it as an insult to your training abilities. I continue to spend many hours perfecting my skills. Maybe one day another will show the same dedication."

Ryven merely smiled and remained quiet. No doubt the trainer took offense at Thorin's words, but it was the truth. After all, Thorin's dedication was more than wanting to be the best—he didn't want to lose control and harm his colleagues.

"I do have a request of you, Ryven."

"Yes, sir?" Ryven asked without taking his eyes off his students.

Thorin lowered his voice. "I want you to start training the female colonists who wish to learn self-defense."

Ryven blinked and met his gaze. "Pardon?"

"We don't know how things will turn out on Jasvar. Our colonists could shed discipline, or the Jasvarians may try to take something they shouldn't. A female should be able to protect herself."

It was something Thorin wished his mother had been offered.

Ryven's expression remained neutral. "I believe we're not supposed to start changing Kelderan traditions or laws until we reach Jasvar, sir."

"I'm the ranking officer aboard this vessel. The females will be trained, and I do mean all females, Xanna. The Barren will be included."

The trainer searched his gaze a second before shrugging a shoulder. "I spent several weeks as a prisoner on Jasvar with female guards for the most part. I no longer hold illusions that females are weak and can't protect themselves. So, I'll do it. I'd rather they learn from me than from the Jasvarians. Otherwise, the humans will lure away our females into their own cities. That is a situation I want to avoid."

"Deserting the Kelderan colony within the first year defies the agreement signed by both sides."

"If I may speak freely, sir?" Ryven asked.

Thorin wanted to drawl that Ryven already had, but merely murmured, "Proceed."

"The colonists making this journey are open to changing Kelderan ways—that's part of the reason they were selected—however, too much too soon will cause strife. I suggest training the Barren separately from the other females. Otherwise, even if they convince their lords to allow them to attend at all, they may negotiate that the females can only go if they stay clear of the Barren. However unfounded, the Barren's promiscuous reputations are notorious."

The notorious reputation referenced their freedom to sleep with many males, as opposed to one and only for fertile Kelderan females.

Vala's words from earlier, about them having two different views on society, came back to him.

He was beginning to see her point. They may both risk discrimination, but at least Thorin had the ability to hide his shortcoming. Vala, on the other hand, was branded with a tattoo for all to see.

He clenched the fingers of one hand into a fist. He wished he had the power to erase her tattoo and allow her true freedom. Too bad it was irreversible, unless she had a skin graft.

Which would never be granted to a Barren under Kelderan law, except for life-threatening circumstances. And even then, it depended upon demand and resources.

Before Thorin could think of how to reply to Ryven's request without showing his anger at circumstances beyond his control, Ryven motioned to the far side of the room and Thorin followed. Once they were far enough away that the others couldn't hear, Ryven whispered, "I know that after all these years, you've finally taken a Barren mistress and no doubt wish to earn her good graces and please her. However, while I may have suffered weeks of first Jasvarian imprisonment and then Princess Kalahn's enthusiastic views of the future, most Kelderans have not. We must move slowly, sir. I have faith in Princess Kalahn being able to achieve equality for all females on Jasvar, even for the Barren. But a millennia of expectations takes time to shift. I advise against causing unnecessary discord."

Thorin noted Ryven mentioning Princess Kalahn several times. He had no idea the two had been friends growing up; he couldn't imagine any other reason for him speaking of the princess so casually.

Still, despite Thorin's desire to change views and show Vala it was possible, Ryven spoke reason. Thorin nodded. "Very well, but then you must offer one class for the fertile females and another for the Barren. I want the self-defense lessons to begin as soon as possible. Update me on the progress and any outrage you detect."

It was illegal for a Kelderan male to harm a female, but it still happened occasionally. Thorin suspected some of the males on the ship might try to persuade their females to stay away through violence.

He resisted a frown. Maybe there was more credibility to Vala's earlier words about warriors poisoning Barren out of jealousy than he had thought originally.

"Yes, sir," Ryven answered, garnering his attention. "Now if you would excuse me, the session is about to wrap up. You can take aside the warrior you wish to interview soon after that."

Thorin grunted his assent. Ryven returned to his students, but Thorin remained where he stood and studied Beltor. Instead of his upcoming talk with the warrior, Thorin's mind only wanted to think about sharing the news of the self-defense classes with Vala.

But she wasn't his female and he needed to remember that fact. Thorin's duty lay in honoring the king's request and rooting out the traitors.

No matter what he wanted for himself, Thorin always fulfilled his duty. That was the way of any Kelderan warrior.

However, for the first time in his life, he sensed honoring that tenet wasn't going to be as easy as it had been in the past. Especially if he claimed Vala and grew even closer with her.

Chapter Nine

Vala had read and reread everything she could find surrounding the Brevkan, but she had found little about what happens when a male claims his possession.

Which made sense since giving a prisoner a female and watching how a Brevkan male took her was dishonorable.

Still, Vala liked to be prepared. Most Barren believed in the power of research—most anything could be solved if one used as many resources as possible and dug deep enough. The lack of data made her want to toss her notescreen onto the floor.

If only she had access to the older Barren who had raised the half-Brevkan children. While there might be a few onboard the colony ship, none of the correct age were from her citadel. The Barren may not try to take out their rivals as the rumors suggested, but each citadel was akin to a single, large family and protecting one's own family was always paramount. She doubted they would talk about such a delicate secret with a stranger.

Still, she could attempt to gather information once she was settled on Jasvar. No doubt the Jasvarians would want information on the Brevkan too since welcoming the Kelderans to their planet meant that the human colonists could become targets as well if the Brevkan ever found out about them.

But for the present, it seemed all she could do was wait and wait some more.

Vala plucked at the sheet with her fingers. She could try another round of exercises to keep her leg muscles from withering, which would keep her mind occupied for at least a short while. It might also help with easing her nerves about Thorin. As much as she wanted him, it would be her first time and she didn't know what to expect.

Just as she leaned over to begin her routine, the door chimed.

While she wanted it to be Thorin, he had sent a brief message that his task was taking longer than it should have. "Computer, allow entry."

The door slid open to reveal Thorin's tall form. The intensity of his eyes made her heart skip a beat.

Never taking his eyes from hers, he stepped into the room and the door slid closed.

With any other male, Vala would bow her head and wait for him to speak. However, Thorin's mere presence gave her the courage to be forthright. "Have you made a decision?"

He took a step closer. "I have." And another one. "Have you?"

She leaned back against the headboard storage unit. "Us being polite and beating around the bush will make this take a lot longer than it should."

For a second, she wondered if she'd gone too far. After all, if Thorin had decided against accepting her help, he may also require her to act as any other Barren would with regards to his rank.

Then he smiled slowly and the butterflies settled in her stomach. "I'm glad you still speak your mind, Vala." He moved a little closer to the bed. "Because if you're to help me, honesty will be vital."

She leaned forward. "You want my help?"

"Of course. It is the logical choice."

"Because the idea has merit or because it means you can finally claim me?"

His eyes flashed a bright blue before the glow faded. He ordered, "I want you to tell me your decision plainly."

Not backing down, she replied, "Only after you answer my question first."

His smile widened a fraction and Vala blinked. The approval reached his eyes. She wondered what it would be like to share emotions freely with him on a regular basis.

Thankfully he spoke up before she could dismiss such a ridiculous thought. "Your idea has merit, but I would be dishonest if I didn't admit to wanting to claim you as well. I've thought about it more than I should have over the last few hours."

Her heart thumped faster. "Then you wanting me should make my request easier."

His smile faded, and she wanted to scream for him to bring it back. "Request? I didn't realize this was a negotiation." His jaw tightened. "What do you want?"

"I don't want any special favors. I'm not that type of female."

"Then what?" he barked.

Not wanting to lose her nerve, she sat taller and blurted out, "You can claim me provided it's done face-to-face."

Any lingering emotion vanished from his face and eyes. "That is unwise."

She crossed her arms over her chest. "I won't budge on this, Thorin. Threaten me with whatever you like, but I want to know and see the male claiming me for the first time."

To make a lasting memory was left unsaid.

He shook his head. "I don't think you understand how dangerous that situation could be for you. I've never taken a possession before. What if my barbaric half emerges and forces you to do what you don't want to? I'm not sure I can stop once the urge takes over. Even the smallest chance of you being hurt or forced is too risky."

She needed a way to convince him that he wouldn't hurt her, but how? Then her eyes fell to the blaster gun at his side. She motioned toward it. "Give me your blaster gun. I'll put it on the stun setting and keep in one of my hands the whole time. If you go too far, I'll shoot you."

Vala couldn't believe she had just suggested shooting a general.

But when Thorin grunted in approval, she let out a breath. He took the blaster gun in hand. "You are indeed a clever female, Vala Yarlen. And yet, you must swear on your Barren Mother's life that you will shoot me if I go too far or do anything you dislike."

Swearing on a Barren Mother's life was the most sacred of vows to one of the Barren. To go against such a vow was also illegal.

Vala didn't hesitate. "I swear on my Barren Mother's life to protect myself if such a situation arises. But I sincerely wish it's unnecessary."

He did something with the blaster gun and handed the weapon to her. Their fingers brushed, and it took everything Vala had to focus on the weapon instead of looking up at Thorin. He murmured, "I set it to the stun mode. Show me that you know how to use it."

He removed his hand and Vala swallowed. She finally tapped just below the trigger. "I simply point and pull this."

"Good. Have you used one before?"

She tested the weight in her hands. "No, but I've read the basics of how to operate one in the past. Even Barren are briefly instructed on how to respond to emergency situations before boarding a starship."

"They should include hands-on training as well, which is something I hope to rectify soon," he replied. "However, since you have little instruction, it just means that I'll try to take you as slowly as possible and hopefully you won't have to use it. But I can't guarantee my actions once I'm inside you, Vala."

Thorin stepped back and Vala finally met his eyes. They glowed a bright blue and she whispered, "They're beautiful."

He grunted. "A male is not beautiful."

"They can be. I'm just glad you didn't close your eyes again. I want to welcome all of you into this bed, Thorin."

"Don't discount the dangerous part of me. Besides, you are a virgin, Vala. You don't know what you're in for."

She raised her chin. "Stop trying to scare me away. If your preview earlier is anything to go by, I will enjoy it."

With a growl, Thorin closed the distance between them and threaded his fingers through her hair. "I'm reaching the limits of my control. This is your last chance to refuse me, Vala."

Never taking her gaze from his, she raised the blaster gun in her hand. "I'm ready when you are."

Thorin closed the distance between them and kissed her.

~~~

Thorin never should've agreed to take Vala face-to-face. And yet, he—the hardened warrior—found it nearly impossible to say no to her.

Maybe a Brevkan's possession had power over her male as well.

But as his lips touched hers, all rational thought fled his mind. All he wanted was more of Vala's sweet taste.

As he entered her mouth and caressed her tongue, Thorin gently lowered himself on top of his female. He moaned at the softness of her breasts and belly against him.

His restraint shattered and he increased the urgency of his tongue as he ran a hand down her side and to her skirt. Images of him moving inside Vala flashed into his mind and he simply gripped her skirt and pulled.

He paid little heed to the torn fabric and gripped her thigh. Her softness was a nice contrast to his firm muscles, and desire flooded his entire body. He wanted more of her softness wrapped around him.

Moving his hand up to where her hip met her ribcage, Vala's muscles tensed under his fingers. Something wasn't right.

He forced himself to break the kiss. He could see his glowing eyes reflected in hers. He had to be frightening her.

Thorin rolled away and sat on the edge of the bed, his elbows on his thighs. While his cock pulsed in need, signaling he had to take care of himself soon or risk an outburst, his memory of Vala's tensed muscles allowed him to say, "I told you this was a bad idea. Touching your skin is dangerous. I can't control myself."

Vala's small hand touched his back. "I'm not afraid of you, Thorin."

He shook his head. "There's no need to placate me. I know what I am. It's best for you to lean over the bed and let me take you with as little touching as possible."

"No."

At the command in her tone, he dared to look over his shoulder. He expected fear, but determination flared in her eyes. She spoke again. "I. Am. Not. Afraid. Is that clear? Because I won't tell you the real reason for my reaction until you accept that."

Despite her mussed hair and one strap of her dress off her shoulder, Vala looked more like an officer than a soft female.

The need to possess her and fill her with his cock surged through his body.

No. Vala deserved honor and respect. He would give it to her. "If you're not afraid, then what?"

She straightened her delicate shoulders; shoulders he could snap if he wasn't careful. "I'm nervous. I like being prepared, but I couldn't find anything about Brevkan mating practices."

The image of Vala searching records about his father's people and their sex lives made him smile. "Not everything can be learned from records."

"I know, but you keep making it out to be rough and terrible. I somehow think you're viewing it through a biased lens."

His smile faded. "Once I'm inside you, something snaps inside me. It has always been so with others."

"Were they possessions?"

"No."

"Then how do you know it will be the same?"

"I—" he paused. "I don't."

Triumph flashed in her gaze. He liked how she was feeling more comfortable around him and showing more of her true self.

Vala raised the blaster gun. "This is my added protection. By taking the vow, I'm required to use it if I feel threatened or risk imprisonment for not honoring my word. Did I use it on you?"

He frowned. "No."

"Then why did you stop?"

~~~

While waiting for his answer, Vala's heart thumped so hard she wondered how half the ship couldn't hear it.

Voicing opinions and being in charge was taxing, but she refused to allow Thorin to hide behind his assumptions and self-hatred. Before she arrived on Jasvar, she was determined to prove he was honorable and worthy of happiness.

It would be her parting gift to him. Then one day he might even find a female who could give him a child and a family.

Her stomach twisted at the thought of Thorin taking someone else as a bride, not that she should think about Thorin's future. Their paths would diverge soon enough.

Thorin rose from the bed. "Let's try this again and I won't stop unless you shoot me."

Before she could do more than open her mouth, he undid the fastenings of his trousers. As his long, strong fingers revealed his lower belly, her mouth went dry. With a few more movements, his erection sprung free. While Thorin had light blue skin, she swore his penis was a slightly darker blue and glowed slightly. Maybe it was another indication of Brevkan ancestry.

He wiggled out of his shoes and trousers and Vala couldn't take her gaze from his maleness. She was both anxious and scared of it. She had seen her fair share of penises when taking care of the sick, but Thorin was thicker and longer than any of them.

Thorin took his hardness in hand and stroked. "Since I bared myself to you, it's only fair you do the same." She swallowed as she looked to Thorin's glowing eyes. He murmured, "I want to see your glorious body, Vala. Show it to me."

For a second, she said nothing. Then her brain switched back on and she raised her gun. "I have to put this down."

He stroked again and she loved how his eyes glowed brighter. "On my honor, I won't touch you until the blaster gun is in your hand once more."

Given how Thorin had moved away of his own free will when she'd tensed earlier, she trusted his word. Laying the gun down, she gripped her skirts. Heat flushed her cheeks, but after taking a deep breath, she wiggled until they were at her waist. Thorin's husky voice filled the room. "Your legs tempt me. Show me the rest, Vala."

Her ears buzzed. But when Thorin whispered, "Please," she found the courage to tug the rest of the material over her head and toss it aside.

He said nothing and her nerve slipped a fraction. She was softer than many of the other Barren. Maybe Thorin preferred their bodies or the toned ones of the Jasvarian warrior females.

Then she heard his groan and she met his gaze. Desire burned hot as he said, "I could come from merely admiring your body." He took a step closer. "But another time. I don't want you to suffer any longer."

Before she could state she wasn't suffering, Thorin covered her body with his. The hardness against her belly made wetness rush between her thighs.

Engulfed by Thorin's heat and muscled body, she oddly felt safe. Almost as if she could face anything with him by her side.

But then he kissed her jaw, and all she could think about was his hot, wet lips on her skin.

When he finally lowered his muscled chest to hers, she moaned at the friction against her nipples. If only she could move her legs, then she would wrap them around his waist and let him know how much she yearned to take him inside her.

Thorin trailed kisses down her neck, her upper chest, and finally stopped just above her right nipple. He darted out his tongue to flick the sensitive bud and Vala arched her back. Thorin's touch was more intense than that from when she'd orgasmed from the ministrations of her own fingers.

Her warrior murmured something she couldn't understand before taking her tight bud into his mouth. Each swirl of his tongue or suckle with his mouth only made her skin hotter. Needing to feel a part of him, she threaded her free hand through his hair and dug her nails into scalp. Thorin lightly bit her when she did, and she screamed as pleasure coursed through her body.

When the wave crested and she came down, Thorin's husky voice filled the room. "You should be ready for me now. Will you grant the honor of allowing me to claim you?"

As she stared into his glowing eyes, Vala played with his dark hair. "You don't need to keep asking me that. I said yes and I meant it."

He lightly licked her nipple before answering, "Then I won't ask again."

He repositioned his body and hers so that he knelt between her legs, his cock in hand. "I wish I could prevent the pain I'm about to cause."

Vala was more than aware of Kelderan female biology and nodded. With a growl, Thorin eased inside her until he reached her barrier. He bowed his head in apology and thrust to the hilt.

She hissed as pain radiated up her spine and down her arms. She had no idea how long the sharp pain throbbed, but eventually it became a dull ache.

Thorin caressed her cheek. "It will get better soon."

As he moved his hips, he pinched one of her nipples in time to his thrusts.

While she wanted to trust him, she scanned his face for any sign of struggle. While his eyes glowed, she didn't notice any straining muscles or clenched jaws.

She was tempted to toss aside the blaster gun but didn't want to distract him or possibly scare him away again.

As the building pressure from before reappeared, she was soon too distracted to scrutinize Thorin for loss of control. Each movement of his body brought more pleasure. When he moved one of her legs and pressed it to the side, he changed his angle and she moaned.

Despite never doing it face-to-face before, Thorin was skilled.

A light sweat covered his body as he reached even deeper inside her. The oddly addictive scent from earlier, right before she'd blacked out, returned. However, instead of falling unconscious, it made her want to pull Thorin closer and ask him to take her harder.

Before she could wonder where that thought had come from, Thorin growled. His eyes were brighter than fire, albeit blue.

They were glorious.

Just as her skin felt as if it would snap in two from the tension, Thorin stilled and yelled. At the same time, he lightly twisted her nipple and waves of pleasure crashed over her again.

Even through the haze, she took in Thorin's towering, glowing body as he found his release. She would never forget the sight of his muscled body radiating light blue. It was one of the most beautiful sights she'd ever seen. Even more beautiful than the lush, sacred valley of Zeevayn on Keldera with its fields of purple wild flowers against the yellow grass.

Thorin's shoulders slumped and a light tingle traveled up her legs.

She moved a toe and felt it. "It worked, Thorin. I can feel my toes at least."

He smiled at her and tucked a stray piece of hair behind her ear. "I'm glad, Vala. I hope to never take anything away from you ever again."

At the sadness in his voice, her throat choked with emotion. For some reason, his words were more akin to a goodbye than a romantic sentiment.

Only wanting to focus on the present, she reached out a hand and lightly brushed his abdomen. "I was right, you know, about it being different with a possession. You didn't lose control, did you?"

"No."

She tilted her head. "You sound less happy than I thought you'd be."

He smiled. "No, I am happy. But I've always wondered what a pure-blooded Kelderan would feel like during a claiming."

"And?"

"It's nice to be in control." He kissed her gently. "Thank you for showing me a different life, Vala. Even if it's just for tonight."

She wanted to frown at his words, but she forced her tone to remain light. "It doesn't have to be for just tonight, Thorin. You could keep me as your mistress."

For a second, hope filled her chest at Thorin's silence. But then he shook his head and she knew his duty would come first. "No, I must dismiss you. I won't risk others trying to harm you out of jealousy. You must appear available."

"Appear available? Why?"

He lightly traced one of her shoulders. "I must go back to Keldera and you will join the colony on Jasvar. It's better to keep our distance, unless it's related to the investigation. Attachments will only complicate matters. Besides, you'll find out more information if you're unattached. That is, if you still want to help me."

Vala had no idea why her chest constricted as if someone had grabbed her heart and squeezed, but she forced a smile. "Of course I'll help you. I won't fail you, sir. I promise to do my best to root out any traitors."

Thorin's expression shuttered. He slowly retreated from her body and stood next to the bed. "I believe you. Now, will you allow me the right to clean your body?"

While Vala knew of the Kelderan ritual to gently clean a female's body after her first time, she had never expected to experience it herself. After all, in the eyes of society, the Barren weren't completely female since they couldn't have children.

Still, she wasn't going to pass up the opportunity to spend more time with Thorin. Strange as it was, she wanted every second she could get with him. "Of course."

As he turned and headed toward the replicator to ask for the necessary supplies, Vala studied his broad back, narrow waist, and tight buttocks. This would probably be her only chance to memorize Thorin's form and she wanted to be able to draw upon the memory for the rest of her life.

Because for a brief moment in time, Thorin was treating her like a fertile female instead of a Barren to be used and discarded.

And who knew if she'd ever experience it again.

Chapter Ten

A few hours later, Thorin sat next to the bed fully clothed and watched Vala sleep.

He wasn't sure why he'd offered her the traditional first cleaning as he never would've thought to give one to a Barren in the past, but it had just seemed right.

And not just because she'd cried out in pleasure and never flinched from his glowing body.

No, he admired who she was rather than her station, much like how she accepted him as a male instead of a half-Brevkan bastard. She should be accorded every honor given to a fertile female.

For a brief moment, he'd yearned to keep her at his side. He hadn't gone rogue or been rough with her. Thorin had been in complete control the entire claiming. It was a first for him and he wished it to be the same always.

But after giving him the gift of her desiring him regardless of his heritage, he wasn't about to steal her freedom away. He would do whatever it took to deliver her safely to the new colony.

She snuggled deeper into her pillow, her white hair sliding over her cheek, and he smiled. He could watch her all night and never tire of it. She was a lightness in the darkness. Thorin may have to return to the torture of his barbaric visions soon enough, but for the moment, he beheld innocence and beauty. He would treasure the view and memorize it to counter future urges and dark moments.

He leaned over and was about to pull the blanket back up over her shoulders when his communicator vibrated at his waist. As quietly as he could, he rose and exited the room.

The room adjacent to his was also secure since it was reserved for a general's mistress, so he entered it and said, "Computer, patch through communications."

The voice of the nighttime command deck officer in charge, Yutven Surrell, filled the room. "Sorry to disturb you, sir. But there's a situation you should see. It's too delicate to discuss over communications."

"Understood. I will make my way directly."

Despite the fact Thorin wanted to leave a message for Vala so that she didn't wake up to an empty room, Yutven's voice had wavered; something made him nervous. Thorin needed to take care of his ship and its cargo. Otherwise, Vala and every other person on board might suffer from his negligence.

He strode down one corridor, took an elevator and finally made his way to the command deck. Yutven sat in the raised chair in the middle. Thorin noted that only males he had served many times over with in the past manned the various stations instead of the usual nighttime staff.

As soon as Thorin stopped next to the command chair, Yutven said without preamble, "There is a problem in engineering. The engines stalled and no amount of contacting the various engineering officers has been successful. Visuals for those parts of the ship won't come online, either."

"Did you send anyone to investigate?"

"Aye, sir. However, once they entered the engineering department, they ceased communications. And before you ask, the computer reports nothing unusual. Rather than risk more warriors, I thought it wise to contact you. Also, due to the sensitive nature of the situation, I replaced the usual night staff with more experienced officers."

Thorin nodded. "Send everything you have about this situation to my personal office. I'm going to go over the facts and put together a team. For the moment, keep the area in question quarantined, complete with force field barriers. Let me know the second anything changes."

"Aye, aye, sir."

Thorin walked to his small office off the command deck. As much as he wanted to trust Yutven, it was only the second mission they had worked together. He wasn't about to divulge the possibility of traitors or even a mutiny as the source of the current situation to anyone he didn't trust completely.

Which meant he needed to assemble a few males he would entrust his life to.

Once his door had locked, he said, "Computer, contact Ryven Xanna."

"Connecting," the computer stated.

After about thirty seconds, Ryven's voice came over the line. "What is it?"

Thorin dismissed Ryven's crankiness given the late hour. "There is a situation. I want you and Syzel to come to my personal office as soon as possible."

Ryven's voice was more alert when he replied, "Understood. I'll pick him up on the way and be there shortly."

The line went dead and Thorin sat at his desk. Pulling up the information, he scanned the readouts and visuals recorded before the investigative team had gone silent. In his experience, there was always some sort of reading, even if miniscule, that occurred right before an event. He needed to find it.

And once he did, he'd lead a team himself. If anyone could find out what was going on, it was him, Ryven, and Syzel.

Although just in case he faced a new type of enemy or threat, he'd also make sure to record a message for Vala and reinstate her security clearance. He wouldn't allow cockiness to possibly cause the female pain.

Quickly setting things up for Vala, Thorin turned back to the data. Only the situation at hand mattered.

~~~

Vala opened her eyes to an empty room. She listened for any noises from the cleaning area, but there was only silence.

Thorin was gone.

She shouldn't care since she had no claim on him, but his absence made her heart squeeze. The one and only time a male would probably ever treat her as if she were a fertile female had come and gone. She would merely be a Barren once more.

Taking a deep breath, she slowly moved her legs until they hung over the side of the bed. The slight pain between her thighs reminded her of what had happened the night before.

Thorin's glorious glowing body above her as he came flashed into her mind.

Vala quickly pushed the vision away. It was time to forget about Thorin and focus on the much more important task of trying to discover any traitors aboard the ship. If there was one thing Vala could do to forget her problems, it was to go to work.

While she'd experimented a little with moving her lower body before falling asleep, Vala had yet to stand since the reversing of her paralysis. She carefully scooted to the edge of the bed and attempted to push herself off. The second she was upright, her legs wobbled and she fell back onto the bed.

After a few more tries, she finally managed to remain standing. Slowly she made her way to the new clothing left for her on the far side of the room. Just as she reached for the brown dress, a flash of red on her ankle caught her eye. Placing a hand against the wall for support, she leaned over to take a closer look.

Vala's normally golden skin had turned red around her ankle, almost like a large cuff. At about her mid-calf, the red faded back to her usual skin tone. She lightly touched the red area, but it felt like any other part of her body; smooth and slightly warm to the touch. Since Kelderans didn't change skin color after a claiming, the result had to be because of Thorin's Brevkan half.

She brushed the skin again with her fingertips. The red had covered the markings on her skin as well, although devoured might be a better phrase since her runic markings had been erased in the red sections. If it were related to being a Brevkan's possession, she wondered why the doctor in her research notes hadn't mentioned it.

She'd keep an eye on it and maybe research it later. For the time being, she dismissed the oddity to put on her dress.

After a little more pacing around the room to test out her strength, Vala stood at the door and gave Thorin's quarters one last glance. For the most part, she'd hated being restricted to the room. But now that she was leaving, she wanted to stay a little longer.

Ridiculous, Vala. Squaring her shoulders, Vala turned and exited the room. Only when she spotted her first warrior did she quickly bow her head and lower her gaze. She needed to remember that the rest of the ship saw her as a Barren. Not only that, the law did as well. If she landed in trouble and broke the law, not even Thorin would be able to assist her.

Keeping her head down, Vala clenched her fingers and headed toward her former room. With each person she passed, she fought the urge to meet their gazes.

And each time she did, anger gathered in her belly.

Thorin had done more than claim her virginity. The male had also started to make her believe she was the equal of others.

In her heart, she believed that. But staying out of jail was her top priority and she needed to be careful.

When she finally entered the designated Barren section of the ship, Vala raised her head again. The first female she saw was Setla, the female she knew from her childhood and the one who had been terrified aboard the shuttle to the colony ship. Vala smiled. "Hello, Setla. Do you remember me?"

The female bobbed her head and whispered, "Sorry, but I must go."

Setla hurried down the corridor. Vala barely had time to frown at her actions when another female voice filled the space, "Don't mind her. She thinks the rumors about warriors wanting revenge on the general through his mistress are true. Someone started a new rumor as well, about how jealous males also take out the mistress's friends and acquaintances."

Vala swung around. A slightly older black-haired female with lavender skin, wearing a flowing, multicolored dress, smirked at her. Since she had a head wrap on, Vala had no idea if the female was a Barren or not. Vala raised her brows and then blurted the question, "Who are you?"

The female snorted. "I had heard how working with the princess had changed you, but I had yet to believe it. I guess it's true."

Vala studied the female but didn't recognize her from her previous assignment. "While I'm flattered to be associated with Princess Kalahn, you still haven't answered my question. Only the Barren are allowed in this section of the ship unless there is an emergency." She waved toward the head wrap. "Without seeing your forehead, I'm not sure how to address you."

The female stood and placed a hand on her hip. She scrutinized Vala a second before replying, "Why does it matter? I can't see you bowing down to me if I turned out to be a fertile female."

Vala dug her nails into her palm to tame her irritation. The other female seemed not to dance around issues. Vala wouldn't mind if she knew if the other female was a Barren. However, until she found out the truth, Vala needed to watch her tongue.

Thankfully the other woman spoke up before Vala could. "My name is Azalyn. The reason why I'm in this part of the ship is because I wanted a respite from my older brother and his bride. They seem determined to find me a lord before we reach Jasvar. My trips to the Barren section over the last week have been the highlight of the journey so far. You all have freedoms I could only dream of."

So she wasn't one of the Barren, then. "Freedom is a subjective word."

The corner of Azalyn's mouth ticked up. "Do elaborate." Vala hesitated and the female rolled her eyes. "You have nothing to fear from me. But if you need formal permission to speak freely without consequence, then I give it."

Vala looked closer at the female. While not an empath, Vala didn't sense any hidden agenda in the female's posture. "Let's confirm your identity on the ship and then I'll speak freely."

Azalyn raised an eyebrow. "You are more commanding than the others. I think we're going to get along well in the future, if you're part of the colony, that is."

She dismissed the part about being friends and said, "You are in our sanctuary. Of course I'm going to vet who you are. Even the law would recognize my right to do so."

Azalyn motioned with a hand. "Then lead me to whatever computer you need to use so that you can scan my retina."

Vala moved to a console nearby. "Here."

The female came and waited. Vala said, "Computer, scan retina for identity and display file. Record of this scan is confidential to the Barren and not to be shared in the public access files."

For a second, the computer said nothing and Vala wondered if Thorin had curbed her access. Then the computer answered, "Ready for the scan."

Azalyn leaned forward. Once the computer finished, Vala read the results:

Azalyn Rippak Sulani. Age 40. Member of the prominent merchant Sulani family through fostering. Officially severed ties with the Rippak family when the Sulanis took her in, and she adopted the Sulani surname at maturity. Passed fertile scan. Single. Special note: access to palace grounds is prohibited. Not allowed within sight distance of any member of the royal family, as decreed by King Kastor. Granted permission to leave Keldera to join the colony on Jasvar.

Vala barely paid attention to the other details and focused on the bit concerning the royal family. She met Azalyn's dark eyes. "What did you do to merit being prohibited from the palace grounds? While few have access, even fewer have an official entry stating they're not allowed inside."

Azalyn smiled. "So, you noticed my record, I see." Vala opened her mouth to press, but Azalyn continued, "I made the mistake of falling in love with a prince. I suggest you avoid doing the same, if given the chance."

While detailed information about the heir to the Kelderan throne, Prince Keltor, wasn't public knowledge, Princess Kalahn had told Vala a little about her brother's youth.

Keltor had wanted to take a shop assistant's daughter as his bride. Azalyn had been told Keltor was betrothed to another and that if she didn't want her father to lose his position, she needed to forget Keltor existed and go into hiding.

The female had disappeared. Not even Prince Kason had been able to find her.

Vala finally made her mouth work. "You loved Prince Keltor."

Azalyn's gaze shuttered. "I don't know how you know which prince it was, but I don't wish to ever hear that name again."

At the anger in Azalyn's tone, Vala debated what to do. For all she knew, Azalyn had ties with the antimonarchy group. More than most, Azalyn had reason to hate the royal family.

However, before she could make a decision, Azalyn walked a few feet away from her and said, "Report me if you like, for invading your space. But I'll leave now and never return. It seems I can't find as much peace in this section of the ship as I had hoped."

With that, the female disappeared down the hallway.

As if Vala already didn't have enough tasks to do, she now had another.

However, she wasn't going to condemn Azalyn before even looking into her. After all, the female had suffered enough pain simply because she'd fallen in love with the wrong person. Another accusation could ruin her reputation forever.

But if she were innocent, that would cause another conundrum. Mainly, if Vala should tell Princess Kalahn about Azalyn's place on the colony. Because if she did, Kalahn would probably share the news with her eldest brother, Keltor.

Vala had never met Prince Keltor and didn't know what would happen if he found out about Azalyn. Vala suspected the female was one of his potential destined brides, which meant she was one of a handful of females who could bear him offspring.

History was full of stories about princes and kings claiming females against their will, all in the name of propagating their lines. While not even a prince could take a female by force and go unscathed, the royal family could imprison or threaten the female into silence and acceptance.

Poor Azalyn had no idea what might be coming her way.

With a deep breath, Vala turned and headed to her old quarters. It was time to return to her old life and get to work.

Chapter Eleven

Thorin looked to Syzel to his right and then to Ryven on his left. He'd worked the most amount of missions with the two warriors and could trust them to have his back against the possible unknown enemy.

Raising a hand to signal it was time to move, they exited the elevator and walked down the corridor toward the main engineering department, where the engines were monitored.

Since there had been little to glean from the reports regarding the disappearances and the ensuing communication silence, Thorin had accessed the most restricted records to scan for similar incidents.

While nothing had matched exactly, there had been a few instances of smaller merchant ships suddenly losing their engines and internal visual monitoring capabilities. In three cases, not long after reporting the troubles, communications went silent and the crew was never heard from again.

None of the ships had been in the same sector of space as the colony transport ship's current position, though. And considering all three disappearances had been dismissed as catastrophic malfunctions, Thorin wondered if something bigger had been in play since no wreckage or any sort of particle disturbances had been discovered by search crews at their last known coordinates.

He wasn't about to let the same thing happen to his ship, if he could help it. Since the colony ship was far larger than the merchant ships, if it suffered the same problem, Thorin should have some time to discover what it was and to research a solution. As a last resort, he would contact the fighter ships accompanying him and ask for assistance from headquarters. He wasn't going to let pride get in the way of evacuating the ship's passengers if things worsened and became critical.

Pushing everything else from his mind, Thorin tightened his grip on the blaster gun in his hand. In addition to his weapon, he and his two warriors wore rare, special protective straps across their chests. The straps projected invisible force fields around their bodies. While not impervious, it would ward off most forms of attack. It also prevented being moved by any sort of teleportation or telekinetic abilities, as well as concealing the wearer's emotions against empaths.

They approached the outer force field to the engineering section. Thorin went to the computer panel next to it and typed in his authorization code. Once the computer scanned both his retina and his thumb, the force field dissipated.

Thorin repeated the computer security scans at each force field barrier until they were just outside the entrance to main engineering. He took his time studying the other side of the field for anything unusual. However, the only thing out of the ordinary was the silence. Usually the hum of the engines and the murmurs of the staff on duty could be heard from his current vantage point.

He looked at his warriors. Each bobbed their head, signaling they were ready. Thorin disabled the final protective barrier.

Nothing jumped out at them, which was a good sign but they were far from safe. Many foes bided their time before striking.

Thorin slowly made his way into the outer engineering control room. Everything was pristine. All the flat panels were whole, and the various engineering instruments were either stowed on the walls or near a console where a staff member would keep it. There was no damage or sign of struggle anywhere.

There also weren't any bodies or remains to signal death at the hands of an intruder.

Thorin pressed onward to the engine control room. As soon as he reached the doorway, he noticed the flickering engine drive. The usual steady green and white lights were purely white, which meant they were being overloaded.

He wasn't an engineer, but all generals were trained to man the various stations aboard the ship, especially in emergency situations. He needed to manually turn off the engine's power source before it became critical and could explode.

Signaling Syzel and Ryven to keep watch as he worked, Thorin focused on the control panel. The second he touched it, his protective force field armor flickered and flashed. While he didn't see anything with the naked eye, something didn't want him to interact with the engines.

Unsure of how long he had before his protective gear failed, he quickly typed in the shutdown sequence. His force field crackled as the engine lights burned a brighter white. Something had to be drawing on the engine's power to attack him.

Crackling behind him told Thorin that his two warriors were being attacked, too. He typed the code as fast as he could. Just as his personal force field started to jump and cut him at random spots because of the strain, the engine's light faded until it was dark.

His protective gear instantly went back to a neutral position.

Thorin studied the readout and the engine lights, but both confirmed all power had been cut off. He turned back toward his men. He looked to Syzel and waved toward the male. "Did anything register on your instrument?"

Syzel raised the small rod in his nonweapon holding hand. "If the data collected from this is correct, someone was trying to teleport you off the ship. When that failed, it tried to take Ryven and me. However, this instrument isn't advanced enough to pinpoint where the teleportation source came from."

Thorin said, "Regardless, I believe it was drawing on the engine's power. As long as it's turned off, this area should be safe. We'll have to cut all major sources of power until we can find the enemy, and quickly, before who or whatever figures out our idea and launches a possible no-holds-barred attack."

Ryven spoke up. "So you'll contact the fighters and let them know what we discovered?"

"Yes," Thorin answered. "I'm afraid our journey is going to be postponed yet again. It's pure speculation, but it's almost as if someone doesn't want us to reach Jasvar."

"Agreed," Syzel said. "Do you think it's related to the asteroid-looking objects from before?"

Thorin grunted in approval. "It had crossed my mind. Until the fighters can thoroughly scan the area and say for certain there are some lurking nearby or not, we'll go into safe mode. Ryven, ensure the top-level and most-trusted warriors receive their order to enforce all necessary restrictions. Syzel, you coordinate with engineering on all aspects of the power shutdown and monitoring. Since Enishi was in this room and is now missing, I need your assistance with engineering matters. You always excelled with them during our training years."

Both males said, "Aye, sir," before Thorin continued, "As for me, I'll look into any and all disappearances. Anyone who hasn't reported to duty will be investigated. As you two are experienced, it should go without saying that this is confidential information. I will inform you of who needs to know the details. When making inquiries, keep them as vague as possible. I don't want to stir panic."

Ryven jumped in. "Excuse me for speaking out of turn, sir, but you should see a medic first."

Thorin glanced down at his body. There were probably twenty or so cuts on his chest and arms. More than a few were deep enough to merit laser stitches.

"I know of a medic who can keep things quiet and I'll visit them," he stated. "Report anything you find to me in person only. I want to know even the smallest detail. I'll call meetings when necessary, so be available at all times. For the moment, you're dismissed."

The two men made a fist with one hand and thumped it over their hearts before exiting the room.

Thorin tapped in one last command to the computer, restricting access to only him and Syzel, before switching the entire room to life-support-only levels of power. If any surge was detected in the room, Thorin's communicator would alert him to the change.

He left the area and headed toward the elevator. As the adrenaline wore off, he wanted nothing more than to sit down.

136

There was more blood on his body than he liked. Thorin needed to have his wounds tended to and take restorative drinks to counter his blood loss.

Since he didn't know the head medic well—many of the officers were staying on Jasvar and had been assigned to the ship rather than Thorin selecting them—there was only one person who he trusted to tend him and keep the secret.

It looked like he would need to visit Vala Yarlen once more.

At the thought of Vala, a quick succession of images invaded his mind. He took her against a wall, reveling in his blood covering her body. After claiming her ten other ways, he then roared and went to challenge every shady-looking crew member.

Stop. If he did any of that, Vala would recoil from his mere presence. He never wanted to scare her.

He took a few breaths and regained control of his mind. He refused to succumb to his disgusting urges.

His temper under control, he finally entered the elevator and typed in a secure message to Vala and then to the temporary Barren Mother aboard the ship. Generals could go into the Barren's section, provided they gave notice so that the Barren could keep to their rooms and out of sight.

And since all the Barren still believed Vala to be his mistress, his presence wouldn't be alarming or cause suspicion.

As he exited the elevator and headed toward the entrance to the Barren's section of the ship, he took a deep breath to further reinforce his calm mind. He would do whatever it took to protect Vala and ensure he didn't touch her again. He'd worked up the nerve to dismiss her once. If he ever claimed her again, he wasn't sure he could do it a second time.

~~~

Vala checked her medical bag one more time, ensuring everything was in its place. Thorin hadn't said what had happened to him, but just that he needed her medical experience. The message had been vague, but her gut said it was Thorin who needed medical attention.

To be honest, she wasn't sure if she was nervous or angry at him coming. If he had truly wanted to sever their connection, seeing her again so soon gave the wrong message.

And yet, touching his warm skin and not having to watch what she said or did around him would be nice.

Her door chimed and she stood up tall before saying, "Enter."

The door slid open and she gasped.

Thorin was covered in gashes and cuts across his chest, arms, and even his face. Blood oozed out of a few of them.

Forgetting everything that had happened between them, she walked up to him, took his hand, and tugged him inside. "You need to sit down."

He grunted. "I can stand. I don't want to get my blood on your things."

She pointed to the simple composite chair to one side. "This can easily be disinfected. Sit before I give you a sedative and you won't have a choice."

For a second, Thorin remained silent. Vala didn't break eye contact. When it came to medical matters, even a general had to listen to their enlisted medical professional. Her case might be flimsy since she was a Barren and not a doctor, but she'd stand by it.

The corner of his mouth moved and she resisted a sigh of relief. His deep voice filled the room. "For such a short female, you have incredible bravery."

She pointed to the chair. Once he finally sat down, she replied, "All Kelderan males are stubborn in medical matters. I once had a male with his lower leg crushed in an accident and he claimed he was fine. I wish more people were honest. I can't help if I don't know what's wrong."

Vala turned toward her medical bag. She picked up a handheld disinfectant light and a cloth. Thorin's voice filled the room. "The deepest gashes are on my upper chest and lower back."

She turned toward him. At the exhaustion in his eyes, she softened. "Thank you for telling me. Let me work so we can get you healthy again."

Vala stepped between his spread legs. As she wiped away the excess blood on Thorin's chest, his warmth caressed her as his scent surrounded her.

Vala's heart thumped faster as memories of being even closer to Thorin threatened to spill into her mind.

Needing a distraction, she asked, "What happened?"

A general had no obligation to tell a mere Barren what had transpired. But Thorin replied without hesitation, "I was attacked by an unknown enemy."

She met his gaze again. "Be more specific. Should I be worried?"

He smiled. "I admire you asking for the facts instead of going into hysterics."

Looking back to his wound, she clicked on the disinfectant light and began cleaning his injuries. "If the situation was life-threatening, you wouldn't be sitting in my quarters. Even with your cuts, you'd be on the command deck giving orders."

"You are clever, Vala Yarlen. I should stop doubting you."

She did look up at his face at that. As they stared into one another's eyes, Vala wished with her whole heart she could have Thorin as her own. She had a hard time believing any other male would see past her status to treat her equally, let alone praise her. "Stating the obvious wastes time. Tell me what happened and maybe I can help."

Thorin snorted before grunting. "Don't make me laugh." She merely raised her eyebrows and Thorin added, "Everyone in the engineering department has vanished. I'm fairly certain they were taken via some kind of teleportation."

She blinked but quickly recovered. "I want to hear the rest, but I need to fix you up. So talk while I work."

He grinned. "Aye, aye, sir."

Shaking her head, she went back to work cleaning his wound so she could stitch him up.

Thorin explained the disappearances, the overloaded engines, and the flickering personal force field armor. She had nearly finished laser stitching the deepest wound on his chest when he stated, "So as much as it pains me to say it, our trip will be delayed. But do not fear, Vala, because I will ensure you reach Jasvar, no matter how long it takes."

At the determination in his voice, she met his eyes once more. Only truth reflected in his blue gaze.

If he weren't in pain and the ship in possible danger, Vala would chance kissing him. Thorin was a more honorable and caring male than she had ever imagined.

Clearing her throat, she nodded her head and moved to his back. "You think someone might be trying to stop this ship from reaching Jasvar. Do you think it's connected to your original secret mission, to find the traitors?"

"None of this technology could be Kelderan. Only if they hired an unknown mercenary force to sabotage the ship could this be related, and that would take more funds than I think they have at their disposal."

She finished wiping the blood away and began cleaning the next gash. "You have spent the past few years mostly away from Keldera and I think you don't understand how tense the situation has become between the anti- and promonarchy factions. Each has been secretly gaining support from prominent businesses and citizens. The funds are possible. All it would take is a merchant trader sympathizer to go into space and meet with pirates to facilitate a deal with a mercenary group."

"That would require a phenomenal amount of planning to keep the plot a secret from the Kelderan Army headquarters and their spies."

"Still, it could be possible."

Thorin looked over his shoulder. "It seems I need to learn more about what's been happening on Keldera in my absence. I will look into your theory."

Bobbing her head, she switched the cleaning light to stitch mode and tackled the large gash on his back. "I hope I'm wrong, but it's always best to check every avenue."

"Of course. And you are right about me not knowing the situation on Keldera as well as you. While you work, will you tell me about recent clashes and tensions between the two factions? I'm sure not all of it was put into the official record."

As she began telling him what she knew, a sense of peace came over Vala. She had to admit being looked to for guidance and knowledge could become addictive.

It could also lead to trouble.

Focusing on Thorin's wounds and updating him on the current faction statuses on Keldera, Vala forgot about everything else.

~~~

Thorin listened to Vala's soothing voice as she told him facts and events surrounding the factions on Keldera. Ever since stepping foot inside her quarters, no vision or urge had made an appearance.

Well, almost none. He was fairly certain she'd been about to kiss him and he had wanted to pull her close and devour her mouth.

He'd resisted, as his duty required. He needed medical attention so he could perform his best, and he would suffer it. But then he needed to investigate Vala's suggestions as well as check in with Syzel and Ryven. He simply didn't have time to steal a kiss.

Still, he reveled in the softness of her delicate fingers as she worked. A male could get used to such a touch.

However, Vala's growl garnered his attention. "I don't think you're paying attention."

"I apologize. I'm having a hard time concentrating."

She moved to in front of him once more and took his chin between her fingers. "Are you ill? Do you feel about to faint? Tell me any and all symptoms. And don't display a brave warrior front, either. This ship needs you."

Thorin should simply dismiss her words and look away. But as if someone else were controlling his body, he raised a hand to touch her arm. Lightly stroking her skin, he murmured, "I'm a little weak from blood loss, but that's not the reason."

Vala's voice was breathy as she asked, "Then what's going on?"

"It's best not to say."

Vala studied his gaze, but Thorin remained silent. She finally sighed. "Stubborn warrior."

On anyone else, the words would make him frown. But not coming from his Vala.

He mentally cursed. The female wasn't his and never could be.

Still, as he took in her assessing, intelligent eyes, he had an idea. But first, he needed to ask Vala a question. "If I gave you personal lessons in defense, do you think you could handle any possible threats?"

"What threats? You dismissed me as your mistress. No one will pay any attention to me."

"Just answer the question."

"No. Tell me the full truth or I'll clear you for duty and you can leave my room."

When all she did was raise her eyebrows, he sighed. "I'm not sure how I ever thought you were meek." She shrugged and turned away from him to clean up her supplies. As much as he liked watching her work, each second that passed was time taken away from solving the engineering mystery. He finally spoke up again. "You have knowledge that can help regarding current events on Keldera. I think you should remain my mistress to the eyes of everyone aboard the ship."

She stilled. "What about finding the traitors? They may be related, and I can overhear information much easier if I'm merely another Barren instead of the general's mistress."

"Perhaps. But there are others who I can enlist to help. I've been keeping this mission a secret, but a good general knows how to lean on those he trusts. My only concern is your safety, but private self-defense and weapons use lessons will rectify that."

Vala placed her last instrument inside her bag and slowly turned to face him. Since her expression was unreadable, he merely waited.

After a few more seconds, she cleared her throat. "I will give my preliminary permission, but once things calm down, I want to go over the rules and expectations."

Thorin stood and took a step toward Vala. "What rules and expectations? Now it's your turn to be specific."

As he closed the distance between them, Vala's cheeks heated. When she spoke, her voice wasn't much more than a whisper. "I-I want to help control your urges and visions."

Memories of Vala's cry as she orgasmed filled his mind. "Anything else?"

"We can talk about it later. There are more important things to worry about."

He raised a hand and cupped her cheek. He loved how Vala leaned into his palm. "Then let's seal our temporary agreement."

"But your duties."

"A few seconds will help keep me focused and my visions away. Isn't that what you offered to do?"

When she nodded quickly, Thorin leaned down and gently kissed her. He took his time nibbling her lips before he stopped and pulled his head away enough to see Vala's eyes. "You need to gather your things and move into my quarters. If anyone looks suspicious, you call me immediately. I'll set up the AI system to recognize your voice and to give you clearance for my emergency line."

He kissed her once more before letting go and walking to the door. "I won't keep you locked up again. But I hope that you'll stay in my quarters until things calm down a fraction."

"I'll try, but if things worsen, I'm going to go where my help is needed the most."

"That I can understand. Until later, Vala."

Thorin forced himself to exit the room.

Once he retrieved a restorative drink at the first replicator machine he came across, he walked briskly toward the elevator. Armed with new knowledge and a lightness to his soul that could only be because of Vala, Thorin was refreshed and ready to tackle the latest threat.

Chapter Twelve

An hour later, Thorin sat in his small office off the command deck and frowned at the view screen displaying General Corvel's upper half. "More of the asteroid like-objects have appeared?"

The senior general grunted. "Yes. We're still double-checking the count, but it's about forty of them."

The same number that had disappeared from Thorin's engineering department. Since the line was secure, he said as much to Corvel before adding, "But if the two are linked, where did the missing ten asteroid-like objects go?"

"That I don't know. We've expanded the probe-ranges and have some of our patrol ships also looking for unusual traces of movement or activity, just as the fighters are doing near your ship. In the meantime, remain in your current position and keep your power sources minimal. We'll check in every twelve hours unless something crops up. While waiting, make sure to have your weapons ready to go at a moment's notice. Since weapons require far less power than engines, have the computer reroute all auxiliary power not being used for life support systems to the ship's blasters and laser cannons. End transmission."

The panel went black and Thorin stood.

For all intents and purposes, he was stranded in space with few options. For the first time, Thorin wished he'd already reached Jasvar. That way, he could talk with the Earth Colony Alliance observers living with the human colonists there. Keldera didn't have an alliance with the ECA and thus didn't have access to their databanks or records. The ECA might have experience with the strange events and possible enemy, which could yield helpful information.

While Thorin hadn't been a fan of humans for most of his life, he'd recently worked with two worthy females. One of them was the current leader of Jasvar. He would reach out to her and see if the ECA would divulge information to her.

A secure transmission to Jasvar would take at least a week, but Thorin decided to chance it. For all he knew, he could be stranded for weeks or months in his current location. The transport ship, while not designed for long hauls, could comfortably support the five thousand colonists and crew for up to six months.

After recording and sending the message, Thorin exited his small office.

Since Syzel and Ryven had checked in that all was going smoothly for both of their tasks, and Corvel hadn't provided any new information, Thorin had some time on his hands to talk with Vala about her theories surrounding the antimonarchy faction hiring mercenaries to interfere.

It may lead to nothing, but he needed the knowledge just in case.

He also wanted to issue her a blaster gun of her own.

Looking to the center of the command deck, he asked his lieutenant general, Jelshi, "Any changes in power fluctuations or in the visual feeds?"

"No, sir," Jelshi replied. "Although there is one matter that needs attention—the ship's counselors are overloaded with session requests. The colonists are becoming alarmed."

"Since they aren't warriors, that's to be expected. Have the counselors give group talks for the time being and have them reference helpful texts and videos to help ease the burden of one-on-one sessions. If there's a problem or specific concern, the chief counselor can contact me in my private quarters. I have work that can't wait. You'll retain command until I say otherwise."

"Aye, aye, sir," Jelshi answered.

Thorin exited the room, fully confident that Jelshi could handle basic discontent. They had worked side-by-side during an intense encounter with illegal traders last year. Being on red alert for ten hours had barely fazed Jelshi, not to mention he'd proven himself quick with effective suggestions.

Maybe Thorin could use him for rooting out any traitors aboard the ship, too.

But not yet. He needed to check on Vala before meeting with his first potential warrior spy. While she was proving to be a capable female, he wanted to give her some basic instruction on blaster guns. He had a feeling she would want to leave his quarters sooner rather than later and she needed to be prepared. The thought of her being injured or worse made his stomach churn.

She may not be his bride, but he would do whatever it took to ensure her safety.

~~~

Vala finished typing up her guide to the main factions surrounding the monarchy on Keldera, the known leaders, and some of their suspected business ties. As she reread the last entry of suspected businesses with antimonarchy sentiments, the name of one stuck out: Rippak Merchants.

According to the database file, the female Vala had met earlier, Azalyn, had previously been part of the Rippak family before fostering with the Sulanis. Vala's initial conclusion was that Azalyn wasn't involved with the antimonarchy group. The records Vala had accessed using Thorin's security clearance spoke of a thoroughly vetted colony candidate, not to mention she'd lived far from any known dissident hotspots. Nothing on the file kept by the Kelderan Army spoke of an enemy to the royal family. The restriction regarding the palace was only to keep her from seeking out Prince Keltor again.

However, while Vala thought Azalyn was innocent, members of her former family might know something. She'd have to investigate and seek out the female again, but on the pretense of the meeting being accidental. That way she could try to learn as much as possible about Azalyn's blood family without giving away her objective.

Vala paused at that thought. Here she was thinking about spies and missions. She'd come a long way from healing the sick inside the citadel.

Not that she'd change a thing. If anything, Thorin would probably bring her deeper into his world. Vala had no desire to be a warrior, but she might just like gathering intelligence for her male.

She blinked. *No.* Thorin wasn't hers. She needed to be more careful. After all, Thorin was a skilled general. One slip up of her emotions or even her thoughts, and he might figure out her deeply hidden desire to spend more than a few days or weeks with him.

As it were, when he'd suggested she be his mistress again, it'd taken everything she'd had not to jump into his arms.

Taking a deep breath, she looked back to her notescreen. She had work to do.

Just as she was about to bring up additional information on the Rippak Merchants, Thorin entered the room. Even though she wanted to rush into his arms and feel his strong muscles around her, she remained on the bed.

There was too much undecided and unsaid between them. She wasn't entirely sure how to act.

Thorin spoke first. "You're still here."

She raised her brows. "Of course I am. And I even have something for you." She held up her notescreen. "This might help you better understand the situation on Keldera, which could help with locating traitors."

He crossed the room and sat on the edge of the bed. His body was a few inches from her own, but his heat still managed to caress her skin.

She clutched the sheets to keep from reaching out to touch him.

Thorin's voice garnered her attention. "What do you have for me?"

Clearing her throat, she handed him the information. "Since always having me at your ear is impossible, you can use this."

He glanced down at the document and nodded. "Thank you."

Silence stretched for a few beats. Vala finally reached out and touched his arm. "Don't be formal with me, Thorin."

"Says the female being cautious around me."

She sighed. "I think we need to decide this situation before anything else. Otherwise, we'll be dancing around each other and won't be able to focus."

He smiled slowly. "Normally, I would like the idea of you thinking about me, but I want to show you how to use a blaster gun, and that requires your full attention."

She scooted a fraction closer to him, never removing her hand from his arm. "Already? Aren't there more important things for you to do? I may have only worked on two ships so far, but generals are always busy."

In the blink of an eye, he tossed the notescreen on the bed and moved her into his lap. As he lazily stroked her back, Vala's heart beat faster. He murmured, "I'd be selfish to keep you sequestered inside this room. You'll better be able to help everyone aboard this ship by going about your duties and keeping your eyes and ears open. However, I won't allow you to do so until you know the ins and outs of using a blaster gun."

With just the two of them in the room, she didn't hesitate to echo, "Allow me?"

"Perhaps I could've used a better phrase. Don't expect me to completely bend when it comes to your wishes, especially if your safety is concerned. I won't have you harmed under my watch, Vala. Ever."

At the fierceness of his gaze, she stopped breathing. She'd never imagined a male vowing to look after her and mean it.

She wondered if this was how a lord acted around his bride.

Focus, Vala. She finally found her voice again. "I know, and I wouldn't expect anything less of you." She hesitated a second, but finally gave in and curled against his chest. She listened to his heartbeat as she added, "But I don't know if I'm to be your mistress in reality or if I'm merely to be used for information."

She left out the part about them going separate ways if they ever made it to Jasvar and continued, "What do you expect of me, Thorin? Tell me that and I promise to pay attention to every word you say about blaster guns."

He gently tugged her hair until she leaned back enough to see his face. She shivered at the intensity in his eyes. "I'm not a poetic male and will speak the truth. I want you as long as I can have you, Vala. However, you know we have different paths once we reach Jasvar. What we do in the interim is entirely up to you."

"Y-you want me to decide the rules?"

He nodded. "Yes. First off, what are your orders surrounding the lord and mistress relationship?"

As she stared in Thorin's blue eyes, she blurted out, "I want to be your mistress in all ways."

He moved a hand to lightly brush her breast, and she sucked in a breath. His voice was husky as he answered, "And so it shall be. But a general's schedule is tight and unpredictable. I don't know when I can claim you again, but I look forward to the moment I can."

The symbol on his neck flashed red, signaling desire. Thorin, an accomplished general in the Keldera Army, wanted her again.

Not holding back this time, she kissed him. Thorin pressed his tongue into her mouth and stroked against hers. With each movement, she softened more against him.

When he finally pulled away, Vala's breathing was labored.

Thorin's eyes glowed blue as he said, "As much as I want to rip off your dress and make you cry out in pleasure, I must teach you about blaster guns instead." He stood and took her with him. Vala took a second to find her footing. Once she did, Thorin continued, "Now, are you ready to learn?"

152

THE BARREN

~~~

While Thorin's cock was hard against his trousers, the visions were absent. It was almost as if the more times he kissed or touched Vala, the more in control he was of the urges and dishonorable images.

He wondered what would happen once he said goodbye to Vala. He might suddenly be overloaded and unable to control his Brevkan half. That would mean resigning his position and isolating himself from others.

Yet as Vala stared up at him with curious eyes and her breathing still slightly erratic, he decided to focus on the present and the gift he'd discovered in the form of one Barren female.

Clearing his throat, he finally released his hold on Vala and stepped back. To prevent himself from closing the distance and tasting her sweet mouth once more, he took his blaster gun from his hip and held it between them, but aimed it away from either of them. "While I know you can pull the trigger, you need to be able to configure every setting and understand what each one does to a person."

As he explained the options of stun all the way to kill, he paused after each one to ensure Vala could do it herself. It didn't take long for him to realize she was a fast learner.

No wonder she'd been able to easily adjust from a flight simulator to a small shuttle ship on their previous voyage, when she'd assisted Princess Kalahn.

He stood behind her and watched her fingers tap out the latest setting. The heat of her back against his chest combined with the scent of her hair nearly made him groan.

Vala turned and ran into his chest. For a few beats, she merely stared into his eyes. Most Barren were trained to keep their markings a deep blue to hide their emotions, much like soldiers. In the eyes of fertile females, the Barren weren't entirely living and shouldn't have emotions.

The thought made him reach out and trace the curves of the marking on her neck. When it flashed red, he smiled. "I was hoping you'd show me your true emotions eventually."

"For a general, you're easily distracted."

The instant the words were out, Vala tensed under his fingertips. He growled. "Don't do that. I meant it when I said I want to hear the truth from you. Hold back and I *will* keep you locked in this room."

"Much like you've kept a secret for so long it's hard to share, it's difficult for me to act myself around any male. Change takes time, Thorin. Maybe one day you'll accept your heritage and I can be myself around non-Barren."

But not together was left unsaid.

"I concede your point."

"Good. Does that mean I can move freely about the ship again?"

"To a point. Until you have logged enough hours of shooting practice in one of the private recreation rooms, I don't want you in any of the soldier-only areas or sections that are mostly empty and isolated. You need more than one session to truly protect yourself from a warrior."

"Does that mean the Barren section and the colonists areas are okay? After all, both areas have tight restrictions on weapons use."

He searched her gaze. "Perhaps. First, tell me why you want to go there." When Vala raised her brows, he added, "Please tell me why."

She smiled and his heart skipped a beat. "I suppose we both need some conditioning."

"Vala," he growled out.

Her laugh chased away his negative emotions. She really was his lightness in the dark.

Vala finally said, "I have a theory concerning a possible financier for the antimonarchy faction. While I know there's no concrete proof that mercenaries were hired, I want to explore the possibility."

"Care to tell me why?" When she hesitated, he brushed her cheek. "I more than anyone know how to keep a secret, Vala."

"Even from the royal family?"

He snorted. "Especially from them. I talk as little as possible with the male bastards as I can."

She tilted her head. "Prince Kason is kinder than he lets on."

A rush of jealousy coursed through his body, but then Thorin remembered Kason had found his bride and wasn't a threat. "I don't want to know how you can say that with such certainty. Please tell me who you're investigating, Vala. That way, if you go missing, I know where to start looking."

After another second, she finally nodded. "I want to talk with Azalyn Rippak Sulani."

As did most Kelderans his age or older, he had heard the tale of Azalyn Rippak and her attempt to wed Prince Keltor.

"Wait a second. The female who tried to win a prince is onboard this ship?"

"Yes. I ran into her earlier."

"Then how did she get aboard if she's part of the antimonarchy group? I understand her disliking the king and his offspring for all but forcing her to abandon her own family, but whoever screened her for the colony must've known who she was and should've scrutinized the female severely."

Although, a small part of him wondered if King Kastor had merely wanted the female off his planet for good. Some said Prince Keltor had never found another female to love after Azalyn had disappeared all those years ago.

Vala shook her head. "From what I can find on her, my initial conclusion is that Azalyn isn't a part of that group. But someone from her previous life may know something, and even if Azalyn is estranged, she might be able to say who might be best to investigate. I've heard rumors about the Rippak Merchants leaning toward the antimonarchists. If I can get her to open up to me, then maybe we'll have a lead."

Thorin's initial instinct was to forbid Vala from talking with the female. Anyone who attempted to marry above her station could only be trouble.

He stilled at that thought. By that reasoning, Vala wasn't worthy of finding a lord to love and cherish her.

Vala was correct in that it was going to take time to change his prejudices and way of thinking. Allowing Vala freedom to talk with the female might be a good first step.

Sighing, he replied, "Talk to her. But if you're going to do so, then I have something to give you."

Thorin moved to one of his personal storage bins, pressed, and opened the door. Gently, he retrieved a small, synthetic pouch. Facing Vala, he offered it to her. "Wear this and I'll be able to find you."

Gingerly taking the pouch, Vala opened it and gasped. "I can't take this, Thorin."

She lifted the silver chain and displayed a dangling pendant in the shape of a purple Kelderan flower. The small petals made of dark and light purple gemstones spread out into a large, circular bloom. In the middle was a small electronic time keeper, which also included a chipped locator.

Vala offered it back to him, but he covered her hand with his and pushed it until it rested against her chest. "My mother gave it to me to do with it what I wished. This necklace will allow me to find you as long as you wear it. Will you allow me the honor of bestowing it upon you?"

"I—" Vala paused and spoke again. "I will accept it temporarily. But it's precious and you should give it to your future bride."

The idea of any female but Vala wearing his mother's necklace made the hairs on the back of his neck stand up. "You deserve it, Vala. If I didn't want you to have it, I wouldn't have offered."

She stared down at the sparkling pendant resting against her lower ribcage. "It is beautiful."

Before he could stop himself, Thorin murmured, "A beautiful necklace for a beautiful female."

He wondered if he'd stepped over a line, but Vala merely smiled. "And to think you claimed not to be romantic." He grunted and she laughed. "I'll wear it for now. But as soon as we reach Jasvar, I'll give it back."

Thorin knew when to hold his tongue in most situations, and he finally seemed to have regained control once more. He remained silent and watched as Vala placed the chain over her head.

Once the pendant finally rested between her breasts, she picked it up and asked, "Do I need to change or recharge power sources to keep it going?"

He dared to pick up the pendant and rubbed the center with his thumb. "No. I check it periodically and it should be fine for many months yet." He turned it over and pointed to the small, slightly darker silver circle in the middle. "If you need to call me, press this area hard against your skin for thirty seconds and it'll send an alert to my communicator."

The necklace had been given to his mother after his conception, in case she ever needed assistance against an enemy. She had always wanted Thorin to find his own female to protect and entrust her necklace to. As much as his mother had loved him over the years, she never wanted another female to suffer the same fate as her.

Thorin gently tucked the flower under the neckline of her dress. "As much as I love seeing the purple against your dress, I don't want to risk a robbery or worse."

"Just how valuable is it, Thorin?"

"That's irrelevant. Just promise me that you'll wear it at all times."

She searched his eyes for a second before bobbing her head. "I will."

"Good." He dared to lean forward and kiss her. "I must return to my office and listen to updates from Syzel and Ryven, in addition to some other meetings. I hope to see you here this evening."

Lightly touching his cheek, Vala murmured, "I'll be here, Thorin. I might even have a surprise for you, too."

"What surprise?"

"If I told you, then it wouldn't be a surprise."

He gave his most intimidating stare, but Vala never blinked. Pride swelled his heart. "Then until this evening."

As Thorin exited the room and headed back to his office to face the real world, all he wanted to do was turn around and find out Vala's surprise.

But then he remembered the ship's predicament and kept his expression neutral. He needed to be strong for the crew and colonists. The last thing he needed was to neglect his duties and cause chaos or panic.

Chapter Thirteen

Vala secured a blaster gun holster around her calf and dropped her skirt back into place. She wished she could wear it at her side like a warrior, but she didn't need unnecessary questions or she'd never find her target. And considering Azalyn had managed to remain out of sight for over two decades—if the public information she'd found were to be believed—she knew how to stay hidden.

Right before exiting the room, she lightly traced the outline of the flower pendant Thorin had given her. She'd never received a gift from a male before, and despite how much it shouldn't matter, the slight weight around her neck made her smile. The fact he'd bestowed something so precious into her care spoke volumes. True, he wanted to be able to locate her. But Vala didn't think Thorin would just give it to anyone so that he could trace them.

And no matter what it took, even if she encountered a thief, she'd fight to protect his mother's legacy.

Lowering her hand, she took a deep breath and exited her room. She was careful to keep her gaze downward as she traversed one corridor and then another. However, each person she passed only increased her irritation. She might end up spending most of her time on the human Jasvarian colony sites instead of the Kelderan ones, where she wouldn't have to worry about her station or tradition.

After taking an elevator to the deck where all members of the Sulani family were staying, she dared to raise her head again. Even though it was midday according to the ship's artificial timekeeping schedule, no one walked about. While the entire Sulani merchant dynasty wasn't aboard the colony ship, enough were that Vala suspected them to be working for the duration of the journey. A number of merchants had been granted permission to set up shops for the new Kelderan colony, and the Sulanis were one of them.

Since chiming one door after another to locate Azalyn was out of the question for a Barren, Vala headed toward the large common area used by the entire floor. As with most ships, quarters were small. Not even a rich merchant family would be granted special privilege, per the terms of the Keldera-Jasvar Colony Agreement. All non-Barren citizens were equal aboard the colony ship, although Vala doubted it'd stay that way once everyone was living on the new planet.

Thinking of the agreement made Vala think of her friend Taryn. The human female had been kind to her when few had, and it only renewed Vala's determination to stop any unrest she could aboard the ship. Taryn didn't need any additional headaches or problems to deal with on her planet.

Vala finally reached the large central area of the floor. Chaises and chairs formed semi-circles to either side, with a small, protected garden in the center. The mixture of bushes and flowers would remind anyone of Keldera and might possibly help them forget that they were in the middle of space, especially since many of the colonists had never been aboard a spaceship before.

Scanning the open area, Vala saw no one. She couldn't hang about without a task, which meant she'd have to turn back and rethink how to locate Azalyn without being noticed.

Just as she was about to turn around, she noticed someone crouching next to the purple blooms in the garden that were similar to the one on her pendant.

While the female she'd spotted wore a head wrap, Vala recognized the multi-colored stripes of her dress. She walked toward the female, who then looked up.

It was Azalyn

The female quickly wiped her eyes and stood. Vala asked, "Are you well?"

Azalyn snorted. "'Well' is a vague term. Health-wise, I'm in the prime of my life."

Vala dared to step closer. "And in other ways?"

Azalyn opened her mouth but promptly closed it. After a few seconds, she finally replied, "What're you doing here? Maybe I should threaten to report you like you threatened to report me."

"You could." She took another step. "But I think your curiosity wants to know why I'm on this deck."

She looked around before motioning with her hand. "Follow me."

Azalyn didn't wait for any sort of confirmation, but merely exited the shared area and headed down a corridor.

Following Azalyn could be a bad idea. But Vala's gut still said the female wasn't malicious in nature.

Besides, she had Thorin's locator and the blaster gun around her leg.

She quickly went down the same corridor. Azalyn stood outside a room at the end of the hall. As soon as she spotted Vala, she entered the room.

Once Vala reached it and did the same, the door slid closed. The room was small with a bed, wardrobe, and cleaning area—the standard issue for any single colonist traveling to Jasvar.

However, the walls were covered with sketches featuring flowers, landscapes, plants, and wildlife being held in place by static holders. The array of colors made the room feel cozy. To be honest, it reminded Vala of Azalyn's dress.

It seemed the female had her own view of the world. Vala had to admit she liked the color and brashness of the pictures.

"So, are you going to stare at my paintings or tell me why you sought me out?" Azalyn demanded.

Vala looked to Azalyn. "I never said I was seeking you."

She shrugged. "Given the slight widening of your eyes when you spotted me, combined with your forthrightness despite being a Barren, it's the only logical guess."

The female was observant. Vala would need to remember that. "Then let me be forthright again. All I wanted to ask was whether you kept in contact with your birth family or not?"

Azalyn searched Vala's gaze. "Why does a Barren need to know that? My public record says it all—I severed ties with them once I was adopted by the Sulanis."

Vala hesitated. She wished she could tell Azalyn the full truth, but she was already walking a fine line.

Then an idea struck. As much as she hated lying, protecting the entire ship and getting it to Jasvar in one piece was her top concern.

It was time to be bold like Taryn Demara. Taking a deep breath, she blurted out, "You may or may not know that I am friends with Princess Kalahn. And when we reach Jasvar, I'll have to tell her you're on the colony."

Azalyn narrowed her eyes. "I've left Keltor alone all these years. I haven't broken any of the stipulations forced upon me to preserve my family's business ties and station. There is nothing for the princess or her other brother, Kason, to worry about. I know they're both on Jasvar and I plan to keep my distance."

Vala raised a hand. "This has nothing to do with Keltor. But you may still be tainted by association in other ways. I'm trying to clear your name, Azalyn Rippak Sulani. And to do that, I need your cooperation."

"Why do you care? Even if you are indeed friends with Kalahn, I don't need your help. I'm not sure why you'd bother anyway. You're breaking several rules by merely talking with me. If anything, you're the one who should be worried."

Vala had known the risk by visiting Azalyn and brushed past the remarks. "You have no reason to trust me, but we have more in common than you may think. I know firsthand what it's like to want someone above their station. But while you had a glimmer of a chance of success, I have none. I merely want to see you have a chance at a bright future. That will give me hope of having my own on the colony as well."

The other female remained silent, but Vala knew to wait. She'd said all she could. If Azalyn was still unconvinced, she would have to leave it to others to dig deeper, provided Azalyn didn't report her to the warriors who patrolled her deck.

As the silence stretched, she was beginning to think the female would never speak up. However, Azalyn sighed and opened her mouth.

But before any sound emitted, a surge of energy coursed through Vala's body and the world went dark.

The Barren

~~~

Thorin had just finished going over Syzel's most recent report when the lights flickered in his office. After a few beats, red lights and the alert chime echoed inside the room. He dashed onto the command deck and his operations officer Fyzar said without preamble, "Life support systems are failing, sir."

"Was there an attack?" Thorin demanded.

"Only on our energy sources. A quick draw of power on our reserves has left them almost depleted."

Since a sudden power draw had happened right before the engineering staff had disappeared, Thorin asked, "Is anyone missing?"

"Due to limited power, we'll have to do the passenger check manually. It'll take some time to account for everyone on board."

While he itched to check Vala's location, he needed to focus on the five thousand-plus people onboard the ship first. If anything happened to them while he tried to find his female, she would probably suffer some kind of punishment that not even Thorin could halt.

In that second, he decided that he would find a way to change the laws one day. Vala had worth, maybe more than any living person, except for possibly his mother.

Not wanting to think about how much the female had come to mean to him in such a short time, he said, "For the time being, I want as much power as possible diverted to the arboretum."

"What about the weapons, sir? If we don't save some energy for them, we might not be able to fire anything if attacked," Fyzar stated.

"Our main concern right now is breathable air," Thorin said. "As long as we maintain environmental controls in the arboretum, we can continue to circulate air throughout the ship, temporarily replacing the artificial air supply."

Fyzar typed something quickly before saying, "Then I recommend moving as many colonists to decks twenty through seventy-five as possible. They are closest to the arboretum, and it'll take the least amount of energy to move the air. Quarters will be close, but it's our best chance at conservation and keeping everyone alive for as long as possible."

Thorin nodded. "Do it." He looked to the male manning the communications terminal. "Where are the army fighter escorts?"

"I've been trying to contact them, but there is no reply, sir."

Maybe whatever had drained his ship's engines had used the fighters' ones as well. He asked Fyzar, "Do we have enough power for a quick sweep of the area?"

"Probably not, but when the warrior units investigate each deck, they can check the surrounding space by sight. At least three ships are supposed to be within visual range at all times, sir."

Thorin cursed. "Then include those instructions with the warriors' other orders. I also want every available engineer working on the power problem. There has to be a way to recharge or draw more than we currently are able." He pointed toward one of the lower-ranked officers. "Go convey the order to Syzel." Once the male rushed out of the command deck, Thorin sat in his command chair. "Is the computer AI system working?"

His operations officer shook his head. "It takes too much power. Only essential functions and programs are running."

"Then tell me step-by-step what happened, and don't leave out any detail, no matter how small."

As the officer recounted the course of events, Thorin frowned. Once the male finished, he said, "It sounds exactly like the previous instance, which means at least one other person is probably now missing."

And the question was why a person or two would be worth the trouble. Surely whoever was draining the power and teleporting individuals had some form of intelligence. The second attack meant risking more data being collected on them, which could lead to their eventual discovery.

Some would instantly blame the Brevkan for their troubles since they had not only been the fiercest adversaries over the last century, but they also had teleportation abilities that were mostly not understood.

Even during the wars, their technology had constantly changed. Or, at least that was what Thorin had read in the records during his officer training.

But Thorin didn't think it was them, and not just because of his own heritage. The Brevkan would rather shoot a ship down and take prisoners to torture than use covert actions.

No, the unknown enemy had a motive. Thorin was certain of it. He just needed to find out what it was.

Of course, he had another major problem on his mind. Due to low energy, he couldn't track Vala's location just yet.

Tapping his fingers against his thigh, he willed for her to be safe. He took his vow to protect her seriously.

~~~

Vala awoke inside a small, enclosed space that glowed a faint orange.

She tried to sit up, but her head pounded as pain coursed through her limbs. Laying back down, she took deep breaths to help regain her equilibrium. She catalogued her body but didn't sense anything missing or injured. The slight weight of her blaster gun around her ankle eased her mind a fraction, too.

While she tried to recover her senses, Azalyn's groggy voice filled the space. "Hello?"

"I'm here," she answered. Realizing she'd never said her name, she added, "Call me Vala. Are you hurt?"

"Just a little pain, but I think I'm okay."

Taking a final deep breath, Vala slowly sat up. Her head still pounded, but at least there weren't any sharp pains in her arms or legs like before.

Her eyes had adjusted to the strange light and she could better see her location. After glancing at Azalyn to ensure she was whole and moving, Vala surveyed the area. It was about three of her height lengths long and about her height tall, maybe less. The curving walls created an oblong shape. They were also pocked with small light sources, which went from the floor up to the ceiling.

At first glance, she didn't see a door. Of course, it could be a hidden one. She had no idea whose technology had brought them to this place.

Azalyn spoke again. "Did you do this?"

She looked back at the other female. "No." She paused, debating whether to share Thorin's confidence with her before finally adding, "The ship was attacked earlier and a few people were teleported away. I have a feeling they did the same thing to us."

Slowly sitting up, Azalyn groaned. "Teleportation isn't supposed to hurt. But the bigger question is why would anyone want either of us? Unless you have more secrets that you aren't telling me."

Since they were trapped together for who knew how long, Vala decided to push aside any hesitation. "There's no reason someone would want me. However, maybe it was you they were after."

Azalyn frowned. "What are you talking about? I can tell you in all honesty that the Sulani family are peaceful merchants with no agenda beyond generating enough profit to live well. They have no political affiliation since that would hurt their businesses. It's one of the reasons I was assigned to them."

"Assigned to them?" Vala echoed.

"I have secrets as well, Vala. But I assure you, none of them would land us here."

"Are you sure? Your birth family is suspected of funding the antimonarchist group."

The older female raised an eyebrow. "Are they? I had no idea. I've been living in the far reaches of Keldera habitable space for over two decades. What my former family does is none of my concern."

Vala wasn't an interrogator and had zero experience with extracting information. However, she wasn't going to alienate her only potential ally in her current situation with threats or firm demands. "Even so, maybe they wish to use you for something. Our main concern is to find out where we are and then find a way out of here."

"And how do you propose we do that?" Azalyn waved around. "I don't see any doors."

"No, but sometimes touch can tell us what we need to know when sight fails us." Vala moved to one of the walls and gingerly touched the surface. A tingle raced down her arm and back up again, but then nothing. "It seems safe. I'm going to look for any sort of compartment or latch."

As she slowly moved her fingertips up and then down the wall, the smooth, cool surface only changed when she moved over one of the orange lights. Even then, the surface was only slightly warmer than the surrounding areas.

She moved to another section and saw Azalyn follow her lead. Vala said, "Thank you. With two of us, it should go a lot faster."

Azalyn paused a second before saying, "I should apologize for my behavior. Today is a difficult day for me and I've been taking it out on you."

Vala shouldn't pry, but she couldn't help but ask, "Does it have to do with you crying near the garden?"

"You saw that?"

"Yes. But if it's too painful, you don't have to talk about it."

They both continued searching the walls. Eventually Azalyn spoke again. "If we get out of this situation, I'll tell you. For all we know, someone could be listening and I don't want to reveal any possible weaknesses."

The female's answer only piqued her curiosity more. "Then consider it a deal."

Working in silence, Vala concentrated on the wall. She had nearly met up with Azalyn toward one end when she found a small bump. Pressing it, a tiny window opened.

Outside was the darkness of space, only broken up by the faint blips of faraway stars.

She leaned closer and finally made out a lot of oblong objects scattered nearby. Judging by the shape, they had to be the asteroid-looking objects Thorin had mentioned.

Which meant they possibly weren't that far from Keldera.

Sitting back on her bottom, Vala took out her necklace and stared at it. If only she knew more about electronics. Maybe then she could use it to emit a beacon to anyone nearby instead of just Thorin. If she and Azalyn were in the same asteroid-type field the colony ship had encountered earlier, then the Kelderan Army would be patrolling this area until they figured out what the oblong objects were and who sent them.

Azalyn moved to her side and looked out the window. "So, we're in the middle of space?"

"More than that. It's possible that we're not that far from Keldera. If so, there should be patrol and research ships close to this area."

"I'm not sure I like the 'if' part of your statement."

"Give me a little time to study the star patterns. Then I might be able to give you better answers."

Azalyn turned and sat across from Vala. "A Barren who knows about star patterns? Not to mention also knowing secret details about the location of the Kelderan Army? Just who are you?"

She decided to stick as closely to the truth as she could without lying. "I'm the general's mistress."

"As in General Thorin Jarrell?" She nodded and Azalyn added, "I think you need to share everything you know, because if we're to find a way out of here, information could be key."

171

She debated how much to share. As Azalyn had mentioned, someone could be listening in.

And yet, if Azalyn didn't have at least a basic understanding of the situation, Vala would have to find a way to escape on her own.

Deciding some risk was worth it, she recounted the events and facts Thorin had shared concerning the asteroid-like objects. Azalyn hung on every word.

Why that surprised her, Vala didn't know. Prince Keltor had a reputation of being an intellectual. Any female who caught his eye had to be intelligent as well.

Vala finished by asking, "I don't suppose you have any skills with electronics, do you?"

The other female shook her head. "You saw my room. I'm an artist in my free time and a merchant by trade." She motioned toward Vala's flower pendant. "Why do you keep rubbing your finger over your necklace? Is it because you're nervous or something else? After everything you've shared, I'm long past dismissing you because you're a Barren."

She smiled. "I'm not a spy or warrior. I just happen to know the right people."

"Like General Thorin. Given the confidences he's shared with you, you're more than a temporary mistress. And sorry to say, I don't think it's going to end well. Take it from someone else who fell for the wrong person."

Vala sat up taller. "He and I will part ways at the end of the journey, I know that. But that's enough about him and me for now. If we get out of here, we can talk about it some more."

"I always liked learning a person's secrets. It looks like we both have motivation to leave here, beyond merely regaining our freedom." Azalyn went to one of the walls and peered at one of the orange lights. "I don't know why, but these look familiar. Maybe my family has traded with this race before. If I can remember who, then it might at least tell us who we're dealing with."

"Let me know if there's any way to assist your memory."

"No, no, it's up to my brain. Let me just study them a second."

Vala glanced at the flower pendant once more. While it probably wouldn't work, she pressed it against the skin of her arm and counted. She had no idea if Thorin was okay or not, but she wanted to believe he was alive and would try to help her. As much as Vala hated waiting for someone else to come to her aid, she had little choice in the matter for the present.

Maybe Thorin would finally prove she could rely on someone other than herself.

Chapter Fourteen

Several hours later, Thorin's command chair beeped and glowed with life.

Syzel and his team must've found a way to harness more power. The trusted warrior never would've spared power for Thorin unless there was enough to keep life support functioning properly, along with a few defensive weapons.

Still, the computer would only be on minimal processing power. Voice commands were out of the question, but Thorin typed in his request for the number of lifeforms aboard.

While the computer calculated, he hoped he was wrong about passengers or warriors being taken. Counting by hand had proven difficult. Some passengers must've gone into hiding because recent checks indicated over a hundred missing persons. Given the amount of power it had taken to teleport forty-odd individuals, it was impossible for that many to have been stolen, even taking into account the use of the fighter ships' engines as additional power sources.

None of the fighters had been spotted or had attempted to contact the colony ship. Even with diminished power, the ship could receive text transmitted messages from ships nearby.

As much as he hoped the pilots of the fighter starships were safe, another person's well-being was on his mind. Vala's lack of communication or checking in worried him. She seemed resourceful, and if she were aboard, he had a feeling she would've tried to let him know she was okay. As it were, he couldn't check her location via her necklace until power was restored to a greater degree.

He was starting to understand why generals never took brides. Yes, they may become targets, but not being able to put their safety and comfort first in any situation was almost unbearable. All he wanted to do was search every deck until he found his female.

Not that she was his forever. But she was his for the present, and he didn't take her trust in him lightly.

On top of that, Thorin's visions had popped up twice already in her absence. He needed Vala's presence to soothe his being. It was selfish to want her by his side to help keep him in control, but after feeling like any other Kelderan for a brief period, he yearned for more.

His chair console beeped and Thorin glanced down. Two people were missing. He typed in a clarification, and his heart skipped a beat at the names: Vala Yarlen and Azalyn Sulani.

Vala. She had better still be alive and well or Thorin would resign his place in the army once the ship was secure and then hunt down whoever had hurt her.

Or, worse.

No. He refused to believe she was dead.

Clenching the fingers of one hand, he took a slow breath and unfurled one digit at a time. She needed him calm and collected.

He looked to the male manning the communications terminal. "Do we have enough power to send a message to headquarters?"

The warrior tapped the flat panel in front of him a few times before answering. "I can risk one typed message at this range, but whether we'll still have enough energy to receive their reply is uncertain."

He stood and walked to the panel. "Their reply isn't that important." He motioned for the male to vacate his seat and he obliged. Thorin slid into the spot. "I'll type the message myself. In the meantime, convey to the necessary personnel that only two people are missing from the ship. Their names are still on the screen at my command chair. The second name listed has a family waiting. Inform them of the situation in person."

"And the other name, sir?"

"I will take care of it."

Once the officer saluted and went about his task, Thorin typed out his message to headquarters. He would give them the most pertinent data available concerning the recent episode. However, he would also include the unique locator code for Vala's pendant. While the locators had become popular during the war with the Brevkan, they had fallen into disuse in recent years. He hoped someone in headquarters could figure out how to use the decades-old technology for a possible long-range pinpointing. The army may not go after a single Barren or even a single fertile female, but if locating Vala and Azalyn could lead to the location of the other missing warriors, the army would most likely jump at the chance.

He only hoped his faith in headquarters wasn't misplaced.

~~~

Vala jumped as her entire prison enclosure vibrated. She'd barely blinked at the motion before energy surged through her body.

She didn't know how long the light filled her vision, but eventually it stopped. She exchanged a glance with Azalyn before moving to the window.

The blackness of space had been replaced with a light composite material.

They must've been teleported again.

In the next second, a section of the wall dematerialized into the shape of a door. The silhouette of a male stood in the doorway. He spoke Kelderan, albeit with a strange accent. "Stand up."

A split second of panic rushed through her body, but Vala quickly pushed it away. If she ever wanted to see Thorin again, let alone reach Jasvar, she needed to be stronger than she ever had been in the past. Without information, she and Azalyn would never have a chance at escaping or devising some strategy to win.

If she could win.

No. She couldn't afford to give up now after everything she'd been through.

Before Vala could think of what to say, Azalyn stood in front of her and asked the stranger, "Who are you?"

"You are Azalyn Rippak, yes?" the male asked. "The other female is too young. Either you come without question together, or I kill the other female and take you by force."

Vala moved to Azalyn's side and whispered, "We need to see where we are."

The message was vague, but Azalyn must've understood her meaning because she squared her shoulders and said, "My name is now Azalyn Sulani and I want to meet the person in charge."

177

The male merely answered, "No. Come with me. If I turn around and don't find you following, I kill the other one."

He turned and strode away from the door. Vala touched Azalyn's shoulder. "It's your choice, but staying together is probably our best option."

She frowned. "Of course it is. I won't let them kill you. It seems that they want me. Let's find out why."

As the pair exited the doorway, Vala blinked a few times to adjust to the orange brightness.

The space was bare except for their large, gray and black former prison vessel and another one just like it sitting on the far side of the room.

The male walking with purpose glanced at them. While humanoid, his bright yellow skin and large eyes meant he wasn't Kelderan. Her knowledge was limited concerning alien races, but Azalyn muttered, "A Tallarian."

The male never stopped moving as he said, "Yes. I expected a merchant to know." He picked up his pace and strode toward the largest doorway at the end of the room. "Now, no more talking. He is anxious to see you."

Vala searched her memories for what she knew about the Tallarians, but the only thing she remembered was that there had been a brief war between Tallaria and Keldera many years ago. The Tallarians had lost, though, and had signed a peace treaty. Keldera currently traded with their planet on occasion.

But she had never seen a Tallarian outside of an image in a text. The male's pale-yellow hair was braided into a single queue that bounced down his back. His top and trousers were made of a leather-looking material in a deep brown, with a large, metallic belt around his waist filled with devices that were probably weapons.

Seeing them reminded Vala of her own blaster gun around her leg. She wasn't foolish enough to think she could win against an entire ship, but she could use it in a life-or-death situation, if it came to it.

They exited what Vala assumed was a shuttle bay and into a corridor made of the same smooth, light gray composite material as the previous room. With the lack of texture or decoration, the construction was less refined than inside the Keldera colony ship. She also didn't see any computer terminals or other technology on the walls beyond a few security cameras, which suggested that the Tallarians weren't as advanced technologically as the Kelderans.

Maybe that was something she and Azalyn could use to their advantage.

Not that either of them had skill with electronics or computers, but if any of the missing engineering staff were aboard, they could help. The trick would be in locating them.

It wasn't long before the Tallarian male stopped next to a door. Once it opened, he pointed inside. "He waits."

Azalyn entered the room first, her head high. Vala took strength from the female's example and followed suit.

The second they were inside, the door behind them closed and clicked with a lock.

Vala's attention zeroed in on the male sitting in a raised chair at the back of the room. While his skin was the same bright yellow and his clothes the same brown leather-looking material, he had several silver-colored bands around his biceps, over his clothing.

He barely glanced at Vala. All of his attention zeroed in on Azalyn. "Finally. It has taken longer than I had expected to find you."

179

"And you are?" Azalyn prompted.

"That doesn't matter. All you need to know is that I hold your fate."

Azalyn didn't miss a beat. "Stop being dramatic. What do you want with me?"

"You are our future. You will find out in time."

Azalyn placed a hand on her hip. "Since we're not negotiating a trade deal, I have no interest in following the Tallarian's long-winded custom. What *exactly* do you need me for?"

The male smiled slowly. The predatory look on his face made Vala dig her nails into her palm to keep from showing any emotion.

He said, "You are wrong. This is a negotiation. Maybe you need to see what we have to trade."

The door opened and a Tallarian guard ushered a Kelderan male into the room. The Kelderan looked to be about ten years younger than Vala, with golden skin and dark blue hair. In a way, his complexion and features reminded her of Prince Kason and Princess Kalahn.

His gaze passed over both Vala and Azalyn without recognition.

Azalyn gasped and Vala focused on her companion. Azalyn whispered, "No."

The Tallarian's predatory look turned smug. "So maybe now you will take this meeting seriously."

Vala whispered, "Who is he?"

Azalyn never took her gaze from the young man. "He's my son."

The Kelderan frowned, but since there was a static gag in front of his mouth, he couldn't say anything.

The Tallarian male steepled his fingers in front of him. "Yes, the son who doesn't know the identity of his birth parents. We only found him when investigating you. Kelderans are disloyal and easily give up their own brethren." He tilted his head. "Even though he doesn't recognize you, your reaction tells me that you're still willing to negotiate for his safety."

A multitude of questions swam inside Vala's mind, but she kept them quiet. She could find out answers later, when she was alone with Azalyn.

"What is it you want?" Azalyn asked. "And I'd prefer a straightforward answer. I don't wish to haggle for two hours to reach an agreement."

"The haggling is the fun part, female. And to truly see what you will deliver, you will stay with your son and your friend in a cell for a few days. The more attached you become, the more you will give me in the end."

Azalyn raised her brows. "What makes you think that's true?"

The Tallarian waved a hand. "I do not need to explain myself to you." He pointed a finger at the guard holding the Kelderan male and said something in what Vala assumed was Tallarian. When he finished, the Tallarian with the silver bands on his arms looked back to Azalyn. "Enjoy the reunion. If you try to escape, I will kill your friend first and torture your son to the brink of death, bring him back and do it again."

He pressed something and a bell chimed. Four guards came through the door. A pair each took hold of Vala and Azalyn and then guided them out of the room.

Vala chanced a glance at her sort-of ally. While Azalyn's face remained strong, she clenched her jaw. Vala had a feeling that Azalyn had never dreamed of meeting her adult son at all, let alone under such circumstances.

But worse, none of them knew what the Tallarians wanted or needed. Not for the first time, Vala longed for Thorin at her side. No doubt he'd possess knowledge to help them or knew people who could procure it.

Once all of this was over—she refused to believe this was the end for her or Azalyn—Vala would take her self-defense and weapons training more seriously. Maybe she'd even start studying survival skills for emergencies.

However, all of that required her escaping. The hard part would be in figuring out a way to do it.

~~~

Azalyn Rippak Sulani had done everything in her power to distance herself from the decisions she'd made during her foolish teenage years, when she'd believed that love would be enough to change how the world worked.

Oh, how wrong she'd been.

To pay for her mistakes, she'd willingly joined another family and severed ties with her birth family; kept away from the Kelderan capital and Prince Keltor tro el Vallen; and even had agreed to give up the son few knew she'd had without a male lord. Joining the Jasvarian colony had been the final step. After all, nothing screamed distance more than moving to a different planet and promising never to return.

Yet as she allowed herself to be dragged down a corridor toward some unknown Tallarian cell, located who knew where in the universe, her heart thundered inside her chest as she tried to think of what to do with regard to her son. Despite her best efforts, her past had finally caught up with her.

In order to protect him from the royal family as well as her power-hungry birth family, Azalyn had quietly endured her secret pregnancy and allowed a family far away, trusted by the Sulani merchants, to raise her only child as their own. Not even they were aware that the boy's father was the current heir to the Kelderan throne, Prince Keltor.

While her son may not recognize her, Azalyn had secretly kept track of the boy over the years. His adopted family had taken her suggested name of Kelzal, and each year he'd grown into a more handsome male than she'd could've ever imagined. Intelligent as well; despite being only twenty-two years old, Kelzal was a top inventor at Keldera's preeminent technological research firm.

And after so many years of convincing herself she'd never see him and that her estrangement was necessary, she was going to be locked in a room with him for who knew how long.

Azalyn only hoped she could remain strong and keep the necessary distance from him. If Kelzal discovered who his father was, it would make him an even bigger target. She had a feeling the Tallarians didn't know the truth, either, or they never would've bothered with kidnapping Azalyn. Because while she had no proof, her past ties with Keltor were the only reason someone would go to such lengths to locate and kidnap her. The Sulanis ending a few contracts with Tallarians wouldn't merit such an elaborate scheme to kidnap both her and Kelzal.

Although the joke may end up being on the Tallarians. Azalyn doubted Keltor remembered her as more than a teenage dalliance.

The guards stopped at a door, opened it, and tossed her inside. She'd barely turned over from being facedown when Vala and Kelzal also landed on the floor not far from her.

The door clicked closed. As both Kelzal and Vala sat up, Azalyn finally stared at the child she'd wished to meet face-to-face for over twenty years.

Although, child was the wrong term. Kelzal was a young man. His close-cropped dark blue hair and golden skin tone were nearly the same as Keltor's. Even the quiet, assessing look the male gave her reminded her of when she'd first met the prince.

But his green eyes and the shape of his nose were just like hers.

A sudden yearning to hug him close and hear his voice surged through her body.

While she wouldn't risk hugging him, Azalyn cleared her throat of emotion and motioned toward his static gag. "I'm going to remove this. Will you allow it, Kelzal?"

The young man searched her eyes before bobbing his head. Careful to keep her fingers steady, Azalyn disengaged the gag. "Sorry I can't take off the cuffs. They require a code."

Kelzal remained silent. Since he probably suspected Azalyn was lying about being his birth mother, she searched her brain for a way to convince him. Then his deep voice filled the room. "How do you know my name?"

At this point, truth was her best tool. "I gave it to you and your adopted parents kept it."

He paused, and his action reminded her of a much younger Keltor, who had always wanted to carefully think things through before making a decision.

At least, he'd been that way until Keltor had met her.

184

Pushing aside memories, Azalyn focused on the present. "Look, I don't expect you to believe me about being your birth mother. And to be honest, you don't have to. All we need to do is work together to survive. Keeping your distance from me is probably the best decision anyway."

"So I can be more easily disposed of?" Kelzal asked.

She narrowed her eyes. "Of course not. You and Vala will live. I'll do whatever it takes to protect you both."

He raised an eyebrow but soon looked away, focusing on Vala. "Who is the Barren?"

"Her name is Vala," Azalyn stated firmly. "In here, we're all equals. Call her by her name or I will put the gag back on. Remember, we're unrestrained and have the advantage over you, even if we're female."

The instant the words were out of her mouth, Azalyn wondered if she'd been too harsh. *No.* Long-lost son or not, she wouldn't allow him to dismiss Vala. Just because she was of a different station didn't mean she was less of a person.

Azalyn knew that better than most.

Vala crawled over to Azalyn and whispered, "All that matters right now is being careful of what we say. They could be listening."

Leave it to the soft-spoken female to keep her wits about her despite everything. Azalyn moved her mouth to Vala's ear and kept her voice low. "If he agrees to work with us, he can help. Trust me on this."

Vala pulled away and nodded.

Azalyn had had her doubts about Vala, but the more time that passed, the more she started to think she could trust the female.

She hated being skeptical of everyone, but her past had shaped her to be that way.

Not wanting to think of Keltor breaking her heart and uprooting her life, Azalyn scooted over to Kelzal. So close to her son, she wanted nothing more than to engulf him in a hug and claim twenty-two years' worth of missed affection.

Instead, she whispered into his ear. "I have a plan, but it requires your help and your skills. If you agree, then I'll answer any and all questions you may have after the fact. For now, escape is our key objective."

She turned her head, putting her ear near his mouth in case he wanted to reply. His low voice finally said, "What do you have in mind?"

As Azalyn explained her plan, she started to relax. Being occupied would help her focus on saving her son's life and getting him to freedom, along with Vala. If her life ended up being forfeited in the process, so be it. Azalyn was tired of running and hiding. It was finally time to own her past and face the consequences.

Chapter Fifteen

The next day, Thorin waited for Syzel to finish giving his latest report before he asked, "So, we should be at half power by tomorrow afternoon at the latest?"

Syzel nodded. "Yes, sir. Without any further energy drains, the power sources are slowly recharging. Combined with every available remaining engineer working on it, repairs are slow but steady."

He grunted. "Good. Although until we find a way to shield from the rogue teleporters, ensure we have enough stored energy to maintain life support systems and self-defense weaponry. I don't want to become an easy target once more." Syzel bowed his head in acknowledgment and Thorin moved his gaze to Ryven. "Do you have any more candidates to help with intelligence gathering aboard the ship?"

"Yes, sir," Ryven answered and recited a few names. With heightened security and a possible enemy onboard, Thorin wouldn't allow his crew to risk sensitive information by sending it electronically. Ryven finished and added, "We should hear back soon from headquarters. I'm sure they'll help locate the missing persons."

Thorin tapped his fingers against his desk. "I appreciate the reassurances, but they are unnecessary."

Ryven studied him before asking, "Are you certain? You may fool a lot of people, but remember, I train warriors. There are few who can trick me."

"I did not give you permission to speak freely, Ryven."

Ryven smiled. "But you did yesterday. 'Always speak freely with me when we're alone or in front of Syzel' was what you said."

Thorin was about to rescind the order when a vision of a battlefield, complete with pools of blood and scattered bodies, flashed into his mind. The sole person standing with an old broadsword dripping with a thick, red liquid amidst the carnage was himself.

He closed his eyes a second, took a deep breath, and managed to pack away the image section by section until only blackness remained. He said through gritted teeth, "Our meeting is finished for now. Resume your duties. Dismissed."

The pair mumbled, "Yes, sir," before Thorin heard the door to his quarters open and close.

Over the last day, Thorin had learned to trust Syzel and Ryven more. No doubt the pair had questions, but they would remain silent while they were still on red alert. The top priority was staying alive and protecting everyone onboard the ship.

To do that, Thorin needed to get a grip on his mind once more. And one way proved more effective than other techniques.

Slowly, Thorin recalled Vala's long, white hair and small, soft form. The concern in her black eyes was genuine and she quickly engulfed him in a hug.

He held onto the memory of Vala's precious body in his arms for a few minutes, until his heart rate slowed. What he wouldn't give to have her with him in reality.

He'd been a fool to think they'd merely share a few nights of passion and could part ways. Somehow, someway, he wanted to find a solution to be with her always. Provided she'd want him, of course. He would just need to show how much he treasured her mind and body when he found her.

Maybe he'd join the colony if Vala was agreeable. As much as he hated to ask Prince Kason a favor, he might have to in order to get a recommendation to remain on Jasvar.

Because, yes, despite everything that had happened, he was determined to deliver the colonists to their destination. Turning back would create more instability on Keldera, which would lend itself to war. In turn, if the palace fell, society might dissolve into anarchy. As much as he disliked most of the royal family, he didn't want to see them executed and replaced with chaos and quests for power for who knew how many years.

His secure communications line beeped and Thorin finally opened his eyes.

The message was from General Corvel. Video communications were still down, so he opened the text-only message and read it:

Message received. Reinforcements and barriers en route. More information later.

With a growl, Thorin stood and paced the length of his temporary quarters near the command deck. While he was glad to have help on the way—the barriers referred to larger teleport shields usually used for the palace and the council's meeting house—the message said nothing about the missing people from his ship. Not even a note to say they were being assumed dead and passed over in favor of protecting the colonists.

Thorin would just need to ensure everything was ready and in place for a transition of command. Because if no word of Vala came by the time the reinforcements arrived, Thorin would resign and go look for her and the others by himself.

After all, the colony transport ship would be protected. Not to mention Ryven and his small team of trusted warriors would continue their work of looking for any traitors.

Yes, the ship would be in good hands. Vala, on the other hand, had no one but herself and possibly Azalyn Sulani to help her. As much as he valued Vala's intelligence and determination, she wasn't a warrior.

But Thorin was. More than that, he was her protector. And he'd use his decades of experience to find her at any costs. Because if not for him, she never would've gone looking for Azalyn Sulani and probably would still be safe aboard the ship.

He seemed to bring trouble and sadness to those he cared about. First his mother with years of shame and hardship; then his aunt with being shunned for openly loving him; and now Vala by placing her trust in his judgment.

But he was done allowing things to happen to those he cared about.

~~~

Vala was about to reach up and touch the outline of the flower pendant through her dress, then remembered it wasn't there. Kelzal was trying to see if he could boost the locator signal.

For all the elaborateness of the Tallarians' kidnapping and teleportation tricks, they seemed to view females as even less of a threat than their Kelderan counterparts. No one had tried to search her or Azalyn. Despite Vala offering up her blaster gun for spare parts, Kelzal had refused. He wanted to try on his own first with electronic components from his containment cuffs, which he'd disengaged after about fifteen minutes, using only his skill and the clasp from her necklace.

While young Kelderans tended to have a better affinity with technology than her, Kelzal was more than adept. She'd hazard a guess to say that he was a genius.

Even though it was Vala's job to watch for any approaching guards or visitors, she chanced a look at Azalyn, who was laying on the floor and trying to take a short rest before relieving Vala's post.

The female had her eyes closed, but Vala doubted she slept. Discovering your long-lost son wasn't an everyday occurrence. On top of that, Vala was fairly confident that Keltor was the young man's father. Vala had never met Prince Keltor or seen more than a passing image, but Kelzal's resemblance to the other royal siblings, Kason and Kalahn, was unmistakable.

The one good thing their current situation had done was to reveal that Prince Keltor had an heir, which should help alleviate some uncertainty concerning the monarchy. Too many viewed the bachelor prince as irresponsible and selfish for not finding a bride and continuing the line. After all, how could the people look to the royal family for guidance and stability if there ended up being a squabble for succession after Keltor's eventual death?

Yet as Vala studied Azalyn, she wondered if Prince Keltor had remained unattached for a reason. Vala had recently learned what it was like to care for someone she couldn't have. Even when she parted ways with Thorin, provided she ever escaped and saw him again, Vala would never forget the kind, strong warrior.

Maybe Prince Keltor still dreamed of Azalyn's spirit.

Kelzal growled, garnering her attention. He ran a hand up and down his leg, muttering something unintelligible. She moved closer to him, albeit still blocking his work from the view of anyone watching. The single security camera pointed into the cell, so most of Kelzal's body was easily blocked if someone sat in the correct position.

She whispered, "Are you doing okay?"

"No." He motioned toward the small pieces he'd extracted from his containment cuffs. "I need more."

Despite his deliberate vagueness, Vala understood his meaning. They'd agreed earlier to speak as little as possible about their plan, to avoid detection.

She pointed to her leg to indicate her blaster gun, but he merely said, "Not the right ones."

A plan formed in her mind. She pointed toward his cuff parts. "Will one more suffice?"

"Yes, but—"

"Then leave it to me." She darted her eyes to the parts, and Kelzal hid them under his crossed legs. He placed the empty containment cuff casings on his wrists.

Vala quickly moved to Azalyn's side and gently shook her shoulder. The female opened her eyes without missing a beat, confirming her suspicions that Azalyn had been awake.

Once the other female sat up, Vala murmured into her ear, "Just in case my plan backfires and you do eventually escape, tell General Thorin I'm sorry and that none of this is his fault. He likes to think he can protect everyone with a mere strength of will, but sometimes, that isn't enough. He did all he could. I know he did."

Azalyn frowned. "What are you going to do, Vala?"

She lowered her voice even further. "Kelzal needs more parts. I'm going to try my best to get them."

"Vala, it's too dangerous. I should be the one to risk whatever you're going to do."

She shook her head. "No, you need to make sure Kelzal escapes safely. Not to mention you have the power to negotiate with the Tallarians. In the end, I'm the most disposable out of the three of us."

Azalyn leaned closer. "Listen to me—you're not disposable. And if I have to pin you to the ground to keep you from acting stupid, then I will."

Vala drew her blaster gun and pressed it into Azalyn's side. "Forgive me, Azalyn. But this is something I have to do. It's time for me to step out of the shadows and be the person I know I can be. You and Kelzal need to survive. Let me help the best way I know how."

As Azalyn searched her eyes, Vala kept her finger near the trigger. She truly didn't want to shoot her sort-of friend, but for once, Vala was going to do what she could to help others. She might've been born a Barren, but deep down, Vala believed she could've made a good female warrior in another life.

If she did die, then it would at least be as a female Thorin could admire.

Before she could think more on Thorin and possibly lose her nerve, Azalyn thankfully bobbed her head. "Okay, I won't try to stop you." She paused and added, "Thank you."

While left unsaid, Vala knew Azalyn was thanking her for the chance to get to know her son.

Vala looked at Azalyn another second before she turned toward the security camera. She managed to aim and get off one shot before someone tackled her from behind.

She crashed to the ground, her knees jarring against the hard floor.

Vala had barely caught her breath before a knee dug into her back and Azalyn's voice whispered, "Sorry, but they'll kill you."

Azalyn swiped the gun from her hand. Vala just managed to turn her head in time to see Azalyn hold the weapon under her chin, up toward her brain.

"No!" Vala shouted, but the guards charging into the room drowned her out.

Azalyn spoke loudly and clearly, "You mistook me for a weak female. Well, maybe next time you'll learn from your mistake and make sure to restrain everyone."

The guards pointed weapons at Azalyn, but she continued, "If you so much as move another inch with one of your weapons, then I'll fire this blaster gun. Without me, I have a feeling all your leader's plans will come to nothing. You need me alive."

A voice came over the intercom system. It was the thickly accented Tallarian male's voice from earlier. "What is it you want, female?"

Azalyn answered, "For you to free the other two."

The same male voice hissed. "I think not. They motivate you. Surrender, Azalyn Rippak. That is your only option to keep the other two alive. I won't offer again."

Vala did her best to keep the confusion from showing on her face. Surely Azalyn hadn't expected the Tallarians to give in to her demands.

Azalyn responded, "So if I surrender the weapon, everyone in this room stays alive?"

"For now," the male replied.

After taking a deep breath, Azalyn slumped her shoulders and spoke again. "I see I have no choice against such a strong opponent, but I still had to try. I'll surrender my weapon and allow you to restrain me, provided you promise on your forebears' honor that neither of my companions will be punished for this transgression, nor separated from me."

194

Vala started to understand Azalyn's actions. Her companion knew something about Tallarian customs and had used her knowledge to procure cuffs. Still, she hoped Azalyn knew what she was doing. The Tallarians didn't seem a forgiving race.

Silence ticked by for a few beats before the male replied, "I swear on the mother of my mother's honor that your request will be honored, although all of you will be restrained for the remainder of your time here, for however long that may be. Now, surrender your weapon."

Azalyn moved to the edge of the containment wall. Vala sat up just in time to watch the guards open up a small retrieval hole in the barrier and confiscate the blaster gun. The instant Azalyn proffered her wrists, a guard slapped on a set of containment cuffs and engaged the forcefield mechanism that made them nearly unbreakable.

Once the guard finished, he pushed Azalyn away hard enough to make her stumble. The guard looked at Vala and waited.

She ignored him slowly perusing her body and made her way to the hole in the barrier. Once he placed the composite containment cuffs on her wrists and engaged them, he accidentally brushed her breast.

The gesture was a reminder that if they upset the leader again, he could give Vala to the guards to do what they wished before they killed her.

The guard pushed her back and closed the hole in the barrier. He gave one last sneer before retreating to stand in line with the other guards.

The leader's voice boomed once more. "A Tallarian never breaks his honor code, but know this—I'm done being lenient. At the slightest sign of trouble, I will kill the other female. Your pathetic attempt at escaping was foolish. Kelderan females are even less intelligent than I originally thought. And to ensure you take my threat seriously, food will be withheld for a day."

The voice signed off in Tallarian and the guards exited the room, except for the one who'd touched her. He eyed Vala, his gaze settling on her breasts for about five seconds before he met her gaze again. It took everything she had not to recoil from the hunger there.

If the guard had any power with their leader, she had a feeling her fate would be worse than death.

The leering guard left and an additional forcefield went up over the door.

Vala turned toward Azalyn and hissed, "You could've been killed."

Azalyn held up her wrists and motioned to hers. "But I wasn't. Besides, my chances of success were greater than yours. Being brave means nothing if you're also being stupid. When you work with a team, you need to confer with them, too, Vala. Remember that." Azalyn whispered into her ear, "Although, I will say good job at taking out the security camera. Even if they come to fix it, it gives Kelzal some time to work freely."

Vala grunted her acknowledgment. She whispered back, "I'm not used to teamwork, but we can talk more about that later. Kelzal needs to get to work. The sooner we can let someone on Keldera know our location, the better. You also need to start talking about the Tallarians. Knowledge can only help all of us."

Azalyn tilted her head. "You are much more than I imagined, Vala."

She touched the intricate tattoo on her forehead. "All I ask is for you to treat me as if this wasn't here."

"I thought I was, but I'll try harder." Azalyn nodded toward Kelzal. "Come. There's much to say about our jailers."

As Azalyn sat next to Kelzal, the male did his best to keep his gaze downward. When he finally did look up at Azalyn, a flicker of longing flashed in his eyes.

But it was gone as quickly as it had come. He murmured, "Move a little closer."

Vala watched as Azalyn and her son sat only a few inches apart from each other. While close in proximity, they were galaxies apart in terms of comfort.

Her heart broke at the pair and any lingering anger about Azalyn's actions faded. The future was all that mattered.

And not just for Azalyn and her son, but for Vala as well. The next time she acted, she would fight for a future where all three of them were alive and well.

In other words, she needed to get used to the idea of working with a team.

Vala moved into position, to block the view of Kelzal to anyone who entered the room, and sat with her back to the pair. Pretending to look dejected, Vala listened as Azalyn quietly recited what she knew of the Tallarians. Even if her voice was picked up over the intercom system, the words were innocent enough.

Or, so she hoped.

Chapter Sixteen

Thorin was in the middle of a quick nap to recharge his synapses when a ping came from his communicator. Without opening his eyes, he barked, "Yes?"

Syzel's voice answered, "Come to engineering quickly, sir."

He opened his eyes and banished the dream of Vala he'd been using to calm his mind. He rose from the bed, dressed, and took the shortest route possible to the ad hoc engineering space being used by Syzel.

For good reason, none of them trusted the old space. Especially since the army reinforcements still hadn't arrived yet.

Thorin arrived at Syzel's office in record time. As soon as the door closed behind him, Thorin asked, "What did you find?"

Syzel motioned toward the flat-screen workstation at waist level. It displayed a map of the surrounding planets and galaxies. A small, faint red dot flashed slowly. He didn't dare hope for it to be Vala.

His fellow warrior said, "You can let out your breath, Thorin. The signal is coming from the device you had me rig to track."

The red light flashed as if mimicking Vala's heartbeat. He willed it to be so.

Refusing to think of the pendant sitting on her cold, lifeless body, Thorin focused on the area with the blinking light. "That's not far from the official Tallarian and Kelderan territorial border."

"Correct, but the light is on the Tallarian side of the demarcation." Syzel met his gaze. "If we step foot in that area of space without prior permission from the Tallarian government or merchants' association, it could be seen as a sign of aggression. The bigger question is why they would want to kidnap our people. I could understand Azalyn Sulani since her family has snubbed some leading Tallarian merchant trading contracts in the past, according to public records, but why take anyone from our engineering department? Let alone forty souls."

"Since the Tallarians haven't bothered us in decades, finding out the why will take some time. However, we can get some answers related to the Sulanis easily enough." Thorin walked to the door. Once it opened, he ordered the low-ranking warrior, "Bring the head of the Sulani family here immediately."

Once the male made a fist and pounded it over his heart in affirmation, Thorin went back inside to Syzel's side and said, "I dislike conjecture, but if the Tallarians or a rebel family from that planet wanted to force the Sulanis' hands, it would require weakening our ship's defenses and ability to fly away before they could kidnap Azalyn. Therefore, taking our crew members and draining our power makes sense. Moreover, they could also use our crew members as negotiating points."

Syzel shook his head. "I'm still not convinced. The Tallarians have suffered a number of Brevkan attacks over the last few years. Their central government would want to prevent a war on two fronts at any costs. If they knew of anyone who planned to take revenge on the Kelderans, they would've tried to contain

JESSIE DONOVAN

the problem. Because if both Keldera and Brevka attacked the planet, the Tallarians would lose handily."

"All of this makes me wonder if there's someone who wants to see Tallaria fall."

Syzel shrugged. "Apart from Brevkan, I can't think of anyone. And the Brevkan always prefer combat to elaborate machinations. Not to mention the Brevkan avoid teleportation since it brings out their rage."

When a Brevkan went into a rage, they usually killed anyone in sight, regardless if the people nearby were their own kind or not.

Thorin replied, "We also know that Keldera has tight restrictions on any teleportation use. But even so, we can rule out anyone from our planet since Kelderan teleportation technology is different from what was used to kidnap our crew and passengers."

"It's true, our capabilities are a bit dated by teleportation standards. Still, I'll dig deeper and see if I can find any matches on nearby worlds. It's always possible someone from Keldera bought it off a space pirate," Syzel stated.

Thorin remembered Vala's theories. "If it can be traced to a space pirate's offering, then look into any antimonarchy connections. It's unlikely, but I want to investigate every avenue."

Since Syzel had been helping Thorin with his list of potential traitors, the warrior merely nodded without question.

"Have you shared this information with anyone else?" Thorin asked.

"Not yet. You're in command, so you deserved to hear the news first."

Thorin studied the male warrior. He'd never gotten along well with his fellow army members, but when Thorin let down his barriers and gave males such as Syzel and Ryven a chance, they came through.

He never would've done so without Vala's influence.

Vala. He may not know if she was alive, but the signal might be one step closer to finding her.

Still, his emotions surrounding her possible location would be kept locked up until a later time. He couldn't afford to make a mistake because of his concern for his female. "Thank you, Syzel."

"Of course, sir."

He motioned toward the map. "Now, let's run through a list of the nearest inhabited planets and see if any of them could possess the teleportation technology used on us. It'll be a good idea to also look for possible hiding spots, in case this has been a multipronged attack with a ship here acting as a go between for whatever or whoever is near the Tallarian border."

As the pair of them studied the coordinates and took note of the nearest planets and moons, the door chimed. "Enter," Thorin stated.

A male with graying black hair and light blue skin appeared in the doorway. It was the head of the Sulani merchant family, Ulrick Sulani.

"You wished to see me, General?" Ulrick asked. "I'm curious as to why, since the young male refused to elaborate. Did you find my niece?"

Thorin decided bluntness was best. "How are your relations with the Tallarians?"

Ulrick frowned. "The Tallarians? I'm not sure what that has to do with anything, but my family has a number of trade treaties with Tallarian artisans and craftspeople. I assure you that we follow the letter of the law on both planets."

"Do you have any Tallarian enemies?" Thorin barked.

Ulrick raised an eyebrow. "Why? Do you think the Tallarians took Azalyn?"

The head of the Sulani family was quick. "Just answer the question."

The older male shrugged. "A few of our former suppliers started to cheat their orders and provide inferior products, nowhere near our required standards. Per clauses in our agreement, I severed the relationship and made sure my fellow merchants knew of the deceit. It's common practice among merchants to share such information. In the end, it bankrupts the deceivers and allows us to better run our businesses and maintain customer loyalty."

Thorin grunted. "Which means the former supplier will never trade with any Kelderan merchant again. Bankruptcy sounds like a motive for kidnapping to me."

"Perhaps, but keep in mind that the Tallarian government receives updates regarding all trade agreements, both when they begin and when they end," Ulrick replied. "The government would've kept an eye on the former suppliers, in case they extended their deceitful practices to Tallaria. If they tried to take revenge, they would've been caught almost immediately."

Ulrick had more faith in the foreign government than Thorin did. "How powerful were these suppliers? What kind of resources did they possess? Could they have done something like kidnap your niece?"

"Unless something has drastically changed in the last few months, they weren't powerful or wealthy enough to launch a full-scale kidnapping plan, let alone incapacitate a Kelderan colony transport ship."

Thorin studied the older male, but he didn't detect any deceit. "Syzel will send someone to your quarters to ask more questions and take names of any potential enemies." He tapped a button and the door opened. "Dismissed."

"What about Azalyn?" Ulrick asked.

"I promise you that once we know more and can ensure her safety, we'll inform you."

Ulrick bowed his head and exited the room. Once the door locked, Thorin turned to Syzel again. "I tend to believe Ulrick Sulani's words and opinions surrounding his former supplier, especially if they only severed relations a few months ago."

"I agree. This plan must've been mostly in motion for quite some time. Even if the colony is a recent development, someone must've been looking for Azalyn prior to our agreement with Jasvar. There must be another reason for the kidnappings."

Thorin remembered something Vala had mentioned. "There is another reason someone could've taken Azalyn Sulani. Her former name was Azalyn Rippak. I'm sure you've heard the stories about her and Prince Keltor."

Syzel's eyes widened. "She's that Azalyn? Do you think someone wants to use her against Prince Keltor? The incident happened over twenty years ago. Surely they don't expect the crown prince to surrender to their demands because of a young dalliance."

"Perhaps. But I'm not about to rule out that possibility just yet. Find everything you can on the Tallarians and the current situation on their planet. Something might enlighten us as to their motives for taking our crew and passengers, if it exists beyond wanting something to bargain with." Syzel bobbed his assent and Thorin continued, "While you do that, I'm going to visit my second-in-command and give him temporary control of the ship.

I need to inform Prince Keltor of the situation so that the royal family can prepare for any contact. It might never come, but I'd rather play it safe. The prince can also grant us permission to enter the Tallarians' territory to verify if the locator is working correctly and that our people are there."

Syzel frowned. "We're out of secure communications range, Thorin. And important points such as those shouldn't be transmitted any other way."

"I know, which is why I'm going to take an exploration shuttle until I reach a place where I can use secure communications again. It won't take me more than a few hours to reach that range."

Syzel crossed his arms over his chest. "That's risky. If the unknown threat senses your engine's power source, then you could become an easy target."

Thorin nodded. "I know, but don't worry. I have a plan. As for this ship, while my second will officially be in charge, I want you and Ryven to keep doing what you're doing. I'm relying on you to help us reach our eventual goal of Jasvar."

"We will, provided you take others with you to assist."

"I thought I was the general?"

Syzel smiled. "You are, but sometimes a general needs reminding that he's not invincible. Considering we might've just located your female, your chances of being foolish have increased exponentially."

Thorin should deny Vala was his, but he couldn't bring himself to do it. "I don't have time to comb through the warriors to find trustworthy ones. Each minute that ticks buy is another the Tallarians, or whoever, can contact the prince and throw him off guard."

"If you trust me and Ryven, then we can provide you with a few candidates."

Thorin studied the slightly older male. His initial instinct was to ignore Syzel's suggestion and make his way as soon as possible to contact the prince. He'd always worked best alone in the past.

However, that course of action would indeed be foolish. He'd never be able to warn Prince Keltor or fight to find Vala if he were dead. For all he knew, someone could attack during his transmission to the prince. Without additional warriors to man weapon controls or defenses, he would fail in that situation.

Syzel spoke up again. "If it helps, Ryven is friends with both Prince Kason and Princess Kalahn. Vala is connected to them both, even if Kason's connection is through his bride. Ryven would never betray either of the royal siblings. His recommendations would be sincere."

Thorin decided to chance it. "I'll take them, but I'll need them quickly. Send five of your trusted warriors to shuttle bay twelve in the next thirty minutes."

Making a fist, Syzel pounded it over his heart. "Yes, sir."

Thorin returned the salute before exiting the area. It was time to find his second-in-command.

Chapter Seventeen

Prince Keltor tro el Vallen wandered through the streets of a city north of the capital, dressed as a craftsman in a long cape and simple brown clothes, and kept an eye out for his destination.

While his father frowned at Keltor walking the streets alone, even in disguise, he found it informative. Advisors and council members could only tell him so much about what was happening on his world. Experiencing it firsthand gave him a much better perspective. So when the time came for him to rule, he'd be better prepared.

Keltor may never have wanted to be king, but as his father's health continued to decline, it was inevitable.

In a matter of months, he would be crowned and forced to deal with any ensuing unrest. And unfortunately, there was plenty of it on Keldera.

As he walked the busy streets of Bakren, everything appeared calm with people buying, selling, and going about their business. To a newcomer, the crowds of people and numerous side streets might be overwhelming. However, it wasn't Keltor's first visit to Bakren. Since it was one of the central areas for those who opposed the monarchy, Keltor had been to this city more than any other, apart from the capital.

With each visit, Keltor had spent his time discovering some of the antimonarchists' gathering locations. He'd stayed away from attending any of the meetings since he couldn't risk someone recognizing him. But once he was king, Keltor would place informants in Bakren to keep abreast of events.

However, keeping track of potential enemies wasn't Keltor's reason for coming to Bakren this time around.

The front of the local Sulani merchants' shop came into view. The two-story building made of a fake brick facade and large display windows harkened back to Keldera's past. Considering the Sulanis mostly dealt in crafts, antique-looking furniture, and handmade textiles, it suited them.

He entered the store and looked around at the collection of wooden boxes, chairs, and jewelry stocked in every color imaginable. He'd barely managed to peruse a quarter of the store before a male approached him with a smile. "May I assist you, sir?"

Confident his temporary blue skin coloring hid his normal golden tones, he faced the male and bowed his head. "I'm hoping you could assist me, sir."

The male took in his clothes. "If you're looking to sell your wares, the normal times for acquisitions is before we open."

"I understand, sir. But this was the only time I could find someone to watch my child. I lost my bride many years ago, and it's difficult to work and raise the child on my own."

Even though Keltor had used the lie many times before, he still waited to see if the male would believe him.

The other male finally replied, "You need to find another bride soon, sir. That will ease your troubles."

"I know, but it's not as easy for a male in his forties as in his younger days."

The male snorted. "True enough." He lowered his voice, even though the shop was empty of customers. "Though why a female would want a young man with no experience when they could have a male in his prime, well-schooled in ways of bringing pleasure, I'll never understand."

Keltor knew to keep his silence, smile, and nod. The male finally slapped him on the shoulder. "Come. I'll fetch our acquisitions partner. She should be in the back."

As the male guided him to a table at the rear of the room, Keltor ignored his thundering heart. Just because he'd learned recently that Azalyn worked with the Sulanis as an acquisitions partner didn't mean he'd find her in this particular store.

His father would say he shouldn't look for her at all. But after hearing the truth from his brother Kason about Azalyn being sent away under false pretenses, he could think of little else but searching for her.

No doubt she'd found a worthy male and had several children of her own. But prince or not, he owed her an apology. Maybe then he could finally forget all about Azalyn and fulfill his duty to find a bride and sire an heir.

A female exited the back room. However, her skin was golden, not lavender.

He resisted sighing in disappointment. It wasn't Azalyn.

Keltor went through the motions of showing images of his wares. The female gave him instructions on how to formally submit them for sale and sent him on his way.

As soon as he set foot back on the street, he walked briskly toward where he'd hidden his transport shuttle. While he wouldn't be able to visit another Sulani shop until next week, his list of potential shops was thinning. For all he knew, Azalyn traveled around from shop to shop and he'd never find her.

If only he still had access to her files. He'd found a few right after Kason had told him the truth about Azalyn, but then they'd vanished, almost as if she'd been erased from the system.

Not even death would erase her completely from the record database, so something else had to be at work. Until he could find out what, he'd continue visiting shops to try and find her.

He'd nearly reached his shuttle when his emergency communicator vibrated. Keltor picked up his pace, not wanting to check the notification out in public, where he could be overheard.

The instant he reached the inside of his shuttle, he tapped his communicator and listened to the message from one of his staff:

Report to the royal consultation room immediately. Level Ten.

Keltor moved to the steering seat and started the initiation sequence. Level Ten was the highest threat level for members of the monarchy. Either his father was dying, there was an attack, or one of Keldera's large spaceships had disappeared.

He only hoped it wasn't related to the colony transport ship. If the colonists didn't make it to Jasvar safely, he was fairly sure a revolt would erupt on Keldera.

And in that instance, even with his father alive, Keltor would find himself leading his people sooner than he'd anticipated.

~~~

Vala's stomach rumbled for the third time in the last few minutes. She had no idea of how much time had passed since her pendant's timekeeper no longer worked, but the Tallarians hadn't fed them in days, if she were to hazard a guess. Only water had been provided.

The Tallarians had merely left them to rot until they became useful again.

Despite sleeping on a hard floor and not having any food, Vala at least took comfort in the slight weight of the pendant against her breast. Kelzal had done what he could to boost the signal. As much as she wished there was more she could do to try to escape, waiting to see if the pendant worked was still their best chance at getting away from the Tallarians. The only downside was that the Tallarians might try to coerce Azalyn's cooperation for their plans before anyone noticed her locator beacon.

As much as she trusted Thorin to find her, Vala still kept trying to think of something else they could do to escape.

She looked over at her two fellow prisoners and resisted a sigh. Azalyn and Kelzal sat at opposite sides of the back wall. The boy would move a little closer toward Azalyn, and she would move farther away again. For what felt like days, they had slowly migrated around the small cell. Vala had stayed out of it so far, but her heart ached for the young male wanting to better know the woman who had given birth to him.

As her stomach made another noise, Vala decided she'd had enough of the pair avoiding each other. Talking with Kelzal would help her forget her hunger and hopefully ease the tension a fraction in the room.

Vala closed the distance between them and sat next to Kelzal. He glanced at her and asked, "Is something wrong?"

She smiled. "No, I just wanted to say hello. I know that in your eyes, I'm merely a Barren. But I can be a good listener, too."

He frowned. "I might've thought of you that way initially, but I hold no prejudices against you now, Vala. You've been helpful."

"Good." She darted her eyes to Azalyn and back. "Do you want me to pin her to the ground so you can talk with her?"

Kelzal looked away. "I don't know what you're talking about."

"You're intelligent. You know exactly what I'm talking about."

"The female over there is none of my concern. I loved my adopted mother until the day she died. She will always be my mother in my heart. Nothing will change that."

She dared to touch his shoulder. "I'm sorry for your loss, Kelzal."

He looked at her again. At the pain in his eyes, Vala realized that even those who weren't one of the Barren experienced their fair share of hardships.

Kelzal murmured, "Thank you."

Squeezing his shoulder in reassurance, she whispered, "But it's not a betrayal to your mother's memory for wanting to know your birth mother better."

He grunted. "She didn't want me and clearly still doesn't. I may not be charming or comfortable in most social situations, but I understand her actions well enough."

"You say that, and yet, she wants nothing more than to save you. I even believe she'd sacrifice her life to protect you," Vala said softly.

Kelzal scowled. "She wouldn't."

Azalyn's stern voice carried across the cell. "Of course I would."

Mother and child stared at each other for nearly a minute before Kelzal finally spoke again. "Then why do you keep moving away from me? Actions speak louder than words."

"Actions do speak louder than words. I'm trying to protect you."

He frowned. "Even if you lost track of my birthdays, you can tell by looking at me that I'm not a child. I appreciate the effort, but if I can run a research department staff of fifteen on my own, I'm more than responsible enough to make decisions concerning my future."

Azalyn remained quiet, and Vala wondered if she should break the silence. However, her friend moved closer and hissed, "I've never forgotten your birthday. In fact, it was the day they first brought me to this ship. Rationally, I know that you're twenty-two years old. But in my mind, you'll always be the tiny baby I held for only a few minutes."

Vala remembered Azalyn crying near the garden back on the transport ship. She had been remembering her son's birthday.

Kelzal paused before finally asking, "Why did you give me up?"

"You aren't going to like the answer."

"Try me."

Azalyn moved a little closer to Kelzal. "It was to protect you."

"From who?"

"Too many people to name."

Kelzal growled. "Is there anything you can tell me at all? What about my father? Who was he?"

"I-I can't tell you that, either," Azalyn answered.

"Because you wish to protect me or him?"

"Both."

Kelzal opened his mouth, but the booming Tallarian male's voice from the first day filled the room. "Since you're so keen to protect the male, it's time to see if you'll uphold that promise, Azalyn Rippak Sulani."

Guards entered the room and stood at the entrance, forming a wall in front of the forcefield barrier. The male with the most armbands spoke. "Come forward, Sulani. It's time."

Vala watched as Azalyn stood without hesitation and made her way to the exit. The forcefield dissipated and two of the guards grabbed her arms and guided her out of the room.

The barrier went back up and the guards left without another word. Vala touched her pendant through her dress once more. *Please find me, Thorin.*

Since wishing and hoping would accomplish nothing, Vala moved a little closer to Kelzal and took his hand. He squeezed hers.

As much as she hated it, the waiting game began anew.

~~~

Thorin tapped his fingers against his thigh. Considering the threat level of his information, he had expected Prince Keltor to contact him straight away.

And yet, fifteen minutes later, he still waited. Apparently, King Kastor was otherwise engaged. One of the king's advisors had suggested reaching out to army headquarters, but it was too risky. A number of high-ranking warriors had betrayed Thorin's former boss, Prince Kason, on his last mission. While the army stated that they'd expunged all traitors, Thorin wasn't as optimistic.

One of the warriors on the shuttle with him, Paskor, came up to him. Thorin ordered, "Report."

"All of the personal forcefield shields are still in place and holding."

Thorin had taken most of the colony ship's personal forcefield supply and attached them to different sections of the ship. While it was guesswork, the field should protect the entire shuttle from any sort of teleportation.

If he was wrong, they'd find out the hard way. So far, there hadn't been any power fluctuations or members of his crew disappearing.

"Good," Thorin answered. "Keep monitoring them and ensure they don't overload. I can't stress how important they are to our survival and to completing our mission."

Paskor made a fist and pounded it over his heart before scurrying to recheck the personal forcefield apparatuses.

He looked toward one of the other warriors in the pilot seat. "Have you completed the latest scan?"

"Aye, sir. The only thing registering with the sensors is normal space debris. Nothing significant in size, until Keldera and its moons. There's also no news from the colony transport ship about any changes."

Just as Thorin opened his mouth to reply, his panel flashed with a secure transmissions request.

After enabling the temporary privacy enclosure to keep the others from listening to his conversation—he had no idea what the prince would reveal—Thorin clicked Receive. Prince Keltor's face appeared on his screen. "What's the emergency, General Thorin?"

Despite his wish to avoid polite protocol, Thorin couldn't risk irking the royal family. "Sorry to disturb you, your highness.

But I assume you are up-to-date on the latest events regarding the colony transport ship?" Keltor nodded and Thorin continued, "There has been another development since our last report. One that couldn't wait."

Keltor raised an eyebrow. "What is it, General Thorin?"

"Two more of our passengers were taken. One of them is a female named Azalyn Rippak Sulani. I dislike probing into your personal past, but I believe you knew her when you were younger. I wanted to let you know of her disappearance, in case someone tries to use her against you."

To the prince's credit, no emotion showed on his face. Maybe the female truly meant nothing to him anymore.

Keltor replied, "And the second person missing?"

Unwilling to allow Vala to be deemed disposable, he told a half-truth. "A female named Vala Yarlen. She has a vital role aboard the colony ship."

"I sense there's more information that you aren't telling me, General. Please disclose everything you know to save us both time."

Thorin explained the tracking signal, slightly altering the truth about why Vala had it, and its current location in the Tallarians' territory. Once he finished, Thorin asked, "May we have your permission to enter their designated area and investigate?"

"Without concrete evidence, I'm unsure of granting your request."

Thorin dug his nails into his palm to keep from saying something he shouldn't. "With respect, your highness, they may also have about forty of my warriors imprisoned along with the females. Are we going to let them remain in captivity?"

"The 'may' section of your sentence is what concerns me." Keltor looked to the side and his brows furrowed slightly. "I'm sorry, general, but I have another priority transmission to receive. Maintain your current position and await further contact from me."

The screen went dark and Thorin growled. If the prince still refused permission to enter Tallarian space once he contacted him again, then Thorin may have to devise his own plan on how to rescue Vala and the others. As long as her locator kept pinging, he would continue to look for ways to save her, even if it ended up costing him his career and his freedom.

Chapter Eighteen

Azalyn struggled to remain on her feet. Between the gash oozing on her cheek, her throbbing ribcage, and the ringing in her ears from being throttled by one of the guards, she wanted nothing more than to crumple into a heap.

And yet, she remembered Kelzal's face and found the strength to stand tall. The Tallarians wanted her to cry and beg for forgiveness. After all, what better way to disarm Keltor than to show him a whimpering female he'd once cared about.

Too bad she'd rather die than give in to their wishes. Surely there had to be a way to ensure Kelzal's safety without manipulating Keltor into whatever the Tallarians wanted from him.

Never did she think it'd come to a choice between protecting her son versus all of Keldera. Maybe her decision to keep Kelzal's birth a secret had been a mistake.

Stop it, Azalyn. A game of what might have been wasn't going to solve anything.

The head guard pulled back his arm and was about to punch her again when the leader's voice boomed, "Enough. The prince has finally responded to our transmission."

The guard moved away and stood with his arms at his sides.

She wasn't sure if she was glad for the interruption or not. After all, Keltor may dismiss her as unimportant. If she had no value, the Tallarians would probably kill them all without thought.

Unless they knew the truth about Keltor being Kelzal's father. She clung to the hope that most Tallarians thought all Kelderans looked the same, except for slightly different skin colors.

Before she could worry about yet another unfavorable outcome, Keltor's face appeared on the screen at the side of the room.

Azalyn must be out of range of the video transmitter as Keltor focused solely on the Tallarian leader. Even if he didn't recognize her, she didn't think he was the type of a male to ignore the sight of a beaten female.

Keltor was older, but she'd known that. Despite her best efforts to block him from her life, the crown prince's face had occasionally surfaced in the media and on public display boards.

However, the view screen showed his face in clearer detail. Not that the lines near his eyes or the worn furrows of his brows made him any less handsome. Keltor's brows hid secrets she'd once been able to ferret out. On top of the mystery and good looks, his confidence only added to his appeal.

She was starting to remember why she'd fallen for him in the first place.

Keltor's voice gained her full attention. "Where is she?"

As the guard pushed her forward, Azalyn's heart rate ticked up. She'd barely managed to keep from tumbling over when she finally caught Keltor's eye.

His expression remained assessing as he took in her appearance. However, if she was expecting anger or any sign of concern for her well-being, she found none.

For the first time, she truly wondered if she'd have to reveal the secret of their son in order to save him. Keltor may not care about her any longer, but Azalyn would do anything to keep Kelzal alive. If Keltor knew the truth, he would go to great lengths to secure his heir. He might even launch an attack on her captors.

Keltor's commanding voice echoed inside the room. "Kidnapping any Kelderan citizen is forbidden by the treaty we signed with your people. Harming any of them is nearly a declaration of war."

The Tallarian leader waved toward her. "We can talk treaties or you can save her life. Declare war on the Brevkan and I will release her."

Keltor didn't so much as blink at the odd request. "I assume your government doesn't know about any of this, am I correct?"

The leader barked something in Tallarian. No sooner had a guard exited, then Keltor asked, "What son?"

Of course Keltor would understand Tallarian. She'd forgotten about his proclivity with languages.

The Tallarian leader hissed, "That is unimportant. Declare war on the Brevkan and I will spare the lives of all my Kelderan prisoners. Refuse, and they all die."

"You believe you have more power than you do, Tallarian. Tread carefully," Keltor said calmly.

But as Kelzal was dragged into the room, she forgot about Keltor and looked to her son. Panic clawed at her throat. For all her talk of protecting him, she was powerless.

A sob threatened to escape, but Keltor's voice cut through her emotions. "Azalyn."

At the steel in his voice, she met his eyes. He gave an imperceptible nod, as if to say he would handle it.

She had no reason to believe him, let alone trust him. But for him to reassure her without even seeing Kelzal's face first gave her some hope that Keltor already had a plan.

The guards finally dragged Kelzal into the viewing area of the video transmission. Keltor's jaw clenched ever so slightly. No one else would notice the action, but even after two decades, she could still read the man who'd once had her heart.

Keltor recognized Kelzal as his son.

The strength in Keltor's eyes intensified as he said, "I'm giving you one last chance to surrender before I contact your government. Tallarian punishments are more severe than Kelderan ones. Refusing me equates death to you and your immediate families."

"I'm doing this to protect my government. You denied our request for assistance against our common enemy. However, if you declare war on the Brevkan, they will fight with you and leave us alone." He flicked a finger and a guard punched Azalyn in the side of the head. She stumbled and fell to her knees. The leader's voice barely cut through the ringing in her ears. "Either agree, or I kill her."

The guard kicked her side. Pain exploded throughout her entire body. She slumped to the ground and struggled to breathe.

There was a roar followed quickly by some kind of alert.

But someone hit her again and the world went black.

~~~

For one of the first times in his life, Keltor was grateful for his years of training to conceal emotions. All monarchs needed to appear calm, regardless of the situation.

But seeing Azalyn's battered face had made him want to kill the males responsible.

Not that he had much time to think of revenge, because soon after, a young male who looked a lot like Keltor during his younger days had come on screen.

Azalyn's son.

And judging by the age and looks, Keltor's as well.

He would have plenty of time to be angry and demand answers later. His main concern was rescuing Azalyn before they killed her.

When a Tallarian male punched her and Azalyn stumbled to her knees, Keltor pushed a button on the panel in front of him.

Time to launch his plan.

Before talking with the Tallarians, he had taken General Thorin's warning seriously. Kelderan fighters near the Tallarian border had been put at the ready and teleportation privileges granted.

The flash of words on the panel in front of him confirmed that the fighters were on the move.

Red alerts flashed on the Tallarian's ship just as Azalyn slumped to the floor. Keltor motioned for one of his top warriors to man the seat. "Continue recording this transmission and keep me updated on what happens. I must reach out to the Tallarian government."

The warrior complied without question. Keltor took one last look at Azalyn's still body and forced himself to exit the room.

He wanted to be the one to rush in and rescue her, especially since she'd only been taken to be used as a pawn against him. However, Keltor's father was too ill to talk with any diplomats, which left diplomacy up to him. Since Keltor was going to accuse the Tallarians of violating their treaty, he needed to be the one to reach out to them.

Despite being the crown prince, Keltor was powerless in situations that mattered to him personally.

Clenching his fingers, he vowed to finish his business as soon as possible. Provided Azalyn and her son were brought back alive, he wanted to arrange things so that he could meet with them in private. His position could afford him that much, at least.

Once at the private comm unit, Keltor keyed in his special access code, followed by the direct line to the High Minister of Tallaria, Bavvixx. After another series of passwords, the computer asked him to wait.

Within a few minutes, the yellow, wrinkled skin of Bavvixx, dressed in shiny black robes, came on the line. Since this wasn't the first time they had spoken, the High Minister spoke in Tallarian without preamble. "Prince Keltor. Your request was flagged urgent. What is it you wish to discuss?"

Keltor replied in the same language, "My concern rests with our treaty. A male who identified himself as Cevniv kidnapped at least three of my citizens and injured one severely."

He hated to downplay Azalyn's abuse, but Tallarians disliked subjective quantifiers.

"And the proof?"

"I have a recording that will be sent to you at your request. As much as it troubles me to ask, I must know if you were aware of these transgressions."

Bavvixx didn't miss a beat. "No. The Tallarians enjoy a peaceful trade partnership with Keldera. We wish no harm to your citizens, despite your refusal to help us drive away the Brevkan."

Keltor wasn't about to reveal the uneasiness among his own people to a hated former enemy, treaty or no treaty. "I regret that we could not assist. However, as you know, we are still recovering from our long war with the Brevkan. I could not bring the same fight back to our planet so soon. But I will try my best to rally supplies to ease your burdens a fraction, provided our treaty remains intact."

In other words, if Azalyn's captors were declared as fair game as far as retaliation and punishment, Keltor would send supplies.

The double-speak of diplomacy wasted time, but he wasn't about to risk challenging tradition at such a critical point.

Bavvixx finally replied, "As soon as we see proof of the transgressions, I will issue a retrieval warrant."

Keltor typed in a few commands on the flat panel, copied the relevant section of the recorded event. "I will send you part of it now."

He hit Send. Bavvixx looked down when it reached him. The audio of the footage came over the transmission. Keltor dug his nails into his thigh at the sounds of Azalyn's pain.

Bavvixx met his eyes again. "I assure you that neither the government nor I endorsed these activities. Please retrieve your people. Any remaining transgressors will be dealt with according to our laws."

"One more thing, High Minister. We suspect the same transgressors kidnapped about forty other Kelderans a little before these three were taken. I request permission for our army to investigate space in the Tallarian zone, to try and find them."

The sound muted as Bavvixx talked with someone off-screen. Keltor may be fluent in Tallarian, but he wasn't skilled enough to read lips.

When the High Minister met his gaze again, the sound returned. "We do not wish to have the entirety of the Kelderan army near our planet. However, two ships may enter and investigate, provided they keep in contact with our own defense forces. If there are any signs of the Brevkan or other possible enemies, they must report it to us immediately."

"Provided my ships are not required to engage the enemies at your command, that is agreeable. However, if any of your people fire or attack them, they will have permission to defend themselves without question."

"None of our respected defenders will attack without provocation, you have my word."

Keltor nodded. "Then we are agreed, High Minister. Once we have rescued our three people from the transgressor, my army will be in contact with your government."

As soon as the High Minister signed off, Keltor strode out of the private comm unit room and back to his temporary command center. He said, "Permission granted for operation. Retrieve and bring back our people by any means necessary."

A number of Kelderan warriors teleported onto the bridge of the Tallarian vessel. He watched each development, anxious to see Azalyn and her son rescued.

While he instinctively knew the young male was his son, too, Keltor wasn't mentally prepared to call him that. For the time being, ensuring his safety was more important. Dealing with the ramifications of a secret child would have to wait.

THE BARREN

~~~

Inside Vala's cell, two Kelderans materialized out of thin air. She barely had time to blink when they took hold of her arms and energy blasted through her body.

In the next second, she stood inside a small room with a few Kelderan warriors furiously tapping on flat panels in front of them. A younger warrior swept her off her feet and carried her out of the room. Vala just glimpsed the two warriors disappearing again before the room vanished from her sight.

Throwing every protocol aside, she looked to the young warrior carrying her. "What happened? Where are my friends? And more importantly, where am I?"

The young warrior grunted. "You will find out soon enough."

The male finally entered a medical ward and gently laid her on an exam platform. A doctor she didn't recognize began scanning her vital signs with the necessary instruments.

Vala looked around the room but didn't see Azalyn or Kelzal. "What about my friends?"

The doctor never ceased his actions. "Others should be arriving soon. That is all I know. Now, lay still and let me do my job."

Doctors were usually friendlier than most other Kelderans when it came to the Barren since Vala's kind often assisted in the worst epidemics. So she tended to believe the doctor wasn't dismissing her out of expediency, but rather that he truly didn't know.

She managed to stay still, but never took her gaze from the door. She only hoped Azalyn was still alive to be rescued.

And while it was foolish, she wondered if Thorin would come.

The doctor injected her with a nourishment supplement. "While your blood sugar levels are low due to malnourishment, you should recover. However, my orders are to keep you in a sick room until otherwise instructed."

"By who's orders?"

The doctor's eyebrows shot up. "I'm going to ignore your transgression and simply answer your question. My orders come from the palace. I would suggest you follow the request and remain here."

After a final check at her vital signs, the doctor exited the room and the door locked behind him.

Vala sat up and clenched her fingers. She was tired of people locking her up one way or another.

But until she knew Azalyn and Kelzal were safe, she would stay in her new cell and not try to escape.

However, she should still have the highest form of access to records and databases, thanks to Thorin; she couldn't imagine him revoking it. Standing up, she waited a minute to ensure her balance before going to the computer panel in the room. Typing in her credentials, she held her breath until the access screen appeared. She might not be able to do anything with regards to the ship she was on since each vessel had its own type of clearance. But she soon found the secure army information hub, used to broadcast unclassified information to all warriors.

Vala scanned the headlines but found nothing related to her case. While foolish, she kept refreshing the screen until her door opened and she quickly exited the program. The doctor from before motioned for her to follow him. "I'm going to need your help."

Not wasting time, Vala went through a few rooms until she came to one where Azalyn's unconscious and bloody form lay on an operating table.

The faint beeping declared she was still alive, but her pulse was weak.

Vala wanted nothing more than to rush to her friend's side and help her. But Vala's knowledge of surgery was limited. She only knew how to assist, with ample amount of instruction from a doctor.

Drawing on years of experience with regards to sectioning off emotion, Vala rushed to the doctor and listened to his orders. All that mattered was ensuring Azalyn survived. The brave, strong-willed female deserved a chance to have a future and get to know her son.

~~~

Thorin was close to punching a wall or two.

It'd been an hour since the prince's last transmission.

However, to act without the prince contacting him again could be considered treason since Thorin had been instructed to wait.

Of course, waiting around meant Thorin couldn't do anything to help Vala or his missing warriors. Maybe his drive to become a general had been misplaced. Giving it up to live on Jasvar, with Vala hopefully at his side, was starting to look like the best future.

When the transmission request rolled in, he quickly hit Receive. Prince Keltor's face filled the screen. "I have a mission for you, one of the most delicate and sensitive in nature. Will you accept?"

"First, can you tell me if the kidnapped Kelderans are okay?"

"The females are fine, although we're still searching for the warriors. Now, will you accept my mission?"

Vala was alive.

He wanted to demand her location and rush to her side. But Thorin bit the inside of his cheek to keep emotion from his face, and most importantly his eyes. He couldn't allow them to glow in view of anyone but Vala.

Since he needed to remain in Prince Keltor's good graces, he answered, "I accept, your highness."

Prince Keltor typed something on a panel in front of him and a privacy barrier descended behind him. "What I'm about to say must remain secret. A slow death awaits if you violate my trust in you, General Thorin."

Thorin bowed his head. "You have my vow of secrecy."

"Good. I'm sending you a set of coordinates, which will put you in teleportation range of one of our fighter ships. Several other vessels will ensure your shuttle's safe return to the rendezvous point."

Panic flared. Teleportation could bring out a rage. Thorin might only be half-Brevkan, but it was still possible.

Then Vala's words about him being a good male and being able to resist his despicable urges came back to him. Maybe he could contain his Brevkan-half if it meant finding a way to Vala's side once more.

If not, Thorin would be gunned down once he arrived on the other side.

It was a risk he was willing to take. "Yes, your highness."

Keltor lowered his voice. "Your task is to bring my son and his mother to me without incident."

He frowned. "You have a son?"

"I don't have time to explain. A few select warriors will be assigned to assist you with the mission, and one trusted general will take over command of your shuttle and the colony transport ship. No one else must find out about my son's existence. Understood?"

"Yes, Prince Keltor."

"You'll receive further information once you're aboard the fighter ship. My brother highly recommended your skills prior to your promotion to general. I hope he was correct. I will contact you again later."

The coordinates came in via a written transmission. Thorin bypassed the pilot's control panel and manually inputted their new destination.

Once complete, he disengaged the privacy screen and looked to his men. "I have a new mission. Once we reach a certain destination, a new general will be assigned to you. I entrust you to return this shuttle to the colony ship in one piece."

All the males saluted him. None of them asked any questions, which displayed their experience and understanding that sometimes a warrior had to follow orders without knowing why.

As the ship changed course and headed to the new bearing, Thorin looked to the most senior ranking member of his team. "In order to recharge, I must meditate before my new mission. You have command, but if we are attacked or in danger, interrupt my session."

"Aye, aye, sir."

Thorin went to the small room toward the rear reserved for meditation practices. Once he sat on the hard floor, he closed his eyes. Piece by piece he brought Vala's form to mind. If the prince had told the truth, he would soon be holding his sweet female in his arms again.

Selfish as he was, he yearned to caress every inch of her body before taking her as many times as she allowed. He wanted to escape to his haven from the madness once more.

For the present, he used his memories to try to prevent any visions for the foreseeable future. As he focused on Vala's smile and the warmth in her eyes, he hoped she would also be able to help him survive the teleportation.

After an indeterminate amount of time, a voice came over the line. Vala's form vanished and Thorin opened his eyes to the dimly lit room. "What is it?"

"A Kelderan fighter ship is in range, sir."

Standing up, Thorin moved toward the door. Once he stood in the main control section, he looked to the view screen.

The familiar reddish-brown color of all Kelderan vessels filled his view. Judging by the length, number of thrusters, and visible weaponry, it was one of the ships used in the most dangerous battlefields of space.

He wondered if Keldera and Tallaria had gone to war.

The incoming secure transmission light blinked. Thorin nodded, and his warrior opened the channel.

The face and upper torso of a warrior in his forties came on screen. Thorin knew the male by name. "General Lorrick."

Lorrick nodded curtly. "General Thorin. Prepare to be teleported in sixty seconds. I will take over command of your shuttle and crew shortly thereafter. End transmission."

The screen turned dark.

Thorin looked to his warriors. "I entrust the care of this ship to you and General Lorrick. May you reach your destination and fulfill your duty."

Each of the warriors saluted.

Moving toward the center of the room, Thorin stood and firmly affixed Vala's image into his mind. He needed to do whatever it took to see her again, even if it meant suppressing a rage.

As the energy danced against his skin, Thorin closed his eyes. In the next second, light filled his vision, along with a rush of heat.

When his skin finally cooled, he could feel a hard surface under his feet.

But in the next second, images of him decapitating fellow warriors flooded his mind, followed closely by Thorin laughing as he ripped off limbs.

His eyes popped open. The warrior standing in front of Thorin took a step back. The male's fear stoked a burning need to cull the weak. A warrior was never supposed to display fear.

With a roar, Thorin headed toward the male. The warrior turned and ran. Thorin pushed himself harder at the man's cowardice, tossing aside anyone who tried to get into his way.

"Thorin, stop!"

The sweet female's voice made him stop in his tracks. She was familiar.

Turning, he saw the silver-haired form of Vala. His possession.

More shouts and gasps filled the air. The males near his female all took steps back.

He should claim her and protect her from the cowardly males.

He moved toward the one currently touching her arm. But before he could reach the male, Vala rushed up to him and pressed herself against his body.

Instinctively his arm went around her, to stake a claim for all to see. She said, "It's me, Thorin. Come back to me or they'll kill you."

Her lips danced against his bare chest, and his rage subsided a fraction. "They will never defeat me. I must protect you."

She looked up and placed a soft hand on his cheek. "You must resist the urges, Thorin. Please."

At the desperation in her voice, his anger lessened a fraction. "But they must understand your worth and respect you." He growled at the nearest warrior. "I am the only one who can do that."

She stroked his skin and murmured, "They don't matter, Thorin. All I want is for you to come back to me. Can you do that? Please."

He didn't like his female's tone. She should never have to beg him for anything.

Vala kissed his jaw and his angered lessened a little more. "Vala? Is it really you?"

She smiled at him. The action banished his violent images. "It is."

Uncaring about the others, Thorin lowered his head and kissed his female.

Chapter Nineteen

The instant Thorin's eyes glowed blue, Vala knew there would be trouble.

No sooner had she calmed Thorin down, he pressed his lips to hers.

For a few seconds she opened her mouth and accepted his tongue. His warm body against hers and his taste in her mouth calmed her mind and eased her tension a fraction.

But all too soon she remembered everyone watching and broke the kiss. One of the warriors spoke up, and Vala turned to see him with his gun blaster raised, pointed at Thorin's head. "Brevkan scum."

One of the other warriors shouted, "The prince ordered us to follow him. Shooting him signs your own death warrant."

The warrior with the gun sneered. "The Brevkan killed my uncle and his two children. By right, I can seek revenge."

"Look at him. He would've been a child when that happened. See reason."

Vala never moved away from Thorin. As she watched the warriors squabble, she feared things would devolve into a gun fight. Matters didn't improve when an older, tougher looking male warrior entered the room with a frown.

Taking a deep breath, she drew on every bit of steel she had and shouted, "Before you kill him, ask Prince Keltor for orders."

Everyone stilled and stared at her in disbelief. The warrior with the gun blaster frowned. "You forget your place, Barren."

Thorin growled. "Watch your tone."

Vala patted Thorin's chest, but she never severed eye contact with the soldier as she jumped in again. "Ask the prince about me as well. It's a logical request. After all, Prince Keltor is the ultimate word of the law and your ranking general. If I am speaking out of turn, he will issue a punishment accordingly."

The older male warrior who entered last moved to a computer terminal and spoke up. "Everyone stand down and give me a moment to contact the crown prince. Defy my order and risk losing your rank."

No one said a word, which meant the older male was some type of leader on the ship. Since Vala had spent almost all her time either in a room or assisting the doctor with Azalyn, she hadn't had time to learn who was in charge.

The warrior typed in a set of codes and instructions. Not long after, the prince's face appeared on the screen. "What is it, General Lorrick?"

The general waved toward Thorin. "We have a situation, your highness. His eyes glowed, denoting Brevkan heritage."

Without missing a beat, the prince answered, "I'm aware of his heritage." Murmurs rose, but the prince ignored them. "My original orders still stand. Question them again and all of your military careers will end with a dishonorable discharge. Am I clear?"

General Lorrick spoke up. "Yes, your highness."

"Good. Stop wasting time and put your orders into motion."

The screen turned blank.

Facing the other warriors in the room, Lorrick barked, "Will you follow the prince's orders? If not, step forward now and I'll walk you to a holding cell myself." When no one moved, Lorrick slowly turned to meet Thorin's gaze again. "All pertinent information related to this ship and its crew is ready for you in the general's personal office. If you relieve me, General, I will go and take over your shuttle."

Thorin tightened his grip on Vala. "You are relieved, General."

Lorrick made a fist and thumped it against his chest. "May your journey be safe and uneventful."

"The same to you."

Lorrick gave one last look at the warriors and Vala noticed that no one still held a gun blaster in their hand.

As soon as the general disappeared, Thorin spoke up. "I'm giving you one chance and one chance only to decline following my lead and willingly be confined to quarters. The prince is trusting us with a special mission and I won't have that trust compromised because of bias or a brewing mutiny."

Vala half expected for some of the men to speak up with General Lorrick gone, but they all bowed their heads.

Interesting how their attitudes changed when their own lives and futures were at stake.

"Good," Thorin stated. "My first order is for all of you to treat Vala Yarlen with respect. She's a vital part of the crew."

A few of the males clenched their jaws, but all of them nodded.

"Return to your stations and prepare for our departure. The prince doesn't like to be kept waiting."

As the males dispersed, Thorin lowered his mouth to her ear and whispered, "There's much I want to say to you, Vala, but it must wait. Just know that I'm happy you're all right. Now, will you take me to the prince's son?"

At the mention of Kelzal, Azalyn's unconscious body flashed into her mind. "Yes. And what about Azalyn?"

"I will check on her briefly as well." Thorin lightly caressed her cheek. "Just know that despite what happened, she is a fighter. I have no doubt that she will recover."

She crumpled a little against Thorin. "I hope so."

He held her and Vala took a few deep breaths. His masculine scent was as addictive as she'd remembered.

What she wouldn't give to have just five minutes alone with her warrior to kiss him and hold him close.

Thorin soon pushed her away a few inches and took her hand. As he squeezed her fingers, she did her best to hide her disappointment at the loss of his comforting heat. "Come. The sooner everything is in motion, the sooner we can talk alone."

Vala couldn't tell from his tone if it was a good or bad conversation coming. Regardless, she hoped to curl up against Thorin's chest and listen to his deep voice beneath her ear. Maybe then she could relax for a moment and even reveal the true depth of her worries.

She might be putting on a strong front out of necessity, but Azalyn's condition was uncertain. The thought of her new, lively friend dying caused her throat to close up.

Clearing it, she tugged Thorin's arm. "This way. And I must warn you that the prince's son still doesn't know the full truth, although I suspect he knows who his father is now."

Thorin grunted. "We shall see. Although it's not our place to say anything. The prince will decide how to handle it."

As she led him down one corridor and then another, she finally murmured, "Thank you for standing up for me."

He stopped and took her chin between her fingers. "No thanks should be necessary. Even apart, you are what has kept me grounded. I spoke the truth when I said you are a vital member of the crew." He lowered his voice, "Although you are much more than that to me, *zyla*."

Zyla was a Kelderan term of endearment, used by males for females they cared about.

There may be a lot left unsaid between them, but that single word gave Vala hope for the future. And not just any future, but one with Thorin at her side.

She decided to risk saying the equivalent term used for males a female cared about. "Then let's hurry, *zylar*. I'm eager to talk with you in private."

Thorin smiled, but it quickly vanished. No doubt he needed to keep up his warrior facade for the other males onboard.

Still, as she guided him toward Kelzal's room, Vala smiled without caring. Even if something happened to drive them apart because of Thorin's heritage or her own recent actions, she would enjoy every second she had with him in the present.

~~~

Thorin only released Vala's hand when they stopped in front of a guarded door. His every instinct was to scoop her up and carry her to a room to show her how much he had missed her.

But if he truly wanted to find a way to be together once his current mission was complete, especially since being half-Brevkan was no longer a secret and the news would surely spread, then he needed to perform to the best of his ability. That meant pushing aside his own desires to protect the prince's son and his mother.

He nodded at the warrior guarding the door. If the warrior had heard of Thorin's recent actions, he didn't show it on his face. The male merely turned and entered the access code to open the door.

"You should enter first, Vala, since he recognizes you," he said.

His female didn't hesitate to walk into the room. Thorin followed and frowned at the male pacing the length of the space.

He realized that he didn't know the young male's name. Thorin glanced to Vala and raised his brows. She smiled and looked at the male. "Kelzal, I've brought someone for you to meet."

The male with golden skin, dark blue hair, and green eyes stopped and looked between him and Vala. "He doesn't look like a doctor."

"My name is General Thorin Jarrell and I'm tasked with bringing you to Prince Keltor."

Kelzal ignored him and said to Vala, "What about...Azalyn? Is she alive?"

"Yes. I told you, if her condition changes, I'll let you know straight away."

Kelzal went back to pacing. "I just feel like a fool. I had days to get to know her, and I was too angry to take advantage."

Vala shared a look with Thorin, and he nodded, giving her permission to keep talking with the male.

Vala walked up to Kelzal. "It was, and still is, a lot to take in. It shouldn't be long until we reach Keldera, maybe a day, and then the prince will sort things out."

"You still won't speak the truth and say that he's my father?"

"I can't, Kelzal. The blood relation must be proven to make the claim. Otherwise, I risk treason for even suggesting it."

When the young male growled, Thorin moved to stand next to Vala. He spoke up. "I understand that you're young, but waiting one more day is reasonable."

Kelzal moved his gaze to Thorin. "How can you speak of reasonable? My life is about to turn upside down."

Thorin grunted. "You are not alone in that."

Kelzal frowned. "What are you talking about?"

"Answers will come. If there's an emergency, you can reach me via the AI system. I'll also have Vala visit you frequently, to keep you current on your mother's status. However, you will remain in your quarters for your own safety."

Before the male could do more than open his mouth, Thorin took Vala's hand and tugged her out of the room. Thorin said to the guard, "Vala and I have access to this room. Until I update you with any other names, no one else is to enter."

"Yes, sir."

They walked and once out of earshot, Thorin murmured, "When did you last check on Azalyn?"

"Right before you teleported. She's sedated and will be for some time."

"Does she have anyone to watch over her?"

Vala nodded. "Yes. Since I assisted with the surgery, the doctor ordered me to rest for a while and come back in eight hours for another shift."

"Then take me to your quarters, *zyla*. It's time for us to talk."

With each step she took toward her assigned quarters, Vala's heart thumped faster. True, she'd been longing to see Thorin and draw strength from his touch, but so much had happened since they had last been alone together. Between her status as a Barren and him revealing his Brevkan heritage, she wondered if a future existed where they weren't ripped apart.

The instant they were inside her room, Vala released Thorin's hand and walked to the farthest point away from him. He frowned at her. "What's wrong?"

"If I stand next to you, I'll be tempted to delay talking and just kiss you. And right now, we definitely need to talk, Thorin."

"What happened to *zylar*?"

She wrapped her arms around her torso. "I slipped up in using it earlier. For all we know, I could be banished to a far-flung Barren citadel on Keldera for the number of times I've spoken up and overstepped my rank. It may be easier to keep our distance until things are more certain."

With a growl, Thorin closed the distance between them. However, he didn't touch her as he leaned his face close. "I will only touch you if you ask, but know this, Vala Yarlen—there has never been a female I would risk everything to see again. Even when the prince asked me to teleport and I knew it would probably bring out a Brevkan rage, I risked it to see you one more time. You, Vala Yarlen, deserve a male so much more worthy than I. But even so, I hope you will choose me as your male and allow me to prove every day how precious you are to me. I love you."

She blinked. "B-but we haven't known each other that long. And surely you know that loving a Barren means a lifetime of sneering looks and harassment, not to mention the fact you have to give up your career."

He moved a little closer, until his hot breath danced against her cheek. "Without you, Vala, life is not worth living. You are my light in the darkness. I know accepting a half-Brevkan male is a lot to ask, but I do ask it of you. No one else will protect and cherish you as much as I will. I promise you that, *zyla*, and I will spend every day proving it to you."

Vala had learned to be strong in many situations, but this wasn't one of them. She needed to see Thorin's eyes.

Reaching out a hand, she touched his cheek and pressed until he met her gaze. She barely noticed the blue glow. All she saw was love mixed with a vulnerability she never would've expected of Thorin Jarrell.

And it was all because of her.

She closed the distance between their lips and wrapped her arms around his neck. Thorin pulled her against his body and caressed her back with his hand. His erection also pushed against her stomach.

He truly wanted her despite her inability to bear children and the possible scrutiny they may face.

Tears cascaded down her cheeks. Thorin broke the kiss to cup her cheek. "What's wrong, *zyla*? Please tell me that wasn't a goodbye kiss."

She shook her head. "No. I just never expected for any male to risk anything for me. After all, not even my birth father wanted to keep me."

He kissed her chin. "Don't ever doubt what I will do for you, *zyla*." His lips brushed her cheek. "I will never take for granted the gift of your feelings for me." Resting his forehead against hers, he murmured, "You are worth any and all trouble."

241

She tried to stop her tears, but couldn't. "Thorin."

"I mean it. Your father was a fool to toss you aside, and no, that's not just pretty words. Remember, my mother kept me despite my shortcomings. A parent should love their child, regardless of what they may or may not have been born with." He wiped away her tears. "Speaking of which, it will probably be harder for you than me once word spreads of my father. Long-held hatred is a difficult thing to put aside."

"You had zero part to play in the Brevkan war. And as I've told you, your mother wasn't alone. If Kelderan society blames children for the crimes of their fathers, then maybe Jasvar will welcome us. A new start is what we all need."

He smiled. "My feisty Vala. We just need to face the prince before we can plan our future. However, I know you have an inner strength strong enough to face anything. Right?"

"If you'd asked me that a few months ago, I never would've answered. I merely would've bowed my head and scurried away. But after not only helping to rescue Prince Kason but also surviving the ordeal with the Tallarians, standing up to the scrutiny of a prince will pale in comparison."

"So does that mean you will be my bride?"

She raised an eyebrow. "I don't remember you asking in the first place."

Thorin stepped away, and Vala wondered if she'd made a mistake.

Then he kneeled on the floor and bowed his head. "Vala Yarlen, once I have completed my current mission, will you do the honor of becoming my bride?"

Tears threatened to fall again. "I want to say yes."

He looked up. "Then why don't you?"

"Becoming a bride when you can't reach the final stage of marriage with a pregnancy will be difficult enough. I want the chance to know you a little better. If you become my lord and then push me away one day when you finally yearn for a baby, I'm not sure I could survive it."

Thorin took one of her hands. "The only children I want are orphans in need of a home."

"It's easy to say now, Thorin."

He shook his head. "I'm not trying to placate you with pretty words. No one should be cursed with the blood of the Brevkan. I never want to pass that on to a child. I would much rather provide a home to one in need, provided I'm allowed to because of my heritage."

A vision of Thorin and Vala hugging two young children, both of which looked nothing like either of them, flashed into her mind. The scene was tempting. "Opinions may change about those like you, who are part Brevkan. That may also change your mind about wanting your own children."

"Vala, I'm not one to change my mind on a whim."

She put up a hand. "I'm not saying no, but I want to know you a little better first. Please give me that."

As Thorin searched her gaze, Vala held her breath. Maybe she was foolish for declining what might be her only offer of marriage.

And yet, she needed to be sure. Thorin's happiness was important to her.

Thorin finally stood. "I will wait as long as it takes. But know this—I'm still going to resign my place in the army once this mission is complete."

"Why? Until you make a declaration, you can merely say I'm your mistress. There's no need to resign."

243

He growled. "I won't take that route and hide my intentions. I'm out to prove myself to you, Vala Yarlen. Just tell me one thing—do you wish to still join the colony on Jasvar?"

Somehow she managed to bob her head. "Yes."

"Good. Then I will find a way for us to both go. That way, if you wish it, you may dismiss me and still live out your dreams."

"Thorin," she whispered.

With a smile, he moved in front of her and cupped her cheek. "You're going to learn quickly how determined I can be, *zyla*. This is just the beginning."

Thorin looked at her like she was the most precious female in the world. She might not be ready to accept being his bride, but she was more than ready for him to claim her once more. "I want to ensure this is reality and I'm not dreaming back on the Tallarian ship. Claim me, Thorin. Take me now."

With a growl, he kissed her.

Chapter Twenty

While Vala may not have said yes to being his bride just yet, Thorin was determined. He would do anything to convince her of how much she meant to him.

True, asking her to be his bride had been rash. But he wasn't about to let her slip through his fingers by being cautious. The time apart had taught him how much he loved her.

As he caressed the inside of her mouth with his tongue, he reveled in every moan and stroke of Vala's tongue. Just knowing that she cared enough about his future to give him an out, to be with a fertile female, only made him deepen the kiss.

He loved her for many reasons, but the time for talking was later. In the moment, he would bring her the pleasure she deserved.

Hugging her against his body, he lifted and walked toward the bed.

Once he finally broke the kiss to lower her down, he took a second to memorize her heated eyes and flushed cheeks. "My beautiful female."

Running a hand down his bare chest, she murmured, "Don't make me wait, Thorin. Claim me quickly, before life threatens to drive us apart again."

He wanted to soothe her fears, but given all that happened recently, she was correct.

Thorin stepped back from the bed and shucked his clothes. When Vala's gaze moved to his erection, his body glowed a faint blue.

The second it did, Vala met his gaze and smiled. "I love it when you glow. I'll never have to worry about being lost in the dark."

He strode toward the bed, took hold of her ankles, and pulled her closer. "In that situation, you'll need to put your hand on my cock. The glowing only happens with intense desire and arousal, or for the brightest light, an orgasm."

A rush of red filled her cheeks. His Vala may be innocent at the moment, but he intended to expand her sexual education quickly. With lots of practice.

He ran his hand from her ankle to up her thigh. The red band around her calf caught his attention. "Did the Tallarians do this to you?"

Vala shook her head. "No, it appeared after the claiming. I thought you might know what it is."

Lightly brushing the red part of her skin, he murmured, "No, I don't. Does it hurt?" She shook her head and he continued, "Then I can research what happened later." He met her gaze again. "How attached are you to your dress?"

She touched the light brown material. "If I never have to wear brown again, I will be the happiest female in the universe."

"I see. I just need to present you with colorful clothes and you'll be my bride."

She snorted. "Thorin…"

Taking her dress, he ripped the skirt in half and pulled harder at her waist until the entire thing was parted down the middle. "I like my name on your lips. Let's see if I can hear it with more feeling."

Before she could reply, he leaned down and took one of her nipples into his mouth.

As he suckled and teased, Vala groaned and threaded a hand through his hair. She dug her nails into his scalp, and he ran a hand down her body to tease her opening.

"Thorin," she murmured.

Releasing her nipple, he blew on her wet flesh and said, "Much better. Although let's see if I can make you sound even more desperate."

Flicking her taut peak, Vala arched her back. With her two beautiful breasts on display, his cock pulsed with need. He wanted her more than anything he'd wanted in his life thus far.

Taking a breast in each hand, he gently kneaded her flesh before running his hands down her soft stomach and to the juncture of her thighs. As he ran a finger down her slit, he growled, "Nice and wet for me." He met her gaze, but never ceased his actions. "Tell me what you want, Vala."

"I-I want you…"

"Yes? Tell me exactly what you want me to do, *zyla*."

The endearment seemed to ease the reluctance in her gaze. "I want you inside me, Thorin. I've dreamed of you for days."

He grunted. "And I, of you." He took his cock in hand and positioned it at her entrance. With his free hand, he lightly pinched one of her nipples. "Will you allow me the honor?"

She frowned and in any other situation, he would've chuckled at the expression. She stated, "Stop asking and just claim me."

She wiggled her hips and her swollen folds lightly brushed his cock.

With a hiss, Thorin thrust into her and leaned down to take her lips again.

He waited a few seconds before he moved his hips. She was tighter than he remembered. With each thrust, he focused on committing the sensation to memory. Even if Vala agreed to be his bride, he wanted as many memories as possible to help push away his Brevkan side.

After all, because of Vala, he might one day have a chance at a mostly normal life.

Vala lightly scratched his back, erasing all other thoughts but pleasing the female in front of him. He increased the rhythm of his hips. While he didn't have any visions or urges coursing through his body to blame for the expedience, Thorin wasn't going to risk life interrupting and denying him his female in this moment.

A female he loved and hoped would love him back one day.

He continued to play with her nipples as he moved. While pressure built at the base of his spine to release inside her, Vala needed to find her pleasure first.

Lightly running his hand down her thigh, he stopped behind her knee and pressed her leg up so he could change his angle. Each forceful thrust made her breasts shake. With a growl, he leaned down and kissed the side of one of them and then the other before taking one of her hard buds into his mouth.

Since Kelderan females usually orgasmed from attention to their nipples, he nibbled and licked the puckered flesh. Each groan and sucking in of breath guided him to do more of what she liked.

His female responded best when he was a little rough.

Biting slightly harder, he slowed his hips to pull out slowly and slam back inside. Vala dug her nails even deeper into his back, so he repeated the motion.

Between her marking his back and her delectable heat gripping his cock, Thorin was close to losing control.

No. His female deserved better.

Determined, he moved to her other breast and worried her other nipple until Vala squirmed beneath him. He raised his head and met her eyes. "My Vala," he whispered, raising her other leg to reach even deeper inside her.

"Yes, Thorin. Like that."

Sweat trailed down his back. He knew teasing her taut peaks would be quicker, but he refused to take his gaze from Vala's. He wanted to memorize the moment and watch her come.

After a few more quick thrusts, she finally arched her back and cried out.

He reveled in each squeeze of his cock. In her own way, his female was claiming him.

When her spasms finally ceased, Thorin waited until she met his gaze again before he let go with a roar.

He was vaguely aware of his glowing body reflected in Vala's eyes, but for the first time, he wasn't ashamed. Vala accepted all of him.

He would only ever bare his true self to his kind, caring female.

The only one he would ever love.

After spending his last drop, Thorin collapsed on top of Vala. He wanted to whisper his love to her, but kept quiet. He might pursue her, but he wouldn't pressure her. Part of loving a female included respecting her right to make choices in affairs of the heart.

The female in question lazily stroked his back. Her delicate touch made him want to growl and take her all over again.

Her warm voice filled his ears. "You glowed a faint purple just now. Do the different colors mean different things, like it does with our Kelderan markings?"

He kissed her shoulder. "I don't know. I always closed my eyes in the past, to block out the glowing, since it only reminded me of my shortcomings."

Her motions ceased. "Look me in the eye, Thorin."

He moved until he met her gaze. The determination in them made him blink. Vala added, "None of us are responsible for how we came into the world. It took me many years to realize that being infertile was only one part of who I am. A genetic predisposition no longer controls my mind or how I view the future. You need to do the same and accept your heritage, Thorin. Because I will tell you right now that if you never even consider the idea, I'm not sure I can ever be your bride. I'm not asking for you to accept things overnight as that's ridiculous, but in time. You are a caring, determined, intelligent male with many other talents that the world benefits from. I only wish you'd see that every time you look in the mirror instead of seeing the half-Brevkan male you believe never should have lived."

Before he could stop himself, he blurted out, "You're brilliant, Vala Yarlen."

Smiling, she touched his cheek. "I know."

The corner of his mouth ticked up. "I only hope the rest of the world gets to see this side of you more often."

"Well, some of them have. I fired a blaster gun inside the Tallarian ship when I was imprisoned."

"What?" he barked.

"Don't be angry. I thought it was the best chance at getting another pair of force field cuffs so that Kelzal could boost the locator signal."

He frowned. "I think you need to tell me the details, *zyla*, and as many of them as you can before you return to your nursing duties and I to my crew."

As he listened to Vala's tale, Thorin reluctantly pulled out of his female to resist temptation. But to make up for it, he pulled her against his chest and simply held her close.

~~~

Laying against Thorin's chest as she told him what had happened with the Tallarians was one of those ordinary moments that Vala wished could happen more often.

A female in the arms of the male she cared for, the world oblivious to them, and a calmness that came from being with someone she trusted.

Vala did much more than trust Thorin, but she wasn't about to face her feelings just yet.

She finished and tried not to laugh at Thorin's furrowed brows. He grunted. "So your plan was to hope they wouldn't kill you, just so that you could get some hardware?"

"Don't trivialize the situation. Without the extra set of containment cuffs, Kelzal never would've been able to boost the signal. From what others have told me, that is how you located us in the end."

"It is, but I must make sure to thank Azalyn for keeping you alive."

At the mention of her friend, Vala's happiness melted away. "Here I am, enjoying the company of a male who loves me and she's lying unconscious in a hospital bed. I'm a horrible friend."

He placed a finger under her chin and raised her face. "You haven't had warrior training, so you probably haven't heard this before. But under stressful situations, it's necessary to find a moment of peace or humor when you have the chance. Otherwise, the tension will impede your ability to do the best job you can. You and the doctor have done all you're able to for the time being. If you did not take a break and had merely cared straight through, never leaving her bedside, you might tire and miss something." He kissed her nose. "However, I still see the worry on your face. Let's shower and you can take me to her room. While you check on her, I'll double-check the security. I didn't investigate the crew assigned to me, and while the prince might trust them, I need to reach that conclusion on my own."

She kissed him gently. "Thank you, *zylar*."

He smiled slowly. "Thanks for the term, *zyla*."

She snorted. "At some point you're going to have to stop thanking me for everything."

"Why? Without you, I would've been doomed to a lonely, self-hating existence. I had never believed how meeting one person could change your life before, but I understand it completely now."

"To be honest, I understand the feeling now, too. I've had a few people change my life recently, and all in different ways."

"I hope that I was the best change."

She raised her finger to smooth Thorin's frown. "And here I thought you were above the usual male ego."

He grunted. "It's not ego. If I'm blessed, I will have you at my side for the rest of my life. The others may be your friends, but I will be your eternal companion and lover. I can further lay out details as to why my claim is accurate, if need be."

It took everything she had not to laugh at his serious expression. If she said the word, he would lay out every reason why his statement was true.

She didn't need to hear it, but she loved the fact that he would do it if she asked. There had been few people in her life who had been honest, let alone took the time to be persuasive with her, apart from the Barren teachers drilling her in how she must act in every social situation.

Not wanting to think of being forced back into that life, she brushed her lips against Thorin's cheek and murmured, "We can keep debating about you being the best change or we can move to the shower. I think washing each other will help save time and give us one more brief spell of peace before we face the world outside of this room."

It took everything Vala had not to blush at her own words. But at the devious glint in Thorin's eyes, she decided it was worth it to tease him. His voice was husky as he replied, "I promise not to miss a single inch of your skin."

Blood did rush to her cheeks at his remark. "Then hurry up and give me another moment of joy."

Thorin rose from the bed, bringing her along with him. "Come. Since I am a warrior, I can be quick and thorough at the same time."

Little did Vala know his words held a double meaning. It wasn't long before she discovered just how quickly Thorin could make her scream his name again.

Chapter Twenty-One

A little while later, Vala stood next to Azalyn's bed in another hated brown dress and took comfort in the steady beeping of the heart monitor.

Her friend hadn't woken up, but at least she was stable.

However, surgery and a few hours of rest hadn't erased the bruises on her face or healed her split lip.

She'd heard about how the Tallarian male had hit her repeatedly, and even now, Vala wished she had the skills to seek him out and make him pay. More and more she was starting to see the wisdom in giving females self-defense training. She'd need to make sure that Thorin gave her regular lessons once they finished dealing with the prince. She hoped things wouldn't be as bad on Jasvar, but she'd rather be prepared than taken by surprise.

The door opened behind her and she turned. Thorin stood with Kelzal at his side.

The young male looked anywhere but inside the room. She had a feeling Thorin's powerful presence was making Kelzal uncomfortable. For all that he was Azalyn's son, he seemed to lack her vivacious personality and way of carrying herself. Maybe the male had inherited it from his father.

Not that Vala would know. Prince Keltor was shown to the public as the palace wished to portray him. No doubt his true personality was a lot different from his public persona of calm, collected, and wise. Not even a royal heir would be void of less desirable traits.

Thorin spoke up. "I'm going to entrust Kelzal to you. We're nearly to Keldera and given the security of this room, it's one of the safest parts of the ships. I want you both to stay here until we land."

She bobbed her head. "I'll watch over them both. How long until we're on the planet's surface again?"

"Less than ten minutes. Don't hesitate to contact me if there are any problems."

Some might take offense at Thorin's distant behavior, but Vala understood that General Thorin had to be cool with everyone. Her smiling and loving version of Thorin would return when they were finally alone once more.

Thorin held her gaze for another moment before exiting the room. The second the door locked closed, she walked over to Kelzal. He finally met her eyes and Vala smiled. "I know this will be difficult, but you seem like a logical male. Know that Azalyn is stable and the doctor is confident she'll pull through this."

Although, the doctor wasn't sure if Azalyn's internal injuries would result in lasting damage or not.

But Kelzal didn't need to know that yet, if ever at all.

Taking a deep breath, Kelzal finally looked at his birth mother's body.

Vala watched as fear and then relief flooded Kelzal's face. In the next beat, he clenched his fingers into fists and growled, "I wish I could've protected her against that bastard."

While she didn't have children herself, Vala had learned when tending to sick warriors that male egos needed to be handled carefully. "Physical action isn't always the best kind. I don't know exactly what type of technological research you do, but you might end up developing something to help Keldera in the future against enemies. Keep working toward that goal, and it will avenge your, er, Azalyn."

If Kelzal noticed her near-mishap of using the term "mother," then he didn't act on it. "I hope so."

She placed a hand on his arm. "Come. Despite the past, she still sees you as her son. Your presence might help her recover faster."

For a minute, Kelzal didn't move or say anything. Just as Vala tried to think of a different approach, the young male strode over to Azalyn's bedside and stared at her face. After another minute, his voice filled the small space. "She must've been young when she had me."

She cleared her throat. "Working out the math from the records, she was eighteen when you were born."

Prince Keltor would've been twenty, but she wasn't about to mention that part since Kelzal's blood hadn't been tested yet.

Kelzal replied, "What do you know about my mother and the prince?"

Public knowledge would be safe enough to share. "They met, fell in love, and tried to marry. However, your mother disappeared not long after the rumor of their intentions spread. I'm positive there's more to the story, but I'm sure Azalyn or maybe even the prince will share it with you."

Kelzal glanced at her. "I want to push aside the anger, but I can't. There are too many unanswered questions for me to make my mind up one way or the other."

She gently laid a hand on his shoulder. "I have a feeling you'll be learning everything soon enough."

He looked back to Azalyn. "That means Azalyn needs to wake up so she can answer all of my questions. If my father is who I think he is, then I don't think he'll be as forthcoming. If she was willing to die for me, then I think she'll also try to keep my birth father honest."

Vala bit back a smile. "But of course. And hearing that, I'm sure Azalyn will wake up sooner."

Kelzal grunted his acknowledgement.

She wished she could leave him alone for a few minutes to say whatever he wanted to say to his birth mother in private, but as the ship's lights flashed three times, signaling their preparation for landing, Vala merely took a seat at the edge of the room.

And not just to give Kelzal privacy. She had a feeling Prince Keltor would be boarding the ship soon after they landed. Even if it was only to see Kelzal and not Azalyn, he would still be coming into the room. For once in her life, Vala wanted to blend into the shadows. She had no idea what the prince's reaction would be, and she needed to be in his good graces if she and Thorin were going to ask him a favor. After all, only the prince could grant permission for them to go to Jasvar.

~~~

Keltor barely paid attention to the royal guards walking in front and behind him. He was moments away from seeing Azalyn in person for the first time in over twenty years.

And after so many years of forcing the female he let get away out of his head, he wasn't sure how he'd react. The way he'd allowed Azalyn to slip through his fingers was one of the biggest regrets of his life. She'd needed a strong male willing to search the world for her. But all he'd done was obey his father's orders and distracted himself with duties.

True, he hadn't known she'd been lied to, but he'd loved her more than anything back then. To date, she was the only person who could make him smile regardless of his mood.

If only he weren't a prince, he would nurse her back to health and try to atone for his actions. Especially since Azalyn had been hurt because of her past connection with him.

But he was a prince. Moreover, Keldera needed his calmness more than ever before.

Even when it came to welcoming a son he'd never known he'd had.

To be honest, he was surprised no one had made the connection between Kelzal and himself. Once Azalyn was awake and deemed out of danger, Keltor would have words with her about the male's name. Talking "Kel" from his name and "zal" from hers was all but pointing for others to figure out his parentage. True, it would require looking into the boy's past and putting the pieces together, but it wasn't impossible.

And yet, he was glad the boy had something from him. If he had known of Azalyn's pregnancy, he would've done everything in his power to ensure the best upbringing for Kelzal, not to mention protect him from enemies and those who would use his son against him.

Although it was easy to make such assertions in the present. At the time, Keltor had barely been a grown male himself. Maybe that had been one of Azalyn's reasons for keeping the boy's existence a secret—to protect him from the easily persuaded young Keltor and his father's councilors.

General Thorin, at the front of the entourage, stopped at a guarded door and keyed in a code. Packing away every piece of emotion and individuality, Keltor readied himself for what awaited inside the room. Until the boy's blood had been tested and they were alone, Keltor would have to treat Kelzal as any other subject. Further answers would have to wait until Azalyn woke up.

He refused to accept that she wouldn't. After all, he'd only just found her again.

The royal guards remained in the corridor as Keltor followed Thorin inside the room. The general went to the side of a Barren female, but Keltor barely noticed. His attention fixated on Azalyn and the male standing beside her bed.

Azalyn's bruised face and split lip made him want to punch the person responsible, if not worse. To abuse an unarmed, innocent female was dishonorable.

However, what affected him more than the sight of her injuries was her still form. The lack of movement and vivacity was the opposite of the female he'd once loved. More than anything, he yearned to see her awake and acting without care as to what others thought of her. He'd merely seen a glimpse on the video feed earlier, but it hadn't been nearly enough.

A deeply buried longing coursed through his body. Azalyn had been the last person he'd truly been himself with, completely unguarded without worry as to his words or actions.

Before emotion could slip through his carefully constructed facade, Keltor forced his gaze from Azalyn to Kelzal.

The male was the same height as Keltor. His golden skin tone was slightly lighter and would be the same hue as Keltor's with more exposure to the sun, but his dark blue hair was exactly the same shade. However, the eyes were from his mother. To the present, Keltor had never forgotten the green-eyed gaze of Azalyn Rippak.

The boy kept his expression neutral, which spoke of his maturity since he was only twenty-two.

Closing the distance to Azalyn's bed, Keltor kept his focus on Kelzal. "You must be Kelzal."

"Yes, your highness."

He disliked the formality from the boy, but it couldn't be helped. "I wish to thank you for the role you played in helping the army to locate Azalyn, you, and the Barren." A brief growl came from Thorin's direction, but Keltor ignored it. "To formally recognize your heroics, you will be staying at the palace until such time I can award you your due."

Kelzal didn't so much as bat an eyelash. "As much as I don't wish to upset the crown prince, I have a research team to lead. I must decline."

Keltor raised his brows. "My request is merely a formality. You will stay at the palace for your own safety." When the male remained silent, Keltor took a chance. "Your blood must be tested, and if it confirms what I suspect, your life will change drastically, Kelzal."

"I don't wish to be acknowledged."

Keltor's opinion of the boy rose a few notches. "The truth will leak soon enough. We'll devise a way for you to continue your research, but it must be conducted within the palace grounds. It is not a request."

As soon as the words left his lips, Keltor recognized how much he sounded like his own father.

Kelzal looked away, to Azalyn's face. "What about her? I just found her and I won't allow you to take her away."

"You won't allow me?"

Kelzal's voice was steely as he answered, "Throw me in prison if you like, but, no, I won't allow it to happen."

From his quiet nature, Keltor had assumed Kelzal was more like him in terms of personality. However, the daring to challenge a member of the royal family, uncaring about the consequences, was most definitely a trait inherited from Azalyn.

Keltor tilted his head. "I understand you are recovering from your imprisonment with the Tallarians and are dealing with your mother being injured, so I will overlook your transgression just this once. However, I won't always be so lenient. Keep that in mind."

Before Kelzal could do more than open his mouth, Keltor said to Thorin, "You have your instructions. Once you've delivered them safely to the palace on Keldera, you and the Barren will come see me."

"Her name is Vala, your highness," Thorin bit out.

"Vala then. Report to me as soon as possible."

Without another word, Keltor turned and exited the room. As his guard escorted him out of the ship and to his own private shuttle, he warred with what he wished he could do and what he must do concerning both Kelzal and Azalyn. He couldn't afford to allow his enemies to use them against him. For their own safety, they would have to remain at the palace under heavy guard.

And yet, he wished he could allow them to make their own choices. Requiring Azalyn to live somewhere that reminded her of how Keltor had let her down, not to mention broken her heart, wouldn't be easy.

Maybe there was another way. Once Azalyn woke up, he would talk with her and look for a solution. She understood the world outside the palace better than he and might offer a suggestion he wouldn't think of.

However, upon confirmation of royal heritage, Kelzal would have to be acknowledged and guarded. The radical arm of the antimonarchist faction wouldn't think twice about assassinating Kelzal to make a statement. The radicals were a tiny fraction of the overall group, but Keltor wasn't about to risk it. He'd only just discovered he had a child. He wasn't going to allow anyone to take him away.

Chapter Twenty-Two

A few hours later, Thorin sat with Vala at his side, outside the prince's private conference room inside the palace. Not caring what the others thought, he held Vala's hand in his. He would fight to keep his female.

A royal guard walked past. He didn't blink in Vala's direction, but he did narrow his eyes at Thorin. As he had expected, word of his Brevkan heritage was already spreading.

Once the guard was gone and they were alone, Vala leaned over and whispered into his ear. "If you allow every person who looks at you with anything less than respect to bother you, the stress will pile up and start to affect your health. You need to ignore them."

He glanced down at Vala. The lines of her face and her kind, dark eyes chased away most of his irritation. "I will try, *zyla*, but I'm not as strong as you in that regard."

She patted his bicep. "I'm confident the prince will reward your services fairly. We'll save this discussion until after our royal audience."

Thorin kept his voice low. "You are far more optimistic than I."

"It's not optimism. We both helped bring his former lover and Kelzal to him. All throughout Kelderan history, such acts have been rewarded. From what I've heard of the prince from his sister, Kalahn, he is fair and not vindictive. He will do the right thing."

Keltor's voice interrupted Thorin's reply. "Your female is well-educated, and also correct. Come. We have much to discuss."

Thorin stood and helped Vala to her feet. Since hope was dangerous to a warrior in an unknown situation, Thorin didn't dare allow it to bloom. The prince's words could merely be a way of easing their tension before he pounced.

Even though Vala didn't speak, her eyes told him to wait and see what happened before worrying.

Never releasing her hand, he entered the prince's conference room. While Thorin had never been inside before, it was unusual for the prince to sit alone at the long, oval table in the middle of the room. The crown prince had always been surrounded by staff and advisors any time Thorin had seen him in the past.

Keltor motioned toward the empty seats. "Please sit. This may take a while."

Thorin released Vala's hand and waited until she was seated before he slid into the chair next to her. Her hand went instantly to his thigh, and he placed his on top of hers.

Time to see what their future held. Keltor tro el Vallen had the power to rip them apart, if he so chose.

The prince steepled his fingers in front of him. "Let me begin by saying this room is free of any recording devices and no witnesses are spying on us. What is said in this room is confidential. I expect for our discussion to remain private."

Thorin clenched his jaw before murmuring, "Of course, your highness."

"Good. Then let's begin." Keltor leaned forward and placed his palms on the table. "As grateful as I am for your roles in bringing Azalyn and Kelzal to my side, I can't change Kelderan customs overnight. Each of you has consequences to face, especially regarding your attachment to one another and with acting outside your stations." Thorin opened his mouth, but Keltor beat him to it. "Let me assure you that you won't be imprisoned. However, you won't be able to remain on Keldera, nor can General Thorin remain in the army."

Vala jumped in. "I can accept that fate, but Thorin shouldn't be punished because of who his father was."

Keltor raised an eyebrow. "There are many who will disagree with me, but General Thorin is innocent in that regard. None of us can select our fathers."

For a second, Thorin wondered about the prince's remark. But then he focused on the warmth of Vala's hand in his. "I understand your usual process of drawing out discussions, so as to not anger any party. However, if you could get straight to the point about our futures, I would much appreciate it."

Keltor smiled. "If only more people were brave enough to ask for such a request." His smile faded. "Then let me tell you bluntly what is going to happen. You two will be sent to Jasvar. The colony ship is already en route once more so you will be taking a separate ship. Because even though you'll have to resign your place in the army, I still have assignments for you. Since my father's previous assignment aboard the colony ship has been handed over to Syzel and Ryven, it frees up your time."

Vala squeezed his thigh, but he focused on some of the missing details. "Being sent to Jasvar doesn't tell us what will happen. Vala is my female, and one day, I hope she'll consent to be my bride. If you intend to separate us to punish her for

265

overstepping her rank, then prince or not, I will challenge you." Thorin wanted to end it there, but grudgingly added, "Your highness."

Keltor put up a hand. "No need for threats, General Thorin. However, you might not like the assignment I'm about to give you. Kelzal's blood test confirmed that he is indeed my son. You will take the news to my brother Kason, which will begin your partnership on the planet. You're going to help him set up the Kelderan colony's army and oversight committee."

Thorin frowned. He and Kason had never had more than a tepid acquaintance. "What?"

"It's a lot to take in, but it's the logical choice. Traditions are meant to be broken on the new colony; it's why colonists with more open-minded viewpoints were selected." Thorin gave a quick nod and Keltor continued, "In addition to news of my son, you will also carry a missive to Kason regarding the policy of anyone with partial Brevkan heritage. I'm aware that there are more of you, who hide in the shadows. It'll take time to allow those in control of their actions to come forward on Keldera. However, the colony will be a good experiment to see how others react to the news. If your female will assist, since I believe the Barren know more about the half-Brevkan than I do, we can start locating and convincing others to come forward on Jasvar."

For the first time in a long time, Thorin was speechless. He might finally be able to meet others like him.

Not waiting for a reply, Keltor shifted his gaze to Vala. "My sister still waits for you on Jasvar. Your record remains free of criminal activity or disciplinary marks so you will accompany General Thorin. On top of helping with the partial Brevkan, you will also work with Kalahn and the Jasvarian leader, Taryn Demara. While most of the restrictions have already been lifted via the colonization agreement, I will personally record a message stating you are free to take anyone as lord that you see fit. Pregnancy will no longer be the final stage of marriage on the colony—a binding ceremony and the necessary legal documents will make it so. This should make your union, if it occurs, easier with regards to the law."

Despite Vala's trembling hand under his, she asked, "While I'm grateful for the changes, what about the Barren on Keldera? Will things change for them as well?"

"Someday," Keltor answered. "But until the succession is secured and most of the unrest is subdued, change will have to wait. I wish it were different, but too much too quickly might bring about another war, albeit a civil one this time." Keltor looked from Thorin to Vala and back again. "I expect that these terms are agreeable?"

Thorin shared a glance with Vala. There was a question in her eyes. Even though he would have everything he wanted, he needed to think of his female as well. Even though he had no idea what else she needed, Thorin nodded his encouragement.

His female took a deep breath and said to the prince, "And what about Azalyn? What will happen to her?"

"I will look after her and Kelzal," Keltor said quickly. "You two should leave and prepare for your journey. The ship taking you to Jasvar will leave in a few hours."

Vala dug her nails into his thigh. "But—" Vala began.

"No," Keltor stated. "I've been more than fair. I vow on my dead mother's memory that neither she nor Kelzal will be harmed. They both will be free to contact you, as long as their messages don't include classified information."

Before the prince could dismiss them, Thorin jumped in with his final question. "What will happen to my mother, your highness? She's currently being taken care of at a small hospital for the memory sickness. Even though she may not recognize me, I don't want to abandon her."

Keltor didn't miss a beat. "I looked into your mother's records before holding this meeting. I'm sorry, but moving her to a new planet is dangerous and may worsen her condition. You may send her messages whenever you like, and I may even be able to schedule visits every few years, but keep in mind her friends and family are here and will look after her."

"Her friends, perhaps. Her family, no," Thorin said through gritted teeth.

"All I can promise is to have a few of my trusted guards keep an eye on her. If her condition ever improves or worsens, you will be notified straight away."

Thorin wasn't sure of what to do. His mother had sacrificed so much to keep him. Abandoning her seemed wrong.

Then Vala squeezed his thigh and he met her gaze. Maybe if he could visit his mother once and introduce Vala, she would better understand why he needed to leave so he could protect his female. After all, his mother had always wanted him to find his own bride and happiness. He wouldn't be able to do either if he stayed on Keldera.

He looked back to the prince. "It is a lot to ask, but I wish to visit my mother one last time before we leave so I can introduce her to my female."

Keltor remained silent for a few beats before he finally answered, "I'll allow a brief visit, but only with royal guards acting as your escort. Since your mother lives outside the capital city and it'll take a bit of time to reach her, your ship for Jasvar will leave tomorrow instead of today. I can't delay your departure any longer than that, especially as word will spread of your heritage and people's opinions of you will change, no matter how undeserved they may be."

Relieved at his request being granted, Thorin bobbed his head. While he had accepted his mother forgetting him, he didn't realize how much her meeting Vala meant to him, until the topic had arisen.

Keltor folded his hands over his abdomen. "Then this meeting is over. Return to your temporary quarters until the guard unit retrieves you for the visit with your mother. You are dismissed."

Not wanting to upset the prince, Thorin stood and took Vala with him. He bowed his head. "I will await your formal missive."

As soon as they entered the corridor, Vala growled, probably still upset at what would happen to Azalyn. Thorin touched her cheek and shook his head. "Not here."

She remained silent as they wound their way through the various corridors to their temporary quarters. Not once did she bow her head or avert her eyes from the people they passed on the way.

He wished he could give his female everything she wanted, which included Azalyn awake and at her side. That was impossible in the current situation; both of them would make sacrifices for a better future. Still, pride swelled inside his chest at her behavior. Vala was becoming the female she was meant to be. To ask her to quietly take a decision without question would mean Thorin not accepting all aspects of her personality.

And given the prince's recent rulings, Thorin hoped to accept all of Vala for a long time to come. He finally allowed hope out of its cage. Working with Prince Kason would be difficult, but with Vala at his side and hopefully as his bride, he would be a happy male indeed.

He would just need to ask his mother's forgiveness and hope she'd understand his choice to leave her.

Even in the present, just thinking it felt wrong. He would need to draw on his rational brain to justify his actions. After all, he'd never be able to visit his mother at all if he remained on Keldera and others started hunting him down, wanting to exact revenge on anything Brevkan-related. As long as he was out of the picture, his mother should be safe. She was merely a victim.

But if he stayed, they might use her as bait to draw him out.

No, in order to protect those he cared about, Thorin had no other choice but to leave Keldera and his mother.

~~~

Two seconds after Vala and Thorin were inside their temporary quarters, Vala released Thorin's hand and frowned up at him. "You aren't going to suggest we leave not only your mother but Azalyn here, still unconscious and solely under the prince's control, are you?"

Thorin raised his brows. "Azalyn is his former lover and the mother of his son. He won't harm her."

She noticed how he didn't mention his mother. Vala would come back to that. "Harm comes in many ways, Thorin. You know that as well as I do."

"And what would you suggest?" Thorin asked calmly.

"I don't know. You're the general. I'm sure you can think of a good idea."

He closed the distance between them and took her face in his hands. "I won't force you to go to Jasvar, but think of the consequences of staying. Prince Keltor won't, or rather can't, change the law on Keldera anytime soon. We'll be forced into hiding and constantly on the run. We can better help Azalyn's future on Jasvar. Princess Kalahn will know how to best handle her eldest brother. She is a powerful ally to have when a crown prince is your adversary."

"He's not exactly an adversary. Prince Keltor seems like a fair-minded male in most situations. But he broke Azalyn's heart, didn't go after her, and forced her to deal with a pregnancy on her own."

"She gave up the child. Did she ever tell you why?"

Vala paused before saying, "No."

"Then she may have given the child up regardless if Keltor knew or not. She was quite young at the time. If anything, we should find out both sides of the story before vilifying one party over the other."

She sighed. "I hate when you're rational."

The corner of his mouth ticked up. "If you truly hate it, then we may have a problem as I'm almost always this way."

"You said almost always. When aren't you?"

He kissed her and murmured, "Whenever it comes to you, logic flees my brain."

She leaned against him and tucked her head under his chin. The steady beat of his heart helped to ease her tension. "Don't ever change, Thorin. I love you just the way you are."

The muscles of his chest tensed under her cheek. "Look at me and say it again, *zyla*."

Vala could distract Thorin or try to change the subject. But she was done being a coward, if she could help it.

Looking up, she drew courage from the love and warmth in Thorin's gaze. "I can't imagine ever being at ease with another male the way I am with you. You not only understand me in a way few would with regards to being an outcast in society, but you were also willing to defy orders in order to find me when I was kidnapped. More than that, you know just how to bring out the best in me and help restrain the worst. Even though there's still a lot of uncertainty for the future, I won't hide from my own feelings any longer. I love you, Thorin."

With a growl, Thorin took her lips. She parted to allow his tongue, and he took his time claiming every inch of her mouth.

Vala clung to her male, trying her best not to cry. She still couldn't believe she'd found happiness.

And if she were lucky, it would be a happy ending she could be proud of. She just needed to work at getting there.

Thorin broke the kiss, his breathing labored. A small part of her was satisfied she could make the hardened warrior lose his breath.

Threading his fingers through her hair, he finally spoke again. "I think I'm doing a good job of persuading you to be my bride."

"I didn't say yes just yet."

He smiled smugly. "You will."

"Such cockiness is unlike you."

"There is little I could be so certain of before. But with regards to you, I know how it will play out."

She raised an eyebrow. "Oh, is that so? Care to tell me what the future holds?"

"I see us together for the rest of our lives, battling the unfair practices and injustices against the Barren, the half-Brevkan, and I imagine other groups on the fringes of society."

She nodded. "Keep going."

"We'll both help the Kelderan colony to thrive. You, through helping the Barren and educating the Jasvarians about our people. Me through establishing the colony's army and ensuing a peaceful existence for all to thrive."

"That is a fairly high goal."

He shrugged. "If I don't fight to keep the second chance at life I've been given, then I don't deserve it."

Placing a hand on his chest, she said, "All of that sounds perfect, but you forgot one thing. If there's a way to bring your mother to Jasvar so she can be closer to you, we'll find it."

His expression shuttered. "I think you should hold off making plans for my mother until you meet her. She doesn't remember who I am anymore and the memory sickness will probably only worsen with time."

"Don't give up on her just yet, Thorin. I've worked with others who have similar conditions at the citadel. Sometimes, new methods help to bring them back. Maybe not always or completely, but their families always took the moments of lucidity as parting gifts."

He shook his head. "Don't, Vala. I know that you're trying to help, but it's been years since my mother last remembered my name. I've learned to accept that the woman who raised me is gone."

"We'll see, Thorin. We don't leave for Jasvar until tomorrow. Between the two of us, we might be able to think of a plan."

Thorin remained quiet a few beats before asking, "Such as?"

She paused a second. Talk of his mother had brought up memories of her own adopted mother at the citadel. An idea struck. "There might be a way to do it. However, I need to call my mother first. After all, you should meet her as well. If I hurry, she'll be able to meet us at your mother's hospital."

Vala moved to the drawer with the notescreen, extracted it, and powered it up. Thorin's voice came from behind her. "Care to tell me your whole plan?"

She glanced over her shoulder. "I don't want to say too much, just in case. Just trust me, *zylar*. Can you do that?"

"Of course," Thorin answered without hesitation.

As Vala called her mother, she only hoped her idea would work. Otherwise, her heart would break at Thorin saying goodbye to his mother for good.

Chapter Twenty-Three

Later the same day, Thorin waited with Vala inside one of the hospital's large rooms used for private meetings between family members and patients. Only because Vala held his hand did he not pace the length of the room.

Vala's calm voice filled the space. "I wish you wouldn't worry so much."

He frowned down at her. "There are many things you should be worrying about."

"I won't disagree, but there are many things to look forward to as well."

He hated their vague comments, but both of them were aware of the royal guards waiting just outside the door. If Vala's plan was to work, none of the guards or even the hospital staff could be the wiser.

Vala stood on her tiptoes and kissed his cheek. She whispered, "Have faith."

He didn't want to rely on faith. But rather than argue, he released her hand and laid his arm around her shoulders. "If you keep this up, I may start becoming more optimistic myself out of habit."

She snorted. "Good. Because starting a new life on a new planet is going to require lots of optimism."

Before he could do more than open his mouth, the door leading to the patient area opened.

The mostly gray-haired, blue-skinned form of his mother sat in a hover chair, with a nurse guiding her.

His mother, Hallyn Jarrell, didn't so much as acknowledge his or Vala's presence. She merely stared in front of her.

Once the nurse maneuvered the hover chair in front of them, she smiled at Thorin. "Hallyn just woke up from a nap, so she might be a little quiet for a while, although she's been having a good day. If you need me, press this button." The nurse handed him a small, wireless device. "I must prepare for the transfer. I'll return when I'm finished."

The nurse was referring to his mother's transfer to Vala's former citadel. The prince had allowed for the Barren to take care of her, as they sometimes did with similarly afflicted patients.

Although, if the plan succeeded, his mother wouldn't be staying with the Barren.

Not wanting the nurse to notice any distractions, he nodded. "Thank you."

The nurse exited the room, and Thorin released Vala to kneel in front of his mother. "Hello, Hallyn."

As much as he wanted to call her mother, her name caused less confusion.

His mother's lavender eyes met his. Every time they did, he wondered if his blue eyes would remind her of his father; they were the only physical trait he'd inherited from the bastard.

Her gray brows knitted together. "Who are you?"

Since his mother hadn't recognized him for a long time, he was able to keep the hurt from showing on his face. "My name is Thorin. I come to visit you sometimes."

276

Hallyn looked to Vala. "Why is the Barren here? Is she helping the nurses?"

Vala kneeled next to him and answered, "My name is Vala. I'm Thorin's companion."

"Oh, his mistress. Even if he's not wearing his uniform, I can spot a soldier. The male who once took an interest in me was a soldier." She looked away. "Until he left."

Her once intended lord had abandoned her over thirty years ago, once he'd learned of Thorin's conception. Thorin still wished to seek him out and throttle him. After all, the male should have protected his mother during the war. Only his promise long ago not to hunt him down kept Thorin from carrying out his wishes.

Vala placed a hand on his arm, and some of his anger faded. He forced his voice to remain even as he said, "She is more than a mistress, Hallyn. Vala will be my bride one day."

"A Barren bride? I've never heard of it."

Vala jumped in. "It's true. See, he even gave me this."

His female took out the flower pendant from under her dress. His mother stared at it for a while, and Thorin remained silent. He had never thought to show his mother the pendant since it had always reminded him of what he'd never have—a bride to give it to.

But Vala had suggested it, saying something about how familiar objects sometimes helped with memory.

Hallyn finally pointed at the jeweled flower. "I've seen that before."

Vala glanced at him and he nodded. She focused back on his mother. "It was yours, once."

Hallyn looked away. "I don't remember it."

Glad that at least his mother was talking today, Thorin took her hand and squeezed. "That's all right. I just wanted to come and say goodbye. I'm not sure when I can visit you again."

She met his gaze again. "You've visited me before? Why?"

He wanted to remind her that he was her son, but too many times before it had triggered a memory of his father and she'd devolved into hysterics.

And he'd never be able to test out Vala's idea if that happened.

"I knew you a little growing up. As a favor to my mother, I visit every once in a while."

As Hallyn searched his face, Thorin held his breath. But no signs of recognition flared in her eyes.

Vala spoke up again. "Hallyn." His mother looked at her. "Another reason I'm here is because my citadel is going to take over your care. You'll have more freedom and activities available with the Barren than here. Doesn't that sound lovely?"

"I don't remember what I did yesterday, so one place is as good as another, I suppose," she said dryly.

The glimmer of his mother's former self made Thorin smile.

However, the moment was short-lived when one of the royal guards opened the door. "The Barren escorts are here," he stated.

The second the guard stepped aside, two older Barren females walked into the room.

~~~

Vala had managed to keep any negative emotion out of her voice and off her face. Seeing Thorin interact with his mother as if he were a stranger tugged at her heart.

So when her own mother appeared in the doorway, Vala couldn't stand up and rush to her fast enough. Her mother engulfed her in a hug and murmured, "Everything is ready."

She bobbed her head and finally released her mother. Looking into her kind eyes helped to keep Vala from crying, because once she started, her mother would, too, and then her plan may never get started.

After taking a deep breath, Vala turned and motioned for Thorin to come. Once he stood next to her, Vala introduced him. "Mother, this is my soon-to-be lord, Thorin Jarrell. Thorin, this is my mother, Lyssa."

Her mother smiled at Thorin. "I would hug you, too, but I don't wish to overstep my bounds."

Thorin bowed his head. "Thank you. Not only for your respect, but also for looking after my Vala all these years."

"I was skeptical of you at first. But I see my concerns were unwarranted. You act as any honorable male would."

Before Thorin could argue the point, Vala stepped in. "Let's not be rude, Mother. Let me introduce you to your new charge."

Lyssa winked and Vala wanted to roll her eyes. Her mother was not as subtle as she would like.

Walking over to Hallyn, she motioned toward her mother and her Barren companion. "Hallyn, I'd like to introduce you to your new nurse, Lyssa. She will take good care of you."

Hallyn ignored Lyssa and focused on Thorin. "Why did she introduce you as Thorin Jarrell? That's my surname."

Oh, no. Vala had slipped up.

She shared a glance with Thorin and he looked to his mother. "We're related, but I didn't want to upset you. It's not important. What's important is settling you in with the Barren."

"Related to me how?" Hallyn asked.

Thorin shook his head. "Let's get you settled into your new home first and then I'll tell you."

"I'll probably forget by then."

"Then just trust me that it's for the best," Thorin stated.

Hallyn studied Thorin for a minute before finally nodding. "Fine. But if I do remember to ask again later, you'll answer me, no questions asked."

From watching their interaction, Vala was starting to get an idea of how Thorin's mother had acted growing up. Despite what had happened to her, she hadn't shied from putting Thorin in his place when needed.

What she wouldn't give to hear stories from Hallyn about Thorin as a child.

That's not important. All that mattered was getting his mother out of the hospital and on her way. Maybe, just maybe, some of the techniques Vala had read about would help Hallyn remember some more of her past. On top of that, there may be medicinal plants on Jasvar that could help with her condition.

They just needed to reach Jasvar first.

Her mother patted the pack on her side. "I need to help you change clothes for the journey. The temperature is cooling and I want to make sure you're warm."

Hallyn shrugged, and Lyssa took that as her cue to guide the hover chair out of the room, to a side cleaning room used for patients in case accidents happened during visits.

Vala was more than aware of the guard still in the room, watching every move. So when her mother brought Hallyn back

280

out, draped in a long cloak, she half-expected for the guard to search Hallyn's person.

But all the tall male did was remain at his post at the door.

As much as Vala wanted to let out a sigh of relief, there were still many obstacles to face before they could get Hallyn off the planet.

Her mother smiled at everyone. "I think it's best to get a move on if we wish to arrive at the citadel before dark."

As everyone murmured their assent and they set on their way, Vala took Thorin's hand in hers and followed her mother to the Barren shuttle waiting just outside.

The next part of her plan was trickier.

Yet as Thorin pulled her against his side, she took comfort in his heat and scent. Together, they would succeed. She refused to believe anything else.

~~~

For the duration of the journey to the citadel, Thorin was aware of his mother's eyes on his face. He resisted staring back since he couldn't risk upsetting her.

But a small part of him urged her to remember him as just her son without any memories of his father rushing forth.

He nearly blinked at that thought. A few months ago, Thorin never would've had an optimistic dream or hope about anything. Facts and the lowest-common denominator had always been his way.

Vala was definitely rubbing off on him.

He stared down at his female snuggled against his side and decided he wouldn't have it any other way.

When the driver announced they were approaching, Thorin did chance a look at his mother. She tilted her head and for a split second, he swore she recognized him.

However, he didn't have a chance to speak with her until he was alone with her, Vala, and Lyssa inside the citadel.

As soon as the door clicked closed, cutting them off from the guards, his mother spoke up. "I know who you are, Thorin. And you're planning something."

For a second, he merely stared at his mother. Then he cleared his throat. "I don't know what you're talking about."

His mother pointed a finger at him. "You may be a grown male, but you have the same determined eyes you had as a boy, when you wanted to run away to save me. What are you trying to save me from this time?"

"Mother, is it you?" he whispered.

She waved a hand. "Yes. Now before I forget, tell me what you're up to."

Thorin opened his mouth, but words didn't come out. After how many years, his mother remembered him without soon screaming afterward.

As much as he wanted to hug her one last time, he was a grown male. Any Kelderan mother would expect better than childish displays of emotions from a soldier son.

Vala, however, didn't hesitate to move to her side. "I'm so glad you remember. It'll make everything so much easier."

"Vala, don't," he growled.

She looked at him and raised her eyebrows. "Remember what happened when you kept me in the dark for my so-called protection? We can't do that to your mother."

He grunted. "That was different."

"Was it?"

Hallyn spoke up. "I can see now why she's going to be your bride, Thorin. Someone has to remind you to be something other than a soldier at times. Behind your muscles and tough expressions is a male with a huge heart."

He grunted. "Mother, I'm a grown male. I can take care of myself."

"Can you?" She smiled. "At any rate, it's good to hear that word again." His mother opened her arms. "Since none of your colleagues are here, give me a hug."

Thorin nearly allowed his markings to change color, but just managed to keep them a dark blue. Still, he closed the space and hugged his mother close.

When he finally released her, his mother asked, "So what are you planning? Tell me."

He decided he'd better talk or she'd just keep asking and waste what valuable time remaining they had together. "Vala and I are about to leave Keldera to join a colony planet. We were going to dress you as a Barren and take you with us."

His mother smiled. "I appreciate the sentiment, but that plan won't work. Go, Thorin. A colony is a new start and one I wish I would've had."

"But Mother—"

"No, Thorin. It's best for me to stay here. Although I have one request."

Curiosity won out over arguing his point. "What is it?"

"You mentioned Vala is to be your bride. Will you have your claiming ceremony now?"

"No, Mother, we can have it later. We'll all be together."

"Will we? You pretended not to be my son. I have a feeling I usually don't know who you are. Do it now, Thorin. And if you discover something that can help me permanently, come back for me. Otherwise, leave me in peace and start your new life with a female who clearly cares for you."

Emotion choked Thorin's throat. Rationally, he knew his mother was correct. She may never remember who he was ever again.

And yet, he wanted to give her a new start, too.

Vala spoke up. "Let's give her this, *zylar*. Then my mother can be present as well. Even if we have to do this again on Jasvar to make it legal there, this is a memory we all can treasure."

He looked at his female. The love and understanding in her eyes made him wonder for the hundredth time how he was worthy of her.

A battle-hardened warrior he might be, but not even Thorin was strong enough to deny the two females who meant the most in the world to him. "We'll do it, but I vow to search for a way to cure your ailment, Mother."

His mother reached out and took his hand. "I know, Thorin. Now, let's hurry. I have no idea how much time I have."

Lyssa spoke up. "Let me get a few more witnesses, just so no one can question it."

As soon as she left the room, Vala moved to his side and touched his cheek. "Thank you for doing this."

He placed a hand over hers. "I will do anything for you, *zyla*. I love you."

He kissed her gently and Vala sighed in contentment. When he pulled away, his mother's voice chimed in. "I'm glad you found a female who loves you, Thorin."

Vala looked over. "Even though I'm one of the Barren?"

"You know about his secret, yes?" Vala bobbed her head, and Hallyn waved a hand in dismissal. "Then the fact you love him is all that matters to me."

Lyssa returned with a few other Barren. She motioned toward them. "Hurry up, then. I'm anxious to see my Vala's claiming ceremony."

His mother finally released his hand. Thorin pulled Vala against his body. "Vala Yarlen is my bride, and she has chosen me. Do you recognize my claim?"

Cheers arose in the room. Once they died down, Vala said, "Thorin Jarrell is my lord, and he has chosen me. Do you recognize my claim?"

The clapping was louder than before.

Thorin took his cue. "Then per the laws governing both Keldera and the soon-to-be colony, I willingly surrender my commission to better protect and take care of my bride."

Leaning down, he kissed Vala. Despite the many kisses they'd shared before this moment, love and happiness surged through his body at the contact.

And for a brief moment, he forgot about everything but the female in his arms. The challenges ahead for them both, not to mention leaving his mother, would be bearable as long as he had Vala Yarlen at his side.

Epilogue

Two Weeks Later

Vala stood with Thorin at her side, waiting for the light to beep twice so that they could open the hatch and finally set foot on Jasvar. As much as she'd enjoyed spending a couple of peaceful weeks with Thorin, she was anxious to get her new life started.

Thorin chuckled. "Shuffling your feet isn't going to make the door open any faster."

She glanced up at him. "Maybe not, but I bet I'll be the first one out the door when it opens."

He raised his brows. "Are you challenging me to a race?"

"Maybe."

"You'll lose, *zyla*. I'm not about to allow you to win just because you're my bride."

Even though she'd heard Thorin call her his bride many times over the last two weeks, it still made her smile. "If I tore off my dress and ran naked, I bet it would distract you."

"Perhaps, if it were a surprise. However, I'm now aware of your plan and can mentally prepare myself."

She stuck out her tongue. "Sometimes your logic is irritating."

He shrugged. "You love me anyway." Taking her hand, Thorin kissed the back of it. "Besides, any male who sees your naked body will soon have a meeting with my fist."

She rolled her eyes. "I'm not sure Prince Kason will take kindly to that, no matter how much his brother wants you to work with him."

"I can handle Prince Kason."

At his clipped tone, Vala turned toward him and laid a hand on Thorin's chest. "Of course you can. But I just want to make sure I have a lord to come home to every night. I can't do that if you land yourself in prison."

He wrapped his arms around her waist. "It won't come to that." He kissed her. "No matter what happens, coming home to you will always be my top priority."

"Oh, Thorin. If you're not careful, you're going to ruin your hardened warrior image."

His eyes glowed blue. "I don't care."

She was just about to kiss him when the doors started to open. After patting his chest, she moved to stand at his side.

Bit by bit the pink daytime sky, the purple trees, and the blue mountains of Jasvar came into view. Once the doors opened completely, Vala scanned the area until she spotted a row of people not that far away. In addition to Kalahn and Taryn, Prince Kason, Ryven Xanna, and a few others she recognized but couldn't name were standing there.

As Kalahn and Taryn waved, her first impulse was to run to her friends. However, she took Thorin's hand and tugged. "Ready?"

He grunted and she led him out of the ship, down the stairs, and toward the crowd.

Her heart pounded with each step. On her previous ship, few people had liked Thorin and his cool, dismissive manner. She only hoped everyone else came to understand why he'd acted that way—to protect his secret—and saw the changes in him that she did. If the news of his role in the Tallarian incident had reached Jasvar, then it should be easier to convince them to give her warrior a chance. After all, everyone who had been kidnapped had been recovered alive.

Kalahn was the first to greet them. "Vala, I'm so glad you finally made it." Kalahn looked to Thorin, their hands, and back to Vala. "It looks like there's a lot for us to catch up on. Good thing I won some wine off Nova. I've saved it for an occasion such as this."

Vala was just about to ask who Nova was when Taryn joined them. "Welcome," she said in accented Kelderan.

Vala's CEL wasn't very good, but she still managed to say, "Thank you. Good to be home."

Taryn smiled. "Yes, home."

Taryn looked over her shoulder and frowned. Kason walked slowly, but when his bride motioned for him to come, he closed the distance in no time.

When Kason reached them, Thorin nodded. "Prince Kason."

"Thorin." Kason looked to Vala. "I hope he hasn't kept you from your flight simulations."

Thorin growled, but Vala squeezed his hand and answered, "It was hard to do when I was detained by the Tallarians, but I practiced on my way here."

Kalahn rolled her eyes and lightly pushed her brother Kason. "Sometimes, Kason, I wonder about you." Kalahn looked back to Vala. "We heard the basics of your capture and a bit from

Ryven about what happened on the colony transport ship. It all sounds so exciting. Hopefully you can fill us in with the remaining details."

Thorin spoke up. "It's been a long journey. We should settle into our new quarters and rest."

Vala looked up at her lord. "Resting is about the last thing I want to do. After all, we've been cooped up in that ship for two weeks." She stood on her tiptoes and whispered into his ear. "Besides, the sooner we not only answer questions but fill in the prince and princess with Keltor's message, the sooner we can visit that waterfall you wanted to see."

Thorin had told her of his fantasy and Vala was determined to make it true, especially since Thorin's violent visions hadn't reappeared since their claiming ceremony. She was convinced that happiness helped to keep them away and she was determined to make as many happy memories as possible.

Her male looked back to Kason. "Actually, my bride is curious for a tour and to visit with her friends. At your earliest opportunity, we also need to speak with you and the princess regarding official matters."

Kason opened his mouth, but Kalahn beat him to it. "Please call me Kalahn here. I'm sure Kason feels the same way about dropping 'prince.' Am I right, Kason?"

Taryn jumped in, her Kelderan accent strange. "He does."

Vala frowned. She didn't think Taryn's Kelderan was good enough to follow their conversation.

Taryn pointed to her ear, "I can understand, but speaking hard."

Kalahn smiled. "What she's trying to say is that she has a device in her ear that interprets. So, she can understand everything we say, but replying is hard. Maybe one day the Earth

289

Colony Alliance will provide us with more of those devices. It would definitely make things easier."

Kason looked to his sister. "It would just get you out of teaching."

Kalahn waved a hand in dismissal. "We can talk about teaching later." The princess moved to Vala's side and threaded her arm through her free one. "Taryn and I can take you on a tour while Kason shows Thorin the warrior things he needs to help set up."

She looked up at Thorin. "What do you want to do?"

Not caring about who was watching, he leaned down and gave a gentle kiss. "Enjoy your friends. I'll be waiting for you when you're done."

Vala hesitated. Logically, she knew she'd have to let Thorin out of her sight once she'd stepped foot on Jasvar. But sometimes she still felt as if everything were a dream and if she looked away, it would fade.

Thorin brought her hand up to his lips. "I love you, Vala, but it's time for you to visit with your friends."

After brushing his lips against her skin one more time, he released her hand. Kalahn sighed at her side. "He's so devoted to you, Vala. It's hard to believe we thought him a bastard. I guess a good female inspires devotion, as well as manners, in her male."

Blood rushed to her cheeks. "He is my lord, that's all. Any lord would do the same."

Taryn shook her head. "Don't like lord."

Kason nodded in approval. "See, it doesn't bother her, Taryn. It's much better than 'partner.'"

As Taryn spoke quickly in CEL and Kason argued back, Kalahn whispered, "They're always like this, but they usually disappear soon afterward to make up. It's going to be just you and me for now, Vala. I hope that's okay."

She shared a smile with Thorin before looking to the princess. "I imagine you'll find the same fire in your life someday, Kalahn."

Kalahn darted a glance to Ryven Xanna, who was laughing at Kason and Taryn's argument.

Vala sensed there was a story there.

However, before she could ask about it, Kalahn tugged her in one direction. Vala looked over her shoulder and managed to mouth the words, "I love you" to Thorin before she had to focus on her feet and matching Kalahn's pace.

As the princess chatted about the colonists and plans for the future, it was hard to believe that a few months ago Vala had merely been a Barren female in awe of her first assignment on a spaceship.

Now, she not only had a lord who loved her but friends in both a princess and a human. Not to mention an important role in helping the colony, other Barren, and any partial Brevkan Kelderans she could find.

Vala Yarlen was lucky indeed. It made her believe that anyone could find a happy ending and she was determined to help as many people as she could to find the same.

Author's Note

Thank you for continuing to support this new series and new subgenre! The love for *The Conquest* has been amazing and I only hope that the second book lived up to the expectations set by the first one. :)

This book took even more world-building and work than the first story, but I think it was worth the effort. After all, I like challenging myself as an author. The last thing we want is for me to get bored! Vala and Thorin are both sort of unusual characters for romances, but that makes them more special in my opinion. Everyone deserves a happy ending.

Of course I couldn't have done it without help or feedback from others. I wish to thank the following people:

—Becky Johnson and her team at Hot Tree Editing. They caught quite a few of my inconsistencies and made the story better. Thank you!

—Clarissa Yeo of Yocla Designs. Every cover she makes for me is amazing and this one is no different. She knows exactly how to portray the genre without making it look like ever other sci-fi romance out there. I really appreciate her talent!

—My three beta-readers: Donna H., Iliana G., and Alyson S. These three ladies found a few more inconsistencies and typos. They helped me polish it up and I appreciate their help immensely.

I also wish to thank my readers. You make my dream of writing full-time possible. I know some of you wish I wrote faster, but deep down you know that long, quality stories take time. Thanks for your patience and support. It means the world to me.

My plan is to have the third book in this series, about Prince Keltor and Azalyn (as well as more on Kelzal), out in January 2018. That book should prove to be a second chance romance a bit different than anything I've done so far. There's also going to be a lot happening on Keldera…the book may be longer because of it! If you're wondering about Jasvar, we'll learn more about what's going on there in Princess Kalahn's story. While I can't control my imagination, her story *might* be the fourth book. Regardless of who the characters turn out to be, I hope to have the fourth book out in Summer 2018.

While I always post updates on my website or Facebook, you can make sure to hear all the latest news by joining my newsletter at www.jessiedonovan.com.

Thanks and I hope to see you at the end of the next story.

Sacrificed to the Dragon
(Stonefire Dragons #1)

In exchange for a vial of dragon's blood to save her brother's life, Melanie Hall offers herself up as a sacrifice to one of the British dragon-shifter clans. Being a sacrifice means signing a contract to live with the dragon-shifters for six months to try to conceive a child. Her assigned dragonman, however, is anything but easy. He's tall, broody, and alpha to the core. There's only one problem—he hates humans.

Due to human dragon hunters killing his mother, Tristan MacLeod despises humans. Unfortunately, his clan is in desperate need of offspring to repopulate their numbers and it's his turn to service a human female. Despite his plans to have sex with her and walk away, his inner dragon has other ideas. The curvy human female tempts his inner beast like no other.

Excerpt from *Sacrificed to the Dragon*:

CHAPTER ONE

Melanie Hall sat in the reception area of the Manchester Dragon Affairs office, tapping her finger against her arm, and wishing they'd hurry the hell up. She'd been sitting for nearly an hour, and with each minute that ticked by, she started to doubt her eligibility. If she didn't qualify to sacrifice herself to one of the British dragon-shifter clans, her younger brother would die; only the blood of a dragon could cure her brother's antibiotic-resistant CRE infection.

A woman dressed in a gray suit emerged from the far doorway and walked toward her. When she reached Mel, the woman said, "Are you Melanie Hall?" Mel nodded, and the woman turned. "Then follow me."

This is it. Mel rubbed her hands against her black trousers before she stood up and followed the woman. They went down one dull, poorly lit corridor and then turned left to go down another. The woman in the gray suit finally stopped in front of a door that read "Human Sacrifice Liaison" and turned the doorknob. Rather than enter, the middle-aged woman motioned for Mel to go inside. She obeyed, and as soon as she entered the room, the door slammed shut behind her.

A man not much older than her twenty-five years sat at a desk piled high with folders and papers. The room couldn't be bigger than ten feet by ten feet, but it felt even smaller since every available space on the walls was decorated with different maps of the UK. Some were partitioned into five sections, while others had little pins pushed into them. She had no idea what the pins stood for, but the map divided into five represented the five dragon-shifter clans of the United Kingdom—two in England, one in Scotland, one in Northern Ireland, and one in Wales.

One of which might soon be her home for the next six months.

The man cleared his throat and she moved her attention from the walls to his face. When she met his blue eyes, he said, "Take a seat."

Mel sat down in the faded plush chair in front of his desk and waited in silence. She had a tendency to say the wrong thing at the wrong time, and while she usually didn't mind, right now it could end up costing her brother his life.

The man picked up a file folder and scanned something inside with his eyes, and then set it down. She wanted to scream for him to tell her the results, but she bit the inside of her cheek to hold her tongue.

The man's almost bored voice finally filled the room. "Ms. Hall, the genetic testing results say that you are compatible with dragon-shifter DNA and should have no problem conceiving one of their offspring. You also cleared all of the extensive psychological tests. If you're still interested in sacrificing yourself, we can begin the final interview."

Mel blinked. Despite her chances being one in a thousand that she could bear a dragon-shifter child, she qualified. Her younger brother would get the needed dragon's blood and be able to live out a long life free of pain; he now had a future.

Tears pricked her eyes and she closed them to prevent herself from breaking down. *Pull yourself together, Hall.* Crying was the last thing she wanted to do right now. She couldn't give the man any reason to dismiss her as a candidate.

THE BARREN

"Ms. Hall?"

Mel opened her eyes and gave a weak smile. "I'm sorry, sir. I'm just relieved that my brother will live."

"Yes, yes, the exchange. But we have a lot to cover before we get to the contract specifics, so if you're quite composed, I'll carry on." Mel sat up straight in her chair and nodded. The man continued. "Right. You are healthy, genetically compatible, fertile, unattached, and not a virgin, which are the five requirements needed to qualify. Sacrificing yourself means that you will go to live with Clan Stonefire for a period of six months, and be assigned a temporary male. You will consent to his sexual attentions, and if you become pregnant, you understand that your stay will be extended until after the child is born. If you have any questions, any at all, now is the time to ask them."

She had heard the basics before, but now that she'd passed all of the tests, panic squeezed her heart. As much as she wanted to save her brother—and she would save him—being assigned to have sex with an unknown male dragon-shifter was more than a little scary. Especially since many human women died in the process of birthing half dragon-shifter babies.

If the death-by-baby aspect wasn't bad enough, she was putting her life on hold to do this. Mel was one thesis away from earning her PhD in Social Anthropology. If she became pregnant and survived the delivery, she wasn't sure she could just give up the child and walk away. Most of the women sacrifices who lived past the delivery did abandon their children, but no matter how different the dragon-shifters were from humans, Mel wouldn't be one of them. Family meant everything to her.

And if she didn't give up her child, she would have to give up her dreams in order to spend the rest of her life with Clan Stonefire.

She took a deep breath and remembered her brother Oliver, pale and thin in his sickbed, and her worry dissipated to a manageable level. Even if she became a mother before she'd planned, she would do it three times over to give Oliver a chance to see past his fifteenth birthday.

Still, she wasn't about to pass up this opportunity to ask some questions. The dragon-shifters were extremely private, rarely sharing anything that happened on their land with the public. "I understand consenting to sexual activity, as my main purpose is to help repopulate the dragon-shifters, but what guarantees are in place to ensure I'm not abused or neglected?"

The man leaned back in his chair and steepled his fingers in front of him. "I understand your concern, but the UK Department of Dragon Affairs conducts routine inspections and interviews. Childbearing-related mortality aside, over the last ten years, only one sacrifice has ever reported harsh treatment out of hundreds."

With colossal effort, she managed not to think about her fifty-fifty chance of surviving childbirth. "And what about my friends and family? Can I communicate with them?"

"Communication is forbidden for the first six weeks. After that, it is entirely up to your assigned male as to whether you can communicate or not. From experience, the women who made the greatest effort to conceive were awarded the most privileges."

Right. So if she became a sex goddess, she could talk with her family. How she was going to accomplish that since her previous boyfriends had told her she was "good enough" but never fantastic, she had no idea. But she would cross that bridge when she came to it. "And lastly, when will my brother receive his treatment and when will I leave for the dragons' compound?"

"Once our legal representative has gone through the contract with you and it's been signed and witnessed, a copy will be sent to Clan Stonefire. They should approve it within a matter of days and deliver the vial of dragon's blood to your brother's physician. Normally, you'd be expected to arrive within a week. However, in the case of dying relatives, you're given two weeks to set your affairs in order and to be assured that your brother is recovering. Our office will notify you of the particulars within the next five days."

The man picked up a pen and signed something inside the manila folder on his desk. He picked up a piece of paper and held it out to her. "Since you've had a rational conversation without breaking down or bursting into tears, I think you're mentally sound enough to be sacrificed. If you have no further questions, you can proceed to the legal department."

Even at this late stage of the application process, she now understood how some candidates might be scared off. Hearing about no communication with the outside world as well as how giving birth to a half-dragon baby might kill you was a lot to take in. But Melanie wasn't doing this for herself. Oliver had had a shitty last few years fighting off cancer only to beat it and end up with a drug-resistant infection that was slowly killing him.

Her funny, clever brother deserved a chance to live and enjoy life.

She reached out and took the paper. She said, "Thank you. I'm still interested. Please tell me where the legal department is located, and I'll go there straightaway."

He gave her the directions. Mel thanked the man before leaving his office and making the necessary turns. As she approached the last turn, she glanced down at the paper in her hands. Toward the bottom of the sheet, the man had checked "approved" and signed his name. Seeing it in black and white made her stomach flip.

In less than two weeks, she would go to live with the dragon-shifters and be expected to have sex with one of their males.

She took a deep breath and pushed back the sense of panic. While she didn't know how her assigned dragonman would treat her, there was one thing she had to look forward to—the men were rumored to be fit and muscled. For once in her life, Melanie would get to sleep with a strong, hot man. She only hoped he wouldn't be a complete bastard.

~~~

Tristan MacLeod knocked on the cottage door of Stonefire's clan leader. When he heard a muffled, "Come in," he twisted the knob and entered.

Bram Moore-Llewellyn, Stonefire's clan leader and Tristan's friend of nearly thirty years, sat behind the old, sturdy oak desk that had been used by leaders of the clan for over a hundred years. It was beat up with more than a few scratches from young dragon-shifters trying out their talons. Tristan thought it looked like shit, but dragons were big on tradition and Stonefire's clan leader was no exception.

Bram motioned for Tristan to come in and sit in one of the wooden chairs in front of his desk. Shutting the door, Tristan complied.

While he had a feeling he knew what this meeting was about, he asked, "You wanted to see me?"

Bram put aside the papers he'd been reading and looked up at him. "It's time, Tristan."

THE BARREN

Fuck. "Can't one of the volunteer males have another turn? Putting me together with a human is a bad idea, Bram, and you know it."

Bram leaned back in his chair and shook his head. "No. I can't risk the gene pool getting too small. Neither you nor your sister has had any young, and since you're the elder, you're first in line. I hate to be a hardass, but if you refuse to pair with the latest human sacrifice, I'll have to kick you out of the clan."

———————

Want to read the rest?
Sacrificed to the Dragon is available in paperback

For exclusive content and updates, sign up for my newsletter at:

http://www.jessiedonovan.com

About the Author

Jessie Donovan wrote her first story at age five, and after discovering *The Dragonriders of Pern* series by Anne McCaffrey in junior high, she realized people actually wanted to read stories like those floating around inside her head. From there on out, she was determined to tap into her over-active imagination and write a book someday.

After living abroad for five years and earning degrees in Japanese, Anthropology, and Secondary Education, she buckled down and finally wrote her first full-length book. While that story will never see the light of day, it laid the world-building groundwork of what would become her debut paranormal romance, *Blaze of Secrets*. In late 2014, she officially became a *New York Times* and *USA Today* bestselling author.

Jessie loves to interact with readers, and when not reading a book or traipsing around some foreign country on a shoestring, she can often be found on Facebook. Check out her pages below:

http://www.facebook.com/JessieDonovanAuthor

And don't forget to sign-up for her newsletter to receive sneak peeks and inside information. You can sign-up on her website:

http:///www.jessiedonovan.com

www.ingramcontent.com/pod-product-compliance
Lightning Source LLC
Chambersburg PA
CBHW020437270626
47155CB00022B/565